BOOK ONE

THE BLACK SIGIL OF NAPHAL SERIES

PAIGE ALEXANDRIA

SAGE HAVEN

Trigger Warnings

This novel contains dark themes and mature content that may be distressing to some readers. It explores past trauma, psychological struggles, and morally complex relationships. Please read with caution. Trigger warnings include:

•Physical, emotional, and sexual abuse (past trauma, implied & referenced)
•PTSD, depression, anxiety, and dissociation
•Graphic violence & torture (including revenge-driven acts)
•Drink spiking & drug use
•Stalking & kidnapping (forced proximity, captivity themes)
•Explicit language & sexual content (BDSM elements, power imbalances)
•Coercion & manipulation (revenge plots, mind games)
•Victim blaming & gaslighting
•Criminal activity (murder, human trafficking mentions)

This is a dark romance intended for mature audiences only (18+). Reader discretion is advised.

For the girl who wasn't supposed to survive.

"The flesh recalls what the soul dares not confess."
— From the Eldritch Verses of the Eiloud Naphal Ascendancy

Certain details within Sage Haven are intentionally left vague or unexplained. These choices are deliberate and serve the larger narrative arc that unfolds across the series. This story concludes on a cliffhanger, with key revelations and resolutions continuing in later books.

PROLOGUE

SAGE

*L*EFT. *RIGHT.*

I forced my legs forward. One foot, then the other, as I staggered deeper into the dense forest. The trees clawed and scratched at my skin, as though the woods themselves had conspired against me.

I had to get out.

There had to be a path away from here.

Away from *them*.

Everything around me seemed to blur into dark streaks of shadows. The forest floor showed no mercy. Sharp stones and broken branches sliced through my flimsy shoes, biting into the soles of my feet. I stumbled again, catching myself against a decaying tree. The bark scraped my palms raw, but pain didn't seem to matter.

At least not right now.

There was no time for it.

The ground shifted, nearly taking me under again.

Focus, Sage.

I would tell myself that. But the name barely felt like mine anymore.

Like it belonged to someone who still had a chance of making it out of this alive.

My body screamed to stop, to crumple into the dirt and let it all end. But I kept moving. Even when fatigue settled on me like a shroud, threatening to cage me.

Because somehow, adrenaline still flickered, stubborn enough to keep me upright.

But it still didn't change the fact that I was failing.

I didn't know how much longer I could take this.

Their laughter had echoed through these woods earlier when I fled. It was gone now, devoured by silence.

Some may think that would have been a relief... and yet it wasn't.

It was more terrifying.

It meant I couldn't hear *them*.

I couldn't tell if they were near me just waiting for the right moment to bring me back.

Defeat began to press against me, suffocating and loud with everything I didn't want to feel.

Were they watching?

Waiting?

That was when I felt bile rise hot in my throat. I swallowed it down, pushing past the nausea and fear because there was no room left for anything but survival.

A few more steps.

Another.

Almost there—wherever *there* was.

I didn't care.

I had to keep going.

I had to believe something waited for me beyond this dark.

Because this wasn't how my story would end.

Not here. Not like this.

Just as I reached the stretch of pavement that should have been the light at the end of my tunnel, reality closed in.

I felt it first like a sickness, seeping deeper with every step.

The night shifted into an undeniable turning point that screamed they had already won.

Already gotten what they wanted and disappeared, leaving behind something far worse that would follow no matter how far I ran.

A mark no one could see but one I would feel in every breath, every waking moment, and every broken piece of memory.

That's what followed.

I wasn't running from them.

I was running from *myself*.

They had remade me into someone unrecognizable. And no matter how many lies I whispered just to stay on my feet...

I knew the truth.

There was no going back.

I wasn't just broken. I was *claimed*.

And now... I was theirs.

Chapter One

SAGE

I stood at the edge of the world, or at least that's how it felt. The horizon stretched endlessly before me, a bleak canvas of muted gray and pale gold, where the sky kissed the earth. I stared out over it, my gaze searching, desperate for something—*anything*—that might anchor me, might offer a sign, a symbol or a fragment of hope pointing me toward a future less suffocating than the past I'd just fled.

But there was nothing.

No answers.

No revelations.

Only emptiness.

An infinite expanse that mirrored the hollow ache twisting deep in my chest, as vast and silent as the thoughts that churned in my mind.

Thoughts too heavy to speak aloud and too sharp to release without bleeding myself dry.

The adrenaline that had carried me this far, that electric pulse that had driven my escape, was ebbing now. It drained from me slowly, leaving in its place a cold, suffocating stillness. And within that stillness, one question took root, pressing hard against my ribs until I could scarcely breathe—*What now?*

My father had always said that life was a choice between two things—*boredom or tragedy*. He would sit at our kitchen table, cigarette smoke curling in spirals above his head, and mutter it like a curse he couldn't escape.

"Boredom or tragedy," he'd say. "That's all it is... Pick your poison."

He was a master of pessimism. Some people called it cynicism. But I knew better.

For him, it wasn't just a belief. It was a truth.

One carved out of bone-deep misfortune. A lesson learned the hard way and over too many years, that was paid for in scars both visible and hidden.

Growing up, I never once doubted his conviction because I truly lived it. Our lives had unfolded like a series of dull, gray days, broken only by brief flashes of something brighter. But even in those moments, the rare fragments of happiness never lasted. They slipped through our fingers like dry sand, no matter how tightly we tried to hold on.

Even when my mother was still there, smiling with that distant look in her eyes, joy was fragile. Almost ephemeral.

One wrong word. One sharp glance. That was all it took to shatter it completely, until one day, she was just simply... gone.

No warnings. No explanations.

She just vanished like dust being taken by the wind, leaving behind only the faintest whisper of her absence, like the echo of a song long forgotten.

After that, my father stopped pretending.

He dimmed.

A man who had once been full of life, in his own strange, dark way, became little more than a shadow draped in old flannel and regret. He carried his grief like a heavy, unshakable weight. And somehow, in the cruel calculus of family inheritance, I took on that burden too.

As if her disappearance wasn't just his cross to bear, but mine as well.

Every day, I woke up beneath the weight of unanswered questions.

Every night, I laid them to rest like ghosts I couldn't quite put to sleep.

It took years before I saw my father smile again. And even then, it wasn't the kind of smile that reached his eyes. It was thin and hollow. A mask carefully placed to make others more comfortable, to hide the ache he carried like an old wound that never fully healed.

Regardless, we stayed close because we were all each other had.

We spent long hours together, sitting in the dark, talking about the things we could not control.

Generally, this consisted of the universe and human nature.

We tried to make sense of the chaos. Tried to stitch meaning into the vacant holes my mother had left behind, but no amount of words could fill that space, and in time, I stopped trying.

By the time I reached my freshman year of college, my father's body had begun to betray him. He grew thinner, weaker and his once sharp mind began to soften at the edges as sickness overtook him.

I dropped everything—school, friends, plans for the future that already felt flimsy at best. I took odd jobs to pay for his treatment and our livelihoods when he no longer could. Anything to keep us afloat and to keep the fragile world we'd rebuilt from collapsing again.

One of those jobs led me to *The Bloodwine*. A club pulsing at the center of the city's rotting heart. It was a place where money and desperation met under red lights and low ceilings, where men whispered promises they never intended to keep.

It was there that I met Klay.

He was everything I wasn't.

Charming. Confident.

Money to burn and no shame about setting it all a blaze, but it wasn't his physical presence or outward show that drew me in.

It was his focus.

He saw me...or at least, he pretended to.

And after so many months of feeling invisible, of being just another girl pouring drinks and counting tips to buy her father's pills, I was desperate to be seen.

Klay became a regular. He always requested me. Always flirted, making me feel wanted and desired. Something I hadn't ever felt before.

Eventually, I said yes to a date.

We grew close, especially as my father's health worsened. He stepped in and paid bills I couldn't cover. He offered me a kind of stability I hadn't known since before my mother disappeared. At first, I thought he was saving me, but in time, I began to feel the invisible chains he had wrapped around me that were soft at first, like silk, out of sight to anyone who wasn't looking.

And I wasn't looking.

Not then. Not at first.

Because I didn't understand that every favor he did for me, every dollar he spent, was a debt I was expected to repay. Quietly without question, like a silent form of bondage. But he still helped, even when he began to act differently towards me and maybe that's why I let him treat me the way that he did.

But then my father died, and everything changed.

I saw Klay for who he was—a master manipulator who had been pulling my strings like a puppeteer, twisting my reality until I could no longer see an escape.

The night of my father's funeral was when I realized who Klay really was, when I came to him, and he dismissed me like I was nothing but trash to be discarded.

But even he wasn't worst of my fears.

That night...

Something worse happened.

Something I still can't find the words to explain.

Something that hollowed me out completely and left me broken, as the ghost of the girl I had once been.

And it was that night I decided to run.

I packed what little I owned.

I climbed behind the wheel of my father's old car.

And I drove.

No plan. No destination.

Only the desperate need to get away from this city, Sanele, and everything it had stripped from me.

The pain.

The memories.

The life that felt more like a sentence than a gift.

The parts of myself that wanted to give up, echoed in my mind that it was all pointless. But there was a flicker of something small and stubborn deep inside me; the last piece of the girl I used to be, and she whispered:

Keep going.

So I did.

I drove north, into a world I didn't recognize.

And five hours later, just as dawn cracked the sky open, I found myself at an empty port.

A weathered wooden sign leaned crooked in the dirt, its peeling letters spelling out:

"Town of Providence, 2 Miles East."

The name stuck in my chest like a hook pulling me in.

Providence.

A promise?

A warning?

I didn't know, but at least it was a direction, and any direction was better than the one I had just come from.

When I arrived, it didn't take long to realize that Providence was nothing like Sanele.

Sanele had choked the life out of everyone within its city limits. Its factories and power plants casted the streets in permanent dusk, compounded by the air that was thick with smoke and something like hopelessness. The people wore exhaustion like it was all they ever knew, all hollow eyes and thin mouths, but Providence...

Providence breathed.

It was old, but not broken.

The buildings were sturdy, their stonework softened by ivy and time. Fields stretched wild beyond the town's edge, full of life, with air that was clean and crisp, filling my lungs in a way that made me dizzy at first, as if I'd forgotten how to really breathe.

And for the first time in years, I felt something stir inside me.

Hope.

Small, fragile, but real.

It made me feel like I could start over here and that maybe I could build something new.

Something better.

A life carved from boredom instead of tragedy.

I knew it wouldn't be easy.

I knew my ghosts weren't finished with me.

They would find me in the quiet moments, slipping through any cracks I hadn't yet sealed, but for now, I could pretend.

So, I found a small apartment days later and took a job at a café, the kind of place where people smiled for no reason, and for a while, I let myself believe I belonged.

And I believed it, until my past found me again, and everything I thought I'd escaped came crashing back.

Chapter Two

REICH

"YOU MOTHERFUCKER!"

The words ripped from his throat, rough and raw. His voice cracked under the strain, breaking apart into something else, something unrecognizable. It was the final, desperate wail of a man who knew his gods had already abandoned him. A sound meant for no one and nothing except to remind himself that he still existed, if only for another moment.

Each scream he unleashed was another note in the symphony I had spent years perfecting. There were conductors of music and conductors of war, but me?

I composed agony.

Orchestrated suffering with precision.

I stood still. Silent. Watching.

He thrashed, limbs spasming against the steel coils of razor wire that encased him like a grotesque cocoon. The more he fought, the more the wire dug in. Sinking deeper into his muscles and tendons. Each jerking movement carved long, jagged tears in his flesh, opening him up like a fruit being split at the seam. Blood seeped from his wounds in dark rivulets, tracing paths over his ruined skin and running rivers to the concrete beneath him in a spreading pool of failure.

He was drowning in his own pain now, submerged in my entrapment of wire, bleeding out from a thousand tiny incisions and dozens of deep gouges. His body shuddered, spasmed with every twitch, every reflexive movement. It only made things worse for him. Every contortion, every desperate thrash, deepened the wounds. Turned cuts into tears. Turned tears into gaping wounds that exposed pale muscle and glistening bone.

I didn't flinch.

Didn't blink.

The screams from his pain didn't unsettle me. It was... *expected*. *Necessary*.

His eyes bulged, red-rimmed and glassy, as his face had twisted itself into something unnatural—a mask of rage and hopelessness, contorted so violently he no longer looked human. More like some malformed exhibit, the kind you'd find behind cracked glass in some backwater carnival sideshow or one of those grotesque displays in Ripley's Believe It or Not, where people paid a few bucks to gawk at the impossible, but this wasn't entertainment.

This was work.

This was *purpose*.

And if I did it right, Ali Parrish wouldn't just be another name crossed off a confidential ENA ledger no one read twice. No, with my hands, I would make him something permanent. The next exhibit in a gallery of consequences.

A warning and a legacy.

I'd hear people always say the most beautiful thing in the world that they've ever seen is either their wife on their wedding day or the first look of their newborn child's face.

But not me.

I've watched the light fade from the eyes of men who thought they could get away with being sadistic predators. Who believed they could devour innocence and walk away unscathed.

That light? When it flickers out for the last time, leaving nothing but the cold, empty shell behind?

That's the most beautiful thing I've ever seen.

Parrish wasn't there yet, but he would be.

His screams echoed off the cold, concrete walls of my basement, otherwise known as "The Pit".

"YOU'LL FUCKING PAY FOR THIS, REICH!" he howled. His voice broke again, splintering into something wet and ragged. Blood sprayed from his cracked lips with the force of it, flecking the floor between us.

He spat my name like it was a curse.

I smiled. A slow, cold twist of my lips. The kind of smile that held no warmth. No pity.

The kind that men saw right before they died.

"Funny," I said softly, unphased. "I think I said the same thing to you… what was it? Thirty-six hours ago?"

I watched the anger hit him. It struck hard and sudden. His pupils flared, blown wide with disbelief and sudden clarity.

Ali Parrish had his chance.

Twenty-four hours to turn himself in to the ENA.

He thought he was clever. He thought he was untouchable.

And he thought wrong.

So, I dragged him here to pay for his mistakes.

My brother, Castor, and I were made for this. From the time we turned eighteen, we were groomed for sanctioned violence. Taught that morality was just another tool in the box, one you could pick up or put down as needed. We were taught to be good soldiers, to serve higher purposes and not ask questions.

By the time I graduated college, I'd traded any major I once cared about and the white-picket-fence life that came with it, for something darker.

Something real.

Something that was supposed to matter.

And I had never looked back.

The ENA's web was deeper than I had ever known.

Once you were inside it, you didn't get out.

Not in one piece. Not alive.

So, I stayed.

Adapted.

I became the thing they needed me to be.

A weapon.

And Parrish? He was easy.

Cocky. Greedy. A predator who'd stepped too far over the line.

The ENA had finally decided to collect his debt.

And that's why he was here in the Pit.

From an outsider's perspective, the Pit was nothing. Just a slab of reinforced concrete buried beneath my house. Twenty-four feet by twenty-four feet of cold indifference. Flickering warehouse lights above and solid clear coated cement floors beneath.

But as an insider and its owner...it was a church, and I was the priest.

The tools lined the walls, neat rows of metal and wood, all polished to a dull gleam. Pliers. Wrenches. Blades. Hammers.

Nothing special. Nothing dangerous in the hands of someone soft.

But in my hands...

They were scripture.

My sermon and an offering to the gods of vengeance and justice.

Behind me, Parrish choked, hacking up blood and bile, the wet sounds echoing to fill the space between us. I ignored it. My fingers drifted over the tools, slow and thoughtful, like a sommelier selecting a vintage bottle of fine wine.

I was in no rush.

The best things took time.

His coughing grew louder. More insistent and desperate. Until finally— "I know who you're after…" he rasped, voice raw and shaking.

I laughed. A low and dark, humorless sound.

"Doesn't everybody?" I asked.

He twisted in his bonds, wire scraping bone. His panic was a living thing now, breathing in the air between us, and taking residence in the emptiness.

I circled behind him, my boots heavy against the floor. Every step was deliberate. Then I grabbed a fistful of his filthy, blood-clotted hair and yanked his head back hard. His neck cracked against the tension of the wire as his face turned up to mine, eyes wide and rimmed in red. His mouth curled into a sneer, but there was no defiance left. Just hate and fear.

"You'll never catch him," he spat. "He's too clever for you."

Wrong.

I smiled, then reached into my pocket and flicked open my knife. The blade gleamed under the harsh light, a flash of silver in the dull gloom of this place.

I pressed it to his scalp, feeling him shudder underneath me as I dug it in.

And then peeled off pieces of his skin, bit by bit.

His screams tore through the Pit, sharp enough to almost make it feel like the concrete would vibrate. His body convulsed, jerking hard against the coils as I worked in precise, practiced strokes.

Justice isn't clean and it isn't quick.

It's slow.

Relentless.

And meticulously carved into the flesh of men who thought they were above consequence.

The ENA called it their spiritual atonement.

I called it Tuesday.

But I still never asked questions.

Didn't care about the reasons.

Especially when I knew by now that with the ENA, the answers were always worse than the nightmares they left behind.

I finished the strip, let it fall with a wet slap to the floor, and stepped back, wiping my blade clean on his shredded clothes.

"Anything else you want to tell me?" I asked, my voice low, casual, like we were sharing drinks at a bar instead of sitting in a slaughterhouse.

His breathing came shallow and labored but his hate still burned.

He glared up at me through cracked lids. "Fuck you, Reich," he hissed. "He's already... won."

Wrong again.

I worked in a methodical and precise rhythm.

Every incision, every cut, brought forth his wails, adding another verse in a new kind of song only I would ever hear. This was my show.

My mosh pit.

And Parrish?

He was just another body in the crowd.

Were these the right choices?

Hell if I knew.

But Castor and I were still breathing and that was all that mattered.

I made the last cut.

And Parrish stilled.

Another masterpiece.

Another monster erased.

I exhaled slowly.

Rinse. Repeat.

Chapter Three

SAGE

I HAD TRIED SO hard to leave Sanele behind. I thought if I drove fast enough, far enough, I could outrun it and outpace its suffocating grip, but I was wrong.

No matter how many miles I put between myself and that place, it followed.

It was there. *Always there.*

I tried to lie at first and tell myself I'd made it out. That I was actually free. That the ghosts of Sanele had been left behind in the smoke and shadows where they belonged. I fed myself that lie like it was oxygen, clinging to it because if I let go… I didn't know what would be left.

But lies, no matter how tightly you hold them, start to rot from the inside out.

And soon enough, I felt it creeping back.

Settling into my bones with the cold inevitability of winter.

It wasn't loud or sudden.

It was quiet and slow, like it was being patient. Like smoke slipping beneath a doorframe, curling through the air until it fills the whole house.

Sanele's shadows weren't something you could leave behind.

They clung to you, seeping into your clothes, your skin, your breath.

They didn't scream. They whispered.

Always there. Always waiting.

People like to talk about trauma like it's the worst part of the story, like the actual wound is the ending.

But they're wrong.

The trauma itself, no matter how brutal, how violent, how gut-wrenching. isn't the hardest part.

It's what comes after.

The echoes that never stop when you beg them to.

The broken pieces scattered across the floor of your life, sharp and waiting for you to try and pick them up.

And you do. You *always* do.

Because there's no one else to clean up the mess.

You gather them with trembling hands, knowing they won't fit the way they used to. Knowing they'll cut you as you try to rebuild.

And you tell yourself you're fine, that you can handle it.

But then you realize you've still been bleeding the whole time.

And the weight of that realization doesn't ease.

It presses down on your chest until every breath is a fight.

It creeps into your veins, a cold coil of despair that winds itself around your heart and waits—*just waits*—for the right moment to squeeze.

Since the day I left Sanele behind, I woke each morning drenched in cold sweat. My body jolting upright before I was even conscious of being awake, lungs heaving, as my breaths forced their way through my body.

My stomach twisted in knots I couldn't undo.

And my mind—my mind was a nest of nightmares.

Except they weren't just nightmares.

They were memories that followed me.

Invading every sleeping and waking moment, crawling under my skin, like something alive and starving wanting to eat me from the inside out.

Reminding me that the past isn't a place you can leave.

It's not a door you can lock.

It's a scar and one that deepens with time.

I wanted to believe a fresh start was possible.

That time and distance could bury the past, could quiet the screaming.

But every time I looked in the mirror, I saw a stranger staring back.

A face I didn't recognize.

A version of me that didn't fit the story I was trying to tell myself.

I wanted time to heal me.

I needed it to.

But no matter how far I ran, I was still running from myself.

Every day felt like a constant balancing act.

I pieced myself together with shaking hands, careful not to breathe too hard in case everything collapsed.

I told myself that no one could see the cracks if I smiled just right and spoke just enough.

Maybe no one would notice.

Because I knew that with one slip, one misstep, one moment of weakness—I'd fall.

Straight back into the ruins of my past and I wasn't sure I had it in me to crawl out again.

So, I kept my head down.

I kept busy.

I pretended.

Routine became my armor.

If I moved enough, worked enough, maybe I could stay ahead of it. Maybe I could even fool myself into thinking I wasn't unraveling.

But that was a long shot, because every night, when the world quieted, I peeled off the mask and it was waiting for me again.

The memories. The fear. The shame.

It never left.

It just lurked beneath the surface, patiently awaiting.

By the third week, I found trails nearby my apartment complex. They were tucked just beyond town, winding through a forest that stretched as far as I could see.

I made a habit of walking those trails every morning, right after the nightmares spat me out of sleep and before the day had a chance to crush me beneath its weight.

It became my solitude.

The trees arched overhead like old sentinels, their branches knitting together into something that felt like protection. The river cut through the woods with a quiet murmur, its voice softer than my own thoughts and the sounds of the bird filled the spaces between with their song.

And for the first time in years, I felt...lighter.

Not whole but less broken.

Each step away from the past, felt like a quiet rebellion.

A middle finger raised against everything that had tried to bury me.

I didn't know where the trail led.

I didn't care.

Forward was enough.

Then, one morning, I found a small clearing

Hidden just beyond a bend in the path.

A meadow that looked like it had been painted onto the world by some gods I didn't believe in. Wildflowers spilled over the earth in every riotous color imaginable—violet, gold, crimson, ivory.

Untamed and almost rebellious.

But *alive.*

The river glittered nearby, its surface catching the light in a way that made it look molten.

I stood there for a long time, just... staring.

It was too perfect. Too beautiful.

I half-expected it to vanish if I blinked.

For a moment, it felt like I'd stepped into another world entirely.

One untouched by the things that haunted me.

I sat by the riverbank, fingers drifting over the petals, tracing their softness as if they might ground me in something real. The water whispered against the shore, and since coming to Providence I felt something close to safe.

Not exactly safe, but close.

And close was enough.

So, I came back.

Every morning.

After the nightmares.

Before the day could catch up to me.

I came back.

I let the breeze skim over my skin, cool and soft.

I let the flowers fill my lungs with their sharp, sweet breath and lost myself in the stillness.

But still a heavy burden was there within me. Something that kept me from feeling completely safe.

Sitting there one morning, knees pulled to my chest, surrounded by beauty that shouldn't have felt like a lie, I found myself asking—*had I really left Sanele behind?*

Or was it still stitched into my veins, stitched into my name, in ways I didn't understand?

Was I free or was I just pretending?

The questions gnawed at me.

They circled like vultures waiting for me to fall still long enough for them to feast.

I wanted to believe something good had come from all of it.

That through the wreckage and the ruin, I had found this—*a sanctuary.*

In the wildflowers, the river, and trees.

Maybe I wasn't fixed.

Maybe I never would be.

But maybe I wasn't just surviving anymore.

Maybe I was starting to understand what it meant to live.

And perhaps, for now, that was enough.

The thought lingered, delicate and fragile, like a spider's web swaying in a breeze.

Too easy to destroy.

Because deep down... I knew it was a lie.

A convenient story I told myself because the truth was too heavy to carry in daylight.

And because if I didn't keep telling it, I might not keep going.

I leaned back, lying in the grass, the cool blades pressing against my skin. I stared up at the sky that was so vast it felt like I could fall into it and never hit bottom.

It was comforting and terrifying.

Just like everything else in my life.

I slipped on my headphones, scrolling through my playlist. The haunting chords spilled into my ears, weaving through me like a pulse I wasn't sure was my own. The song echoed something I didn't have words for.

Something I refused to face.

But it became my anchor and my burden.

A reminder of the lie I needed to survive the next day.

"I'm okay."

I whispered it aloud.

A hollow mantra that I repeated it until it almost sounded true.

But it wasn't.

And I didn't know if it ever would be.

Chapter Four

REICH

L**AST NIGHT HAD BEEN** a constant battle without end. An excruciating war waged not only against the clock but against the brittle edges of my own sanity. Every passing hour had carved something away from me, left me hollowed out in ways I didn't yet have the courage to examine.

The task was finished. Another name crossed off the list, another obligation fulfilled. But each completion came at a cost.

Always at a cost.

And the aftermath? It was patient. It waited until the work was done, then it came to collect. I could feel it now—the toll it exacted on my mind, my body and even my soul. The ache that settled in afterward, spread through me like a cold frostbite, further numbing me and disconnecting me from my reality.

Sleep remained as elusive as ever. No matter how heavy my eyelids grew or how deep the exhaustion ran through my core, I couldn't find rest. The night clung to me; its cold hands pressed against my throat leaving me reaching for breath.

Every time I closed my eyes, I saw it.

What I'd done.

What I'd become.

When the first light of dawn began to seep in through the blinds of my bedroom window—thin streaks of pale gold against my neutral walls—I felt the pull. A sharp, insistent urge, like an itch beneath the skin I couldn't reach. I needed space. Air. A moment alone before the weight of another day could settle on my shoulders, dragging me back under.

I slid out of bed, moving carefully and deliberately. As if I feared waking someone—or something—that still lingered in the walls of this house. Ghosts. Regrets.

Names I couldn't remember. Names I could never forget.

The house was silent as I moved through it, feet bare against the cold wood floors. Every shadow was familiar. Every corner memorized. It was all mine, yet there were days it didn't feel like a home. More like a monument. Or more like a mausoleum.

I pushed through the glass door and stepped outside, onto the deck that stretched wide before me.

Out here, the world was still.

The deck overlooked everything—the river winding far below, carving its restless path through the valley before merging with the lake in the distance. On the other side of the water, my field of wildflowers had begun to bloom again, a riot of color splashed across the earth like an abstract artist's reckless brushstroke. It looked peaceful.

But I knew better.

I always knew better.

Beneath that wild beauty was soil that had swallowed my secrets. My buried truths.

The earth had taken them in and, like the rest of this place, gone still. So, to an outsider, it was nothing more than a field—a picture-perfect stretch of untouched land.

But to me?

It was a graveyard.

A reminder.

I stood there for a long moment, unmoving, letting the cold bite of morning air settle against my skin. There was a pureness to it. Something crisp and clean that loosened the mess inside me.

Sometimes I let myself believe that this place held something sacred.

As if the land itself was capable of forgiving.

As if absolution was something more than a story, we told ourselves to sleep at night.

I wanted to believe it was possible. That redemption was waiting somewhere just over the ridge. That I could move forward.

But belief had never been my strong suit.

The house behind me stood like a fortress, perched on the edge of the mountain, almost invisible to anyone who didn't already know where to look. It sat nestled inside an old part of the nature reserve that few ever ventured into unless they had a reason. It was a secret tucked in and hidden into the folds of the landscape.

Like my home. Like my life.

Seclusion was a comfort we'd learned young.

My brother, Castor, and I knew the value of shadows. We understood the danger of being seen.

Although Castor had a girlfriend now.

One who asked too many questions.

I had warned him—*more than once*. The risks of curiosity. The weight of knowing. The less people involved, and the cleaner things stayed. The fewer questions asked and the fewer answers we were forced to give.

I exhaled slowly, my breath a thin mist in the cold air, and watched the sunrise as it spread across the horizon. The sky was streaked with amber and gold, the kind of beauty that felt unearned.

And then I saw it.

A glint.

Sharp and Sudden.

Something caught the light, flashing just enough to pull my attention from the horizon and snap it to the far side of the river.

A striking figure stood there.

Crouched among the wildflowers.

Delicate fingers plucked one from the earth as if it was a sacred thing.

A woman.

I watched her carefully, instincts tightening.

She wasn't from town.

I would have known.

In towns as small as this, everyone knew everyone.

But her?

She was a mystery.

An unknown.

Someone that didn't quite belong.

Her bracelet caught the morning light again, the gleam pulling at my focus like a lure dragging a hook through dark water.

I should have looked away.

Should have walked back inside, but I didn't.

I couldn't.

Something about her kept me tethered.

She was the ripple across still water.

Something I didn't want to acknowledge but yet couldn't ignore.

She moved slowly, with a kind of peace and gracefulness that I didn't understand, and then I watched her as she laid back in the grass, letting her body sink into the earth.

She stared up at the sky and smiled softly.

Quiet. Serene.

And I stood there, watching, frozen by the weight of something stirring inside me.

I didn't understand her peace or this illusion of it.

Before the thought could settle, Castor's voice cut through the quiet.

"Hey, Reich…"

I didn't turn.

I felt him step up beside me, his gaze tracking where mine was locked.

His presence was grounding.

His tone, less so.

"What do we have here?" he asked, casual but probing.

"Just another tourist," I replied, flatly.

The words were more for me than for him.

Castor arched a brow, his suspicion bleeding through, "You need me to take care of it?"

The question hung there, heavy with implication.

It would be easy.

Quick. Clean.

And the temptation was there.

To hand it off and let him deal with this new found complication before it unraveled into something worse.

But not this time.

Not with her.

"No." I shook my head, slow and measured as I responded. "She's probably just lost."

The words tasted wrong in my mouth, as I continued, "She'll leave soon enough."

Castor wasn't convinced.

I felt the weight of his stare, the doubt in his gaze. "And you haven't forgotten that a certain somebody is only thirty feet from her right foot?"

He didn't have to say more.

I knew exactly what he meant.

I was already counting the distance in my head, already tracking the probabilities.

Last night's work was buried there.

Close enough that if she wandered, she'd find something she shouldn't.

"If she gets too close, I'll handle it," I said.

My voice was even.

Controlled.

I didn't have the energy for an argument.

And Castor let it go, for now.

He exhaled, a slow breath.

Before I asked, "How's our current assignment going?"

A pivot.

"Nothing yet," he said. "He slipped through my radar, but I'm still looking." He paused before continuing, "I'll track him down after the music festival. You're still going, right?"

The music festival.

I hadn't gone last year.

Hadn't left this house for anything that didn't involve blood or orders.

Maybe that was why the restlessness sat so deep inside me.

"I'll try. I don't want to miss seeing Nerv perform live again."

My next words slipped out, unguarded, a hint louder than I intended.

I winced as soon as they passed my lips, worried we were being too loud and signaling our presence.

"It was complete bullshit that I missed them last year."

I shifted my attention back to the field.

But when I turned back my gaze—she was *gone*.

An unease settled deeper in my chest, cold and sharp.

I should have been relieved.

But instead, there was a question gnawing at me.

Heavy.

Unanswered.

Who was she?

Chapter Five

SAGE

I CLUNG TO ROUTINE like it was the only thing keeping me upright.

A rigid, self-imposed structure meant to keep the chaos at bay and my mind from unraveling thread by thread.

Every morning, I woke up at precisely six.

I walked the trails behind my apartment, pacing the same worn paths until my legs ached and the rhythm of my footsteps pounded some semblance of quiet into my skull.

I read one chapter of a book—fiction only. Nonfiction hit too close to home.

I clocked in at *Java-dence*, my corner café where I hid behind the espresso machine and memorized regulars' orders to avoid actual conversations.

Dinner was the same most nights, whatever was on special at the local market.

Rest was elusive, especially with the constant night terrors, but I laid down anyway.

And then I did it all over again.

Some days, it worked, where the noise in my head dimmed to a low hum I could ignore. The tension in my muscles softened just enough to let me move through the world without feeling like I was dragging chains behind me.

But then there were other days.

Days when the routine wasn't enough.

When it felt like I was sprinting in place, stuck in a loop that pressed down on me like a vice I couldn't slip free from.

On those days, I swore I could feel Sanele breathing down my neck.

And then everything changed.

Like the universe decided to flip the script and see what I'd do when someone else disrupted the cycle I'd clung to for dear life.

It was a morning like any other.

Gray sky.

Car parked in my usual space in front of my apartment building.

I was on autopilot, about to step out and start the routine all over again when something—or rather, someone—cut through the haze.

Out of the corner of my eye, I caught movement.

A figure stepping out of the leasing office, the morning light catching in the tousled, bleach-blonde waves of her hair. She walked like she was carrying the warmth of summer with her, shoulders relaxed, head held high, the faint bounce of her steps completely unbothered by the world around her. She had an energy that couldn't be ignored, like sunlight in motion, and I was the shadow watching her from behind the safety of a car window.

Before I could make sense of it, she was waving.

Ribbon bracelets in every color fluttered wildly from her wrist, catching the light and throwing flashes of bright hues in all directions.

She smiled—wide and unrestrained.

Like we were old friends.

Like we hadn't missed a single day.

And then she was walking toward me.

Straight for my passenger-side window.

For one wild second, I thought she was about to open the door and climb in like she belonged there.

Instead, she tapped on the glass with two knuckles.

I hesitated, but before I could decide if I was ready for this, my anxiety lowered the window.

"Hey! You're the person who just moved into the third-floor apartment, right?" she said, her voice bright and unapologetically enthusiastic. "I think we might be neighbors!"

I blinked at her, momentarily caught off guard.

People didn't greet me like this.

Hell, people didn't greet me at all unless they had to, but there she was—this radiant, unstoppable force of nature standing inches from my car, acting like I was the best friend she'd been looking for her entire life.

I nodded, because I didn't know what else to do.

Her eyes sparkled with something wild and untamed, like she was constantly on the verge of letting me in on a secret too good to be true.

She radiated joy. Pure, unfiltered joy. That was the best way to describe her.

In an attempt to not scare the butterfly off, I reached for the volume knob, turning down the blaring guitar riffs that had been my soundtrack that morning—a raw, guttural metal track pounding through the speakers, but then she surprised me.

"Oh, don't turn it down for me! I love this kind of music." Her laugh bubbled out, light and easy, as if we were sharing a joke, I hadn't realized we'd made. "In fact, I'm pretty sure your apartment only became available because of a few noise complaints. You're welcome, by the way."

Her teasing grin was infectious.

Against every instinct that had kept me alive this long, I smiled. Really smiled.

Not the tight-lipped thing I offered to customers or a passerby out of politeness.

This was something closer to real. More vulnerable.

"Not that I'm a noisy and unbearable neighbor," she added quickly, throwing her hands up in mock defense. She bit her bottom lip, as if considering whether or not she should say more, and then her grin widened like she'd made a decision.

"I'm Sam," she said. "And you are...?"

"Sage," I replied, my voice softer than I intended. So, I cleared my throat and tried again. "Sage."

She nodded like it was already the most familiar name she'd ever heard.

"Well, Sage," she said with certainty, "you're officially stuck with me. We're going to be friends."

And that's how I met the one who would pull me out of my routine.

By the end of that week, Sam was everywhere.

Like sunlight finding all the cracks in my armor, no matter how carefully I'd patched them. She dragged me out of my shell with a force I couldn't fight—not really.

Her energy was relentless.

Her kindness was disarming.

I found myself saying yes to things I never would have before.

Concerts that left my ears ringing and my lungs sore from screaming.

Late-night drives with no destination, just music blasting from the speakers and the wind tangling our hair.

Lazy Sunday mornings curled up on her couch, laughing until our ribs ached at terrible movies that made no sense but felt like home.

She was a whirlwind I didn't realize I needed until I was already caught in it.

And when I wasn't with her, my old routine was still there—waiting.

But it felt different now.

Less like survival.

More like something I could return to when I needed to steady myself and needed space to breathe.

Sam became a regular at my work.

I pretended not to notice when she started timing her visits to match my shifts.

But I noticed.

One afternoon, she showed up at the counter, her usual grin firmly in place but with something sharper lurking behind it.

"Sage," she said, leaning in dramatically. "I need a double hitter fix today. Caffeine. Now."

I raised a brow, already amused.

"What happened?" I asked as I grabbed a cup and marked her order.

She sighed—long and theatrical—and rolled her eyes, as she began, "One of the partners at my firm got caught embezzling money and guess who gets to clean it all up?"

She jabbed a finger at herself.

I smirked, "Wow. What a scandal."

"Truly," she agreed, her lips twitching like she was trying not to smile.

Then, just as quickly, her face lit up again.

"Oh! Sage, I almost forgot, you have to come to the Sacrifice Tomorrow Festival. It is happening tonight!"

I blinked. "Sacrifice Tomorrow?" I repeated. "That sounds... a little cult-y."

She laughed, bright and unbothered. "I promise, it's not! It's called that because it starts at sunset and goes until sunrise. Everyone in town comes out for it. There's music, dancing, food trucks, bonfires. It's a tradition, so I guess maybe it is a little cult-y."

She winked before continuing, "Trust me. You'll love it."

I hesitated.

I always hesitated.

But the truth was, I was already intrigued, and Sam made it hard to say no.

It was one of her talents.

"It does sound amazing," I admitted.

Her grin widened. "Then it's settled. I'm picking you up at eight."

Then she got that look. The one that meant something was coming. Something I may or not be ready for.

"What?" I asked warily.

She tapped her fingers against the counter, feigning innocence. "So... you know that guy I've been seeing?"

I narrowed my eyes. "The one you've basically told me you're in love with?"

She nodded, eyes bright. "He's going to be there tonight. And I want you to meet him. You know, just to make sure he's not secretly into... questionable things."

I snorted. "You want me to vet him?"

"Exactly," she said, grinning. "You're my backup. Just in case he's secretly into nipple clamps or something."

I choked on a laugh. "Especially nipple clamps," I agreed.

We laughed until tears pricked the corners of our eyes. And for the first time in a long time, something warm bloomed in my chest. Something I hadn't realized I was missing until that exact moment.

A friend.

I swallowed hard, my voice quieter than usual. "Thank you, Sam."

She tilted her head. "For what?"

"For being you," I said honestly. "For saying hi to me in leasing area parking lot a month ago."

Her expression softened, and without hesitation, she reached out and hooked her pinky through mine.

A silent promise.

A vow.

"I saw something in you," she said, sincere and certain. "Something special, and I'm so glad I trusted my gut."

I smiled, the smallest, realest thing. "Till the bitter end?"

Her grin widened. "Till the bitter end."

Chapter Six

REICH

THE WORKLOAD WAS CRUSHING.

Over the past week, the assignments had tripled—more targets, more names, more blood. The directives from the ENA came faster than we could process them, stacking on top of one another like bodies in a shallow grave.

We didn't ask why.

We never did.

But that didn't make the weight of it any easier to bear.

The pressure mounted with each passing hour, heavy and smothering.

I pushed myself harder, worked longer, because someone had to.

Even as Castor started falling behind.

He was slower now, distracted in ways I hadn't seen in years. I'd catch him staring at his phone too long, running a hand through his hair like it might steady him.

But it didn't.

He was slipping, and I knew why.

He was trying to live a life outside of this.

Something... *more*.

And I was the one who had made that nearly impossible.

I was the one who led him into this life.

I was the one who handed him the blade and told him where to cut.

I promised I'd protect him. Promised I'd shield him from the darkness that had been swallowing me whole since I first ended up with the ENA but promises like that are built on lies.

I hadn't saved him.

I'd dragged him under.

But even now, standing in the fallout of those choices, it was impossible to tell whether there had ever been another path, though at times I feel like I could have carved out another for him.

The guilt gnawed at me.

Every hour. Every minute.

Relentless as a dull knife twisting under the ribs.

I should've been his protector.

Instead, I became his undoing, and yet, he stayed.

He could have left me in this house, this life, in the graveyard of men we used to be, but he didn't.

He stayed, and that haunted me more than anything.

I ran a hand over my face, fingertips digging into my temples like they could dislodge the pressure building behind my skull.

I needed air.

I needed something else—anything else to keep the walls of this house from closing in on me.

I stepped out onto the deck, shoving the door open harder than I meant to as the wind carried it.

The air held the scents of pine and earth and the faint tug of something distant and wild. I inhaled deeply, holding my breath until my chest ached before letting it out slow.

Trying to clear my head and feel something other than this mental fatigue I found myself in.

The valley stretched out below, quiet and still.

From here, I could see everything.

The river carving its restless line through the valley floor. The lake catching the light like a glass reflection and across the water to the field of wildflowers.

Beautiful.

Deceptive.

I hadn't stood out here in days. Maybe even weeks.

But I knew she had.

That woman.

The trespasser.

Every morning, without fail, she emerged from the trees on the far side of the valley.

At first, I thought it was a fluke. A random hiker who'd strayed too far.

Until it happened again. And *again*.

Then eventually, I knew her routine as well as I knew my own.

I'd been watching her.

Not directly—*not yet*.

But through the lenses of the surveillance cameras mounted discreetly in the trees.

Their daily feeds kept on repeat would glow faintly on the monitors in my study when sleep wouldn't come.

I observed her movements.

Kept track of them.

She always paused at the edge of the field, standing still like she was drinking it in, committing the view to memory. Then she would settle down, sitting cross-legged in the grass with a book in hand, thumbing through the pages while the wind tangled her hair. When she finished her books, whether it was reading or writing, she wandered among the wildflowers, plucking a few before tucking them carefully into the pages she brought with her.

She never stayed longer than an hour.

Never deviated from her schedule.

Precise and predictable.

Too predictable.

But there was something about her... something that held me captive.

Her quiet presence. Her solitude.

The way she existed so completely within herself, untouched by the world that had ruined the rest of us. It was a strange kind of comfort and something more.

Something I didn't dare to name.

Something I didn't trust because it was foreign.

I didn't know if it was how she truly was or if it was merely a mask she hid behind.

Though if it was a mask, she wore it damn well.

I found myself waiting for her to appear on the cameras, even when I didn't have the time to see for myself.

Every morning.

I told myself it was curiosity.

Precaution.

A necessary awareness of anyone who might be a threat—anyone who got too close to a body that needed to stay buried, but that wasn't the truth, and I was tired of lying to myself.

I couldn't look away.

Not from her.

Until she would leave my vision.

I would stand there, hands braced against the railing, eyes fixed on the distant line of trees where she would eventually disappear. And when she did, when her silhouette would eventually slip through the forest's edge like a shadow returning home, I knew I'd go back to feeling empty.

"Are you going to talk to her," Castor's voice cut through my thoughts, sharp and unexpected, "or just keep watching like some creep?"

I turned, not startled by his presence but by how long he must have been standing there without me noticing.

He leaned against the opposite side of the railing, one brow arched in lazy amusement, but his eyes were sharp.

Always sharp.

"I'm trying to figure out what she's up to," I replied, defensive without meaning to be. Like I was justifying something I didn't fully understand.

Castor smirked. "Easiest way to do that? Walk down there and ask her."

I didn't answer.

Didn't look at him.

Just stared back at her as she knelt among the flowers, running her fingers over the petals like they were something sacred.

"What's the matter with you?" Castor asked.

There was a cadence in his voice I didn't hear often.

One that sounded like concern.

"Nothing's the matter with me," I snapped.

And he didn't push.

Didn't need to.

The silence that followed between us after said everything.

After a long moment, he sighed, "I've got errands to run before the festival. You're still coming, right?"

I exhaled, slow and tight.

"I can't—"

"You can," he said, cutting me off, "you said you weren't missing Nerv play again. I'm holding you to it." He nudged my shoulder with his before continuing, "I need this. And so do you. One night." He held up his index finger. "One night won't kill you."

I clenched my jaw.

Felt the resistance crumble in my chest.

But the truth was, I wanted to go.

If only to prove I could still do something normal.

If only to feel something else for a little while.

"Fine," I muttered. "I'll be there."

Castor's grin was fast and sharp, satisfaction flashing across his face. "Good," he said. "You won't regret it."

He turned to leave, pausing at the door.

"Oh," he added, almost as an afterthought, "I still haven't found anything on the last Ovitt son. Slippery bastard."

The mention of the Ovitts sent something sharp twisting in my gut.

A familiar burn.

"Keep searching," I said, voice low. Steady. "No one's beyond our reach."

And I meant it.

I would find him.

No matter how long it took.

No matter how far he ran.

Even if I had to drag him from the depths of hell, I'd make him face what he'd done.

This wasn't just a mission.

It never had been.

This was personal.

Harry Ovitt had poisoned everything he touched. A man who treated his daughters like garbage and forged his sons into monsters. I had started with Harry. Severed the head of the snake. Then I took his sons. One by one. Five pieces of shit. Until there was only one left. The youngest and the one who'd managed to stay ahead of me.

For now.

But sooner or later, everyone answers for their sins, and his time was coming.

Castor disappeared back inside the house, leaving me alone with the valley and the ghosts I'd made here.

I turned back to her.

She moved differently today, lingering longer than usual. Her gaze fixed on the sky in a way that felt heavier. Her fingers tightened around the flowers in her hand, as if she was holding on to something she didn't want to lose.

And for the first time since I'd started watching her, I wondered—Was she running toward something or was she running away from something?

The question stuck in my throat.

I exhaled, slow and steady.

But the emptiness she left behind when she finally turned and disappeared into the woods was sharper than I expected.

I realized then that I didn't need the festival for the music.

Or the noise.

Or even the distraction.

I needed to feel something.

Anything other than this.

Chapter Seven

SAGE

As the festival drew closer, something subtle but undeniable shifted within me.

It wasn't a sudden, groundbreaking moment that changed everything. It was gentler than that—a quiet recalibration beneath my skin, like the slow, steady turn of a dial I hadn't even realized was off.

For the first time in months, maybe longer, I felt balanced... like a newfound rhythm took hold.

The days no longer felt like punishments to endure. Instead, I moved through them with an ease that surprised me. There was a fragile equilibrium between my tedious job, the cautious steps toward a social life, and the restless chaos still lurking in my thoughts.

The nightmares still came.

They still clawed at me in my sleep, pulling me back into the dark places I'd desperately tried to bury but their grip was weaker now. Their relentless cycle had softened into background noise, something I'd grown used to.

And numbness?

Numbness was manageable.

I knew avoidance wasn't healthy. Logically, I understood that. A part of me—*the part desperately clinging to sanity*—recognized it clearly. But feeling nothing had become infinitely easier than feeling everything. Exhaustion had long since stolen my ability to choose otherwise.

Yet... beneath layers of disconnection and apathy, a flicker of something vibrant stirred.

Excitement.

The past somehow felt lighter. Its hold around my throat had eased just enough for me to breathe freely again or at least pretend to breathe for a time.

Just enough to let myself want something new—to finally look forward.

Tonight, I wasn't going to drag my shadows around like chains.

Tonight, I would spend a night out with Sam—my best friend, my accidental salvation—and finally meet the elusive boyfriend she'd been raving about for weeks.

And for once in my life...I wasn't dreading it.

When the knock came at my door, I exhaled slowly before opening it.

And for a few seconds, I forgot how to speak.

Sam stood there on my doorstep like a vision conjured from some fever dream of light and color.

Electric and radiant.

She caught the porch light in just the right way, her skin shimmering like moonlight caught in motion. Every small gesture, every tilt of her head, seemed deliberate—mesmerizing in a way I couldn't quite explain.

Her platinum blonde pigtails, each one streaked with vivid aqua and hot pink extensions, flowed like the ribbons, she always wore on her wrists, every time she moved. The butterfly corset she wore clung to her frame, its iridescent sheen shifting between shades of teal and fuchsia, the colors alive with every breath she took. A distressed denim skirt hung low on her hips, her legs bare save for a pair of high boots laced to perfection.

She looked like she belonged under neon lights or in the middle of an EDM parade.

Then there was me.

I glanced down at myself: an old dark concert tee, ripped jeans worn soft with time, and a pair of battered sneakers that had seen better days.

It started to feel like I'd missed a memo for the attire of this event. Like there was an unspoken dress code I hadn't realized existed.

"I hope this is okay," I muttered, my fingers tugging absently at the hem of my shirt. I shifted on my feet, the weight of comparison settling across my shoulders like something physical. "I haven't really had time to go shopping."

Not entirely true.

I could have made time, but I hadn't.

Sam's sharp gaze flickered over me, catching my discomfort instantly. She didn't hesitate.

Didn't give it time for that feeling I had to take root.

"You look fantastic," she said, her tone warm, certain, but then she tilted her head, that familiar gleam lighting up her expression. "But... I think I have a trick or two to make your outfit pop."

And just like that, she was analyzing my apartment, moving with practiced ease like she'd lived here for years instead of just visiting when she felt like it.

She swept through the space, eyes searching, until they landed on the bundle of wildflowers, I'd gathered earlier that morning.

"May I?" she asked, though her grin told me she'd already decided the answer.

There was something in her expression—mischievous, yes, but also reverent.

Like the flowers meant something.

Like she saw something in them I hadn't.

"Sure," I said, stepping closer without really knowing why.

She crossed the room in two strides and unpinned my hair, letting it fall in loose waves around my shoulders.

Her fingers worked quickly, but there was a tenderness in the way she braided the flowers into my hair, like she was weaving in more than petals and stems.

Like she was stitching pieces of my self-esteem back together.

When she finished, she spun me toward the mirror by my door.

The girl who stared back at me was softer somehow.

"Thank you," I murmured.

I couldn't help but catch a glimpse of her—*the other side of me*—staring back from the mirror.

Sage from Sanele.

The shattered version.

But I didn't let Sam see that reflection. That version was mine alone to carry, crystal clear only to me.

The words felt small, but they carried weight. "It's perfect."

Sam beamed. "Makes sense," she said, without missing a beat, "because you're already perfect."

I smiled—real this time, not forced—and she looped her arm through mine.

"Now," she said, practically vibrating with excitement, "let's rock and roll!"

The festival was sprawling. Massive tents and stages rose out of the hills built for chaos and sound.

Four stages.

Four worlds.

Folk and country to the left—acoustic melodies floating on the breeze like smoke. R&B and rap nearby—bass heavy and thrumming, every beat a pulse in my bones. An emerging artists' stage set far off to the right, full of raw voices and electric hope.

And at the center, towering over everything else, the main stage.

The reason we were here.

Point North. Archers. Nerv. Traceless.

Names that had lived in my playlists and headphones for years. The thought of hearing them live sent a thrill racing down my spine.

Sam and I linked arms and plunged into the crowd. Everywhere I looked, people were alive with the kind of reckless joy I'd only ever envied from afar. Neon lights flashed in dizzying arcs against the darkening sky, painting us in streaks of all different colors.

As we made our way to our viewing spot, Sam called out to me over her shoulder, as she let go of my arm, "Hold tight! I'm grabbing drinks. Might even indulge a little on the way back." Then she winked and disappeared into the crush of people.

I stood there, alone but not lonely, knowing my friend would return soon.

My gaze drifted over the crowd, watching strangers laugh and dance, when I felt it.

Eyes on me.

I turned and found him easily.

Sun-kissed skin. Beachy blonde hair. A surfer-boy smile that seemed perfectly at home in this chaos. His aura was relaxed, easy in a way that felt practiced.

He closed the distance between us, moving with the confidence of someone who had never been told no.

"You're absolutely stunning," he said, like it was fact. Like he wasn't used to his words being questioned.

"Thank you," I replied automatically. "That's sweet of you."

He chuckled, a warm, practiced sound.

"You shouldn't be shy," he said, eyes sweeping over me. "Most of these women don't hold a candle to you."

Before I could respond, he held out a drink.

A vibrant purple concoction in a clear plastic cup.

"It's our special mix," he said. "We make it at tailgate parties. Here...it should help."

I hesitated.

My fingers brushed the side of the cup as I took it.

It smelled sweet, fruity, harmless, but something in my gut twisted tight.

My past's ghost whispered in my ear. A lesson I thought I'd already learned. I had promised myself—never again. Never take a drink from a stranger.

But I didn't want to make a scene.

So, I smiled and took the drink.

He grinned like he'd won something. "Enjoy the show," he said. "Maybe I'll see you later."

And then he was gone, swallowed by the crowd.

I stared at the drink in my hand, the condensation slick against my fingers.

Was I being paranoid?

Overly cautious?

I wanted to not worry, to learn to trust again.

So I took a sip.

It tasted fine.

Sweet and harmless, but deep inside I knew better and for some reason I didn't care if I risked it.

Before I could think too hard about the war in my mind, a voice cut through the noise. Low and unyielding. "You shouldn't take what isn't yours."

I turned and found him there.

Dark hair. Eyes like a storm. Inked arms crossed over his chest. His presence was effortless. Commanding. Like the earth shifted to the ground beneath his feet and we all moved to his rhythm.

Before I could react, he reached out. Took the cup from my hand and poured it onto the ground.

"What the hell?" I snapped, adrenaline spiking.

His gaze didn't flicker.

"A warning," he said.

My stomach knotted, as I asked, "What's that supposed to mean?"

"It was spiked."

Flat. *Certain*.

Cold dread slithered down my spine. I tried to process it but before I could, the lights began to blur and the music swelled.

All of a sudden I couldn't focus on what I was supposed to be doing. I could only focus my body towards him, away from the stage, and opposite to where everyone was staring.

He stood behind me. Close, like a wall between me and everything else.

Then his hand was on my arm, gentle but firm. He turned me toward the stage. "You came here to enjoy the music," he said, his breath warm against my ear. "Let's make sure you can."

His proximity should have unsettled me, but it didn't.

For the first time since leaving Sanele, I felt safe, safer than in the fields, even with Sam, and that continued for what I remembered of the rest of the night.

The night blurred.

Music.

Adrenaline.

His presence beside me, steady as stone, and when the crowd surged, when the mosh pit exploded into chaos, I found myself keeping close to him. Clinging to the strange foreign security he was offering me.

I felt alive, until something shifted, the end of the set and a song coming through the speakers that took me back to where I had come from. Back to that night.

A wrongness bloomed in my gut.

Heat pooled behind my eyes.

The world tilted.

And when the darkness swallowed me whole, his arms were the last thing I felt and a familiar song—the last thing I heard, before everything went black.

Chapter Eight

REICH

I NAVIGATED THROUGH THE crowd, my focus sharp, eyes locked on the main stage ahead as if it were the only thing anchoring me to the moment. Bodies swayed and collided around me, a living sea of heat and motion, but I moved through it like a current against the tide—fluid, purposeful, unbothered. I had the advantage of height, and I used it without thinking, slipping between dancers and drinkers with the kind of practiced ease that came from years of navigating far more dangerous places.

Music throbbed through the air like an electrical current, the heavy bass vibrating under my skin until it felt like a second heartbeat—louder, more insistent than my own.

For a brief, reckless moment, I let myself feel it.

The pulse of life outside duty.

Outside blood and obligation.

Up ahead, I spotted Castor. He was leaning against the edge of one of the vendor tents, half-hidden in shadows, a drink in one hand and his attention fixed on someone I couldn't quite see.

I didn't blame him.

This was our one designated night to forget—to escape the weight of everything we carried. A night off from the kill lists and surveillance footage. A night where we could pretend we were nothing more than men with nothing to run from.

I'd never admit it out loud, but I was glad he'd convinced me to come.

Maybe I needed this more than I thought.

As I neared the front row, I stopped, dead in my tracks.

A girl stood directly in my path.

Small and Petite.

Her shoulders were tense, hunched ever so slightly forward like she was bracing herself against something invisible. Her fingers absently twirled a lock of her hair—nervous, distracted.

And then, without warning, she yawned.

The most exaggerated, over-the-top yawn I'd ever seen.

Like she was doing it on purpose, and I smirked before I could stop myself.

But it wasn't the yawn that caught me.

It was her hair.

A mesmerizing blend of deep coffee brown and warm caramel streaks, as rich and wild as something you'd see on a canvas. The ends were dyed a bold green, the color vivid even in the low light, and woven through those thick, wavy strands were wildflowers—tiny blooms in soft whites and muted pale colors.

And then I saw it.

A glint of light catching on the bracelet at her wrist.

A simple thing, but it struck me like a hammer to the ribs.

Recognition was instant.

My trespasser.

It was her.

The woman I'd been watching from the deck.

The woman who walked through my territory as if it belonged to her.

The woman I'd told myself was harmless—until now.

Before I could process these thoughts, a man approached her.

Blonde. Beach-boy swagger.

I knew the type.

Knew the false ease, the practiced charm, the easy grin that didn't quite reach his eyes. I knew exactly who he was, and I knew exactly what was in the drink he offered her.

And when she accepted it without hesitation.

Without any question.

That made my stomach clench hard.

A sharp, brutal twist of heat and something darker had churned in my gut because she had no idea what she'd just done.

No idea the kind of monsters she was inviting into her life and the danger she'd just let that close.

I moved before I had time to think.

Instinct.

No strategy or calculation.

I closed the distance between us in seconds, sliding through the crush of bodies until I was close enough to catch the scent of her—earth and musk, like wildflowers after a rainstorm.

I was close enough that if I reached out, I could touch her.

Close enough to feel the low, steady hum of tension in her spine.

"You shouldn't take what isn't yours."

The words came out sharper than I intended.

Cold. Controlled.

But it got her attention.

She turned, startled, her green eyes flashing as they locked on mine.

Green.

Brilliant and sharp, like new growth cutting through cracked brick.

For a split second, I forgot why I was there.

Forgot what I was doing, until I remembered the cup and took it from her, spilling its content onto the ground. It was then she scowled.

The confusion in her expression twisted fast into defiance, her chin tilting up in a challenge.

"What the hell?" she snapped.

I didn't answer. Didn't give her time to react.

She gasped, jerking back in anger.

Eyes narrowing as her hand flexed by her side.

"A warning," I said.

My tone was cold. Colder than I meant it to be but it was the only way I knew how to keep control.

She straightened in front of me, trying to shake it off, trying to mask the ripple of fear attempting to poke through. "What's that supposed to mean?"

I met her gaze without flinching. "It was spiked."

For a heartbeat, there was nothing.

Then the color drained from her face. Her fingers trembled at her sides. Not from fear of me it seemed—but of the truth settling into her bones.

The crowd around us erupted into cheers as the next set hit the stage, but she didn't move.

She stood frozen, caught between fight and flight.

I shifted closer.

Not to crowd her.

To shield her.

I was close enough to feel the shudder in her breath.

I reached out—slow, deliberate—and slipped an arm around her shoulders. Her body tensed for half a second before she relented, letting me turn her toward the stage.

She fit against me too easily.

Too perfectly, and it unsettled me more then I initially thought it would.

"You came here to enjoy the music," I murmured, my breath brushing her ear, "Let's make sure you can."

For a long moment, she didn't move.

And then... she leaned into me.

A quiet surrender.

Her body softening against mine like it had always been meant to be there.

Her hair brushed against my chin, the wildflowers woven through it brushing my skin like a memory I hadn't lived yet.

Like something alive, wild and untouchable.

And somehow, I felt... calm.

We stood there as the music poured over us, as the crowd surged and swayed like an ocean caught in a storm, but she was still.

She moved only when I did.

Her body syncing with mine as though we shared some rhythm only the two of us could hear.

For a while, I let myself believe the moment could last.

That we were just two people lost in music.

That nothing else mattered, but then the set ended, and that spell seemed to shatter.

She turned towards me; her green eyes clouded with something I couldn't quite name.

Fear.

Confusion.

Maybe both.

Then, without warning, she bolted.

Slipped from my grasp like water through clenched fists.

Vanished into the crush of bodies before I could catch my breath.

I didn't hesitate. Didn't think.

I moved after her, relentless.

The crowd was thick, but I knew how to move through it. I was a predator in their midst, and she was the only thing I saw.

What was she running from?

Me?

Herself?

Then I found her.

Collapsed on the ground, trembling, hands fisted in her hair like she was holding her head together, and Sam, my brother's girlfriend, was already there.

Kneeling beside her, whispering softly, "Are you okay, Sage?" Her voice was gentle, coaxing.

Sage.

Her name was Sage.

Sage shook her head.

"I can't do this," she whispered. "I need to go home."

Sam glanced at me, then at Castor who appeared behind her like he'd always been there.

Such a dutiful little boyfriend.

"I'll drive you," Castor said. Ever the optimist. Like he didn't know the weight of what had just happened.

I didn't argue.

When Sage tried to stand, her legs buckled.

And instinct took over within me again.

I caught her before she hit the ground.

Lifted her into my arms like she weighed nothing.

She melted against me as we all made our way back to my car.

By the time we reached her apartment, she was barely conscious.

I carried her inside.

Laid her down on her bed like something precious I wasn't sure I was meant to touch.

For a moment, her green eyes fluttered open.

She stared up at me, pupils wide, lips parting in a whisper, before she spoke, "You shouldn't take what isn't yours."

A faint smile overtook my lips before sleep claimed her.

I stayed longer than I should have.

Watching her breathe.

Watching the tension fade from her face.

She looked peaceful, but I knew better.

Peace was an illusion.

She was just between storms.

When I finally felt like I had overstayed my welcome, I left.

As soon as I made my way from her door, Castor was waiting outside.

Leaning against the railing, grinning like he'd figured something out before I had.

But I didn't bother with engaging in whatever was reeling around in his brain. I did what I do best instead—deflected.

"I can't believe I missed Nerv again," I muttered.

He clapped me on the shoulder. "Worth it, though, wasn't it?"

I didn't answer.

Just kept walking.

But Sage's green eyes followed me long after I left, and something told me they always would.

Chapter Nine

SAGE

THE NEXT MORNING, I woke to fragments.

Imperfect pieces of memory, floating through the fog in my mind and slipping through my fingers like I was trying to grasp water.

A futile effort.

There was nothing coherent about it.

Just flashes of blurred lights. The echo of bass thudding against my ribs. Lots of hands, eyes, and faces.

But one detail remained sharp.

Sharper than it had any right to be.

The melody.

It threaded itself through the haze, a haunting refrain looping over and over inside my head until I couldn't take it anymore. Until I had to just leave.

It threatened to pull me back to the night everything changed—the second my world had tilted beneath me and never quite righted itself again.

A weight pressed against my chest.

I gasped, struggling against it, but there was no relief.

No breath.

Only the melody but it was somehow also clouded by the memory of him.

His face emerged from the fog, cutting through it like a blade.

A man with dark eyes and what seemed like even darker intentions.

A man who had stood like an immovable force in a world that refused to stay still.

I tried to follow the thread of memory, but it unraveled in my hands.

Flashing lights. The crush of bodies. The pulse of music thudding louder and louder until it felt like my heartbeat.

And then... just him.

"You shouldn't take what isn't yours." His voice was low and unforgiving.

I squeezed my eyes shut, but the memories of him clung to me and started to trickle back.

His hand on mine, strong but careful.

His arm around my shoulders.

The way his presence had steadied me when everything else had spun out of control.

Not even the music could accomplish that.

Not the crowd of people and feeling of community.

Not even Sam, my best friend.

Just him.

A man I hadn't even known until that night and yet, he'd been the only thing holding me together in one of my most fragile moments.

Later, I met Sam at the café before my shift.

I needed normal.

I needed something grounding.

Java-dence was always busy at this hour and there was something comforting about the noise—the soft hiss of the espresso machine, the clatter of cups against saucers, the low hum of conversations blending into white noise. It smelled like roasted beans, vanilla and something warmer, something softer that just drew you into its comforting atmosphere.

I settled into a corner table near the window, where sunlight filtered through the glass in lazy streaks.

My hands wrapped around a mug of black coffee, fingers tight on the ceramic, as if the heat could thaw the cold pit that was heavy in my stomach.

When Sam arrived, I spotted her before she reached me.

There was something different about her this morning.

A glow beneath her skin that gave a quiet radiance that hadn't been there before. She practically floated toward me, all wide eyes and soft smiles.

"You're positively glowing," I said, tilting my head as I watched her slide into the seat across from me.

She grinned, cheeks flushing the prettiest shade of pink. "I guess that's what a great man can do for you."

I smirked, because she was being coy on purpose, probably because I was the one who ruined the whole evening.

"Castor seemed kind," I offered carefully. Then, after a pause, I added with a dry note, "Not that I remember much. Given my embarrassing exit."

Sam laughed, and it was light and easy, giving me a smile that told me I didn't need to worry about what happened. Like it was already water under the bridge in her eyes. "Oh, Sage, don't even worry about that. We all have our moments." She brushed a strand of hair behind her ear, her gaze softening. "And Cas... is amazing. He sees me. Really sees me. I've never felt so... understood. I'm not at all upset we cut the night early to have some time together, uninterrupted." She chuckled, then exhaled, her fingers fiddling with the handle of her cup. "I am just ready to take things to the next level with him."

There was hope in her voice. Vulnerability.

Before I could respond, she waved it off with a little laugh.

"Enough about my guy," she said, mischief returning to her tone. "I want to hear about yours."

I froze for a heartbeat too long. My fingers tensed on the mug.

Why was I so self-conscious?

Why did I suddenly feel like I was caught in a lie I hadn't even told yet?

The time I'd spent with this man from the crowd clung to me.

Half-remembered.

Half-imagined.

Like a dream I couldn't quite wake from.

"There's not much to tell," I said, keeping my voice casual. "He barely spoke to me. And when I woke up, he was gone. I barely remember much from last night."

The words sounded hollow.

Like something was missing.

Like I was leaving something out.

And I was.

The whole drink debacle. I certainly remembered my stupidity on that one.

Sam's expression faltered, just a flicker, but it was there.

She'd expected a different story.

Something exciting and romantic.

Some reckless adventure she could live through me.

"Oh," she said quietly. Then, after a breath, she added, "Well, Castor mentioned his brother. He's not much of a talker. He can be... difficult."

I sat up straighter.

A spark of something sharp lit in my chest.

"His brother?" I repeated the words like they were foreign because they were.

Sam nodded. "Yeah. Reich. That's who was trailing you out of the festival when we found you."

His name landed heavy.

Solid and unforgiving.

Like the man himself.

I hadn't even known his name.

And somehow, hearing it made him more real.

More dangerous.

I murmured it under my breath, my fingers tracing the rim of my coffee cup.

Reich.

Why was this stranger leaving such an impression on me?

"I didn't even know that was his name," I admitted. My voice was quieter than I intended. Almost reverent, and I hated myself for it.

Sam frowned, puzzled. "Really? He didn't talk to you at all?"

I hesitated. "All I remember is him in the crowd. He didn't say much… just seemed like another brooding man but he stuck by me while we were in the crowd."

I kept my voice steady.

But the unease curling in my stomach was harder to ignore.

I didn't tell her about the man with the drink.

Didn't tell her how Reich had appeared from nowhere and taken the danger from my hands before I even understood it was there.

Didn't tell her how I'd felt safer in his arms than I had in years.

That part was too raw.

Too humiliating.

Another mistake to tuck behind my mask.

Sam scoffed and stirred her drink. "So, that's Reich, I guess," she said with a shrug.

But the casual dismissal made something twist in my chest.

Like I was missing something.

Why hadn't Reich said more?

Why had it felt like we shared something deeper than a fleeting moment?

Was I imagining it?

Was I losing my mind?

Sam's voice softened, thoughtful. "He's a mystery. I've met him a dozen times, maybe more. He's polite, but distant. I've never seen him with any other women. Now that I think about it... Cas has never mentioned it either."

I exhaled slowly. "He seemed... standoffish."

It felt like an understatement.

But she nodded, "That doesn't surprise me. The Davidian brothers have always been enigmatic. People in my office, the ones who've lived here their whole lives, they talk about them like they're some kind of local legend." Her voice dropped a little, conspiratorial. "They moved here after their hometown burned down several years ago and apparently have kept to themselves ever since."

The words slid under my skin like cold water.

Burned down?

How much of that was rumor?

How much of it was true?

And why did it make something deep inside me recoil?

I glanced at her.

"How did you even meet Castor?"

She never told me before.

Never volunteered much on their history.

She shrugged, but her smile was tight, "He came to my rescue when I was in a... messy situation."

These brothers seemed good at that.

Rescuing women in messy situations, but they also seemed untouchable, like they belonged to a world we weren't supposed to enter.

Sam's voice broke into my thoughts again. "Reich seemed taken aback by you, though." Her eyes searched mine. "Do you remember anything else from last night?"

I swallowed hard. "I remember meeting him in the crowd," I said slowly. "Staying close to him."

But after that...

Nothing.

Only impressions.

The blur of the music.

The feel of his body shielding mine.

The sense of being anchored when I was falling apart, and I didn't understand why. Why I felt safer with him than I ever had with anyone.

I cleared my throat, forcing something light into my tone. "I probably got dehydrated."

Sam didn't look convinced. Which was probably why she said what she did next. "Take care of yourself, Sage. I'm here for you. Whether you want to dive headfirst into the chaos or step back from it. But maybe try to take it easy for a bit, if you need to."

I smiled, grateful. "I will."

She met my smile. "And I have no problem keeping your ass hydrated from now on."

I laughed softly. "Thank you, Sam. I appreciate that."

Moments later, Castor appeared. The effortless charm radiated from him, like sunlight pouring through cracks. Tousled blonde hair, an easy smile, a kind of magnetism that made people instinctively lean closer.

His gaze flickered between us, amusement flashing behind his eyes. "Trouble in paradise?" he teased.

Sam smiled as I fumbled over my words, suddenly aware of how tangled I was in this Davidian web. "I—I'm sorry if I ruined the evening for everyone.", turning to Castor, "Please tell Reich I'm sorry, too."

Castor chuckled, waving it off. "No need. Reich is... *private*. Don't take it personally."

Private.

No kidding.

But how could I not take it personally?

How could I not feel the pull of him, even now, like a current under the surface?

As the conversation shifted to other things, I couldn't stop the weight of Reich's presence from settling back into me.

He was a puzzle I wasn't sure I should solve.

But despite myself—*I wanted to try*.

Chapter Ten

REICH

I STOOD IN THE kitchen, braced against the counter with one hand while the other lifted the glass I was holding to my lips. I drank greedily, desperate gulps of cold water sliding down my throat as I tried to force the raw ache in my body to fade.

It didn't work.

My chest still burned from the punishing pace I'd set on my run, but the exhaustion wasn't just physical.

It never was.

No amount of distance on the trail could outrun the storm in my head.

I had tried.

Harder today than most.

Each pounding footfall on the cracked pavement had been an act of defiance, an attempt to drown it out—the chaos, the noise, the relentless pull of things I didn't want to feel, but it didn't work.

Nothing did.

Because no matter how far or fast I pushed myself, I couldn't escape her.

Sage.

Her name was an echo, soft and sharp all at once, whispering through the back of my mind even when I told myself I didn't want it there. She was a slow, creeping presence in the edges of my thoughts.

Always there and waiting.

The more I tried to shake her, the more she stayed.

A sharp pang of frustration tore through me, hot and fast. I clenched my jaw, draining the glass before slamming it down on the counter harder than I meant to. The sound cracked through the stillness of the house like a small gunshot.

I forced myself to breathe.

Steady.

In and out.

I needed to get myself under control and then Castor strolled in, radiating that effortless confidence he wore like a tailored suit. His presence filled the room before he even spoke, walking in with that infuriating grin like he didn't have a care in the world.

Like none of this mattered.

"I take it you had a pleasant night of debauchery," I said dryly.

My voice was unimpressed and flat, but Castor thrived on that.

He smirked as he dropped onto one of the barstools, sprawling with the kind of easy arrogance that made people underestimate him.

"Pleasant?" he echoed, lips curling. "No, brother. It was fucking transcendent." He stretched, his joints popping. "Sam and I's time together? It borders on depravity. You ever see two mental patients fuck each other's brains out to the point of temporary sanity?" He winked. "A lobotomy fuck?"

I scoffed as I rolled my eyes, grabbing the pitcher and refilling my glass. My throat was still parched but my patience was drier.

"Always such a poet, Cas."

He chuckled low, the sound vibrating in his chest as he rested his elbows on the counter. "And you?" he asked, tilting his head as if he didn't already know. "How was your night?"

I could have lied.

I should have but what came out was worse. "She wasn't worth it." I sharply said.

A reflex and Castor knew it.

He smiled. That slow, knowing smirk that meant he was about to fuck with me purely for sport. "Really?" He asked.

I turned away, setting my glass in the sink as if that would close the conversation, as if he'd ever make it that easy, but Castor was relentless.

He always had been.

"Since you're not interested," he drawled, "and she seems to be struggling to fit in... maybe she'd like to join Sam and me for a night." He gave a thoughtful pause. "She's easy on the eyes, isn't she?"

The heat that surged through me was instant.

Hot. Irrational. All-consuming.

My hand flexed at my side, fingers curling into a fist so tight I felt the pull of the tendons in my wrist.

He wanted a reaction.

And fuck him, because he was getting one, but I wasn't going to give him the satisfaction of seeing it.

Not all of it.

I forced my voice into indifference. "She's alright."

Flat. Cold. Deceptive.

But it didn't matter.

Castor wasn't fooled.

I started to walk away, needing space.

Needing anything that wasn't this conversation, but Castor wasn't finished. "She was smitten with you, you know?"

I stilled.

Just a fraction of hesitation, but it was enough.

"What makes you say that?" I asked, working to keep my tone even and controlled.

He leaned back, casual as ever. "I had a little chat with Sam and Sage this morning," he said, voice light but his gaze sharp. "Sam's worried. Says Sage keeps asking about you."

I hated when he did this.

Dropped information like breadcrumbs, daring me to follow.

Tossed out scraps of truth like weapons, waiting to see if they hit their mark.

I shouldn't have cared.

I told myself I didn't.

And yet, there it was.

The crack.

The twist deep in my chest that told me I was lying.

I shrugged because I had to. "She's not my concern."

"That's odd," Castor mused, his voice too casual. "Considering she looks an awful lot like that girl we've seen hanging around the back field every morning."

My jaw tightened.

So he'd noticed her too.

"I'll take care of it," I said, the words clipped and final.

They left no room for argument, but Castor wasn't arguing.

He was watching, and that was worse.

"Right," he said slowly, pushing off the stool. "Well, I've got a blondie waiting who needs some taking care of."

He made it sound casual, but as he moved toward the door, I stepped into his path.

Blocking it.

The air between us shifted—sharp and tense.

"Whatever you do," I said, my voice low and even, "make sure this girl doesn't mess with our work."

For the first time in hours, Castor's grin faded. His expression hardened. Eyes locked on mine, cool and calculating, "I could say the same to you, brother."

A silent beat passed between us.

An understanding.

A warning.

Then he left, and I was alone again, but not for long.

Because every morning after my run, I still found myself standing on the deck.

Watching her.

Sage.

She didn't move through the field like she was passing through.

She moved like she belonged to it. Like the earth had claimed her long before she stepped foot on it. And I—I started to feel like I was the trespasser. Like I didn't belong here.

I told myself to look away.

I told myself this was nothing, but it didn't shake the pull of her, that was so damn magnetic and irresistible.

Every day it seemed to get worse.

And after meeting her, and getting so close, my desire for her was like a wildfire, spreading unchecked.

And I wasn't sure how much longer I could contain it.

Fuck.

Castor returned late that night, but his usual confident demeanor was gone, like it had been stripped away.

He was grim when he walked through the door, dropping his laptop bag and a thick file onto the coffee table with a heavy thud.

I didn't move and didn't speak.

Just waited.

"I found something," he said.

His voice was quieter than I liked. "You're not going to like it," he continued.

I exhaled slowly.

"I don't like most things," I muttered. "What is it?"

He didn't answer. Just flipped open his laptop and started navigating.

His fingers were quick and precise, and when the screen loaded, I felt the weight of what was coming settle deep in my gut.

A dark web site.

One of the worst.

A twisted marketplace.

A place where people were bought, sold and hunted.

Bounties. Contracts. Blood for hire.

Castor clicked a listing.

The page loaded slowly.

And then—*her*.

Sage.

Her photo stared back at me.

Frozen. Unaware. Exposed.

NAME: Sage Holquinn

AGE: 27

LAST SEEN: Sanele

HUNTING FEE: Negotiable

Every detail of her life was laid bare.

Her car. License plate. Copies of her identification.

Her life reduced to data points on a screen.

I skimmed further, pulse pounding in my ears.

DESCRIPTION OF JOB: She's unstable. She ran away. Needs to be returned. Breathing preferred, but not necessary.
USER: K.O. King

The world around me went silent.

The weight of recognition hit me like a punch to the gut.

K.O. King.

The initials, K.O.

Klay Ovitt.

The man we'd been hunting.

My hand gripped the edge of the table, turning my knuckles white.

Why her?

"What do you want to do?" Castor asked, watching me.

The answer formed before he finished the question.

A perfect, terrible clarity.

A slow grin pulled at my mouth as I met his gaze. "This couldn't have worked out better if we'd planned it."

Castor blinked, "What the hell are you talking about?"

I exhaled. Steady. "We use her."

His expression darkened. "Use her?"

"She's our bait," I said, leaning forward. "To get to Klay."

Castor's disbelief hardened into something colder. "You're insane."

"Maybe," I allowed. My grin widened. "But better us than some other lunatic."

I let the words settle and watched the realization click into place.

"We'll keep her safe," I said, my voice dropping lower. "Relatively speaking."

Castor exhaled sharply. "You're playing a dangerous game, brother."

I smirked, but it didn't reach my eyes. "Good."

I already knew what I was doing, and I didn't care.

Because I had just found my way to her.

She was mine now.

Even if she didn't know it yet.

Chapter Eleven

SAGE

My routine had spiraled completely out of control since the festival.

Everything I'd built—the carefully ordered days, the rituals that once kept me grounded—was unraveling like frayed threads slipping through my fingers.

I'd tried. I really had.

I'd taken Sam's advice. Told myself to slow down. Take it easy. Breathe.

But the longing inside me refused to loosen its grip. It only sank deeper, winding itself through every thought, filling up the hollow spaces I had fought so hard to keep empty.

And it wasn't restlessness.

Not really.

It was sharper than that.

A gnawing ache for something more.

More than routine.

More than the hollow predictability I'd convinced myself was safety and now, I was starting to see it for what it was.

I hadn't been protecting myself.

I'd been hiding.

Mistaking comfort for stability.

Mistaking numbness for peace.

I'd carved out this careful version of myself and locked myself inside it. Told myself I needed control. That surviving was enough.

But I was wrong and all I could feel was the burn of that realization.

The irony of it.

This life I thought I'd built to keep me safe had become a prison.

And I was the one holding the key.

Me.

I didn't know why I did that.

Why I'd spent so long folding myself into the smallest version of who I was.

Especially when I had always dreamed of something bigger.

Wilder.

Outside these walls of normalcy. Even when it was dangerous.

Even when it hurt.

I wanted a life with purpose. To wake up with a fire I couldn't smother. A hunger that pulled me toward something, instead of always running away.

But since I'd moved here, that dream had thinned into a mirage.

Always close enough to see.

Never close enough to touch.

At the festival, just for a moment, I thought I felt it.

That pulse of possibility.

The music in the air, the blur of lights, the way strangers laughed like they belonged to each other.

I thought maybe I could belong too.

But the feeling slipped through me like smoke, and I'd been chasing it ever since.

I kept hoping it would find me.

That one day, it would just... happen.

That something would click into place and make it all make sense.

But hope like that is dangerous.

It keeps you waiting.

And the longer I waited, the heavier the ache became.

I was stuck.

Caught between the safety of predictability and the pull of something wild I couldn't name.

And maybe the question wasn't whether I was ready.

Maybe the question was:

What was I still so afraid of?

That afternoon, the sun hung low on the horizon. Dragging the day out, stretching the light thin before the dark came. The sky was bruised with color—soft golds bleeding into purples and oranges.

I watched it from my window for too long.

Fingers restless.

Heart pounding in my ears, and then I moved, because if I didn't, I would implode.

I followed the pull.

Out the door. Through the trees. To the field.

The air buzzed with life.

Fireflies floated around me, tiny stars flickering in the growing dark.

Their light was delicate, faint and beautiful, like something that could easily be dimmed.

I took a breath, letting it expand in my lungs.

For a moment, the world slowed.

I smiled softly, my fingers brushing the tops of the wildflowers as I passed.

I had never come to the field this late.

Never this close to night, but I was glad I did.

It wasn't part of my routine and that was the point.

The risk made me feel alive.

The danger of the woods at night—

The memories it stirred—

They didn't scare me in the same way anymore.

They made me feel something and I was tired of feeling nothing for so long.

I let myself wander deeper.

Drawn to the flowers swaying in the wind, their colors vivid even in the low nightlight.

They stretched toward me like an invitation.

I bent down, gathering them slowly.

Gentle and careful, as if I was afraid that they might vanish if I wasn't.

The sound of crickets filled the air.

Soft and constant, like a lullaby spun from the hush between breaths.

I closed my eyes. Let myself just be there.

Let myself exist.

But it was only for a brief moment, because suddenly I felt like I wasn't alone like I thought I was.

I could feel it, even though I couldn't quite see it yet.

The unmistakable weight of being watched.

The air started to shift.

Colder and Thicker.

And I knew.

I didn't need to turn.

I knew it was him coming from behind me.

Reich.

A towering silhouette framed in twilight.

And every nerve in my body lit up.

My breath hitched in my throat.

I froze, but not from fear, from something else.

Something that didn't make sense to me.

He closed the distance between us slowly.

Deliberate steps. Giving me time to run. To step away.

But it was almost as if he knew I wouldn't.

And I knew it too.

My pulse raced in anticipation; each beat harder than the last as my peripheral caught his hand that lifted from behind me.

Before I could react, fingers ghosted along the frame of my cheek.

Feather-light.

I leaned in, breath catching, even as I told myself not to.

And I let his touch drift lower.

Down the curve of my arm over its skin that prickled in response to him.

His hands continued to drift, as I stood frozen, while his fingertips brushed the bouquet of wildflowers I had in my hands.

He held them with me for what felt like a heartbeat too long.

Like he was weighing its worth or mine.

He leaned in.

His breath warm against my ear and his voice low and commanding, "You shouldn't take what isn't yours."

The words hit me hard causing a shiver to chase itself down my spine.

Not just because of what he said.

But because he was here.

In this field.

At this time.

Why?

Then it slammed into me hard.

I was trespassing.

I tried to save face when the realization hit, "I—" I stammered.

But his voice cut through me, as sharp as a fresh blade. "Stay away, Sage."

He said my name like it meant something.

Like it burned his tongue.

But his hand on mine told a different story.

A little too tight and too reluctant to let go.

"I didn't know," I whispered. "I thought this was part of the preserve. The flowers... they're beautiful. I wasn't trying to—"

"Leave."

Cold. Final.

I swallowed hard. "Why are you being like this?"

My voice was thin. Barely holding. "I'm just trying to explain—"

"Because I don't care."

His voice— his voice cut deeper than I expected.

I sucked in a sharp breath, the bouquet trembling in my hands.

I gripped it tighter like it could anchor me.

Like it could hold me together but then—he caught my jaw.

Fingers strong, steady, bringing my face to his. Firm. Unyielding.

My pulse skipped as his eyes darkened, trapping me there and locking me in place.

His other hand drifted lower, brushing my wrist.

Barely a touch. Too light to be restraint but far too deliberate to ignore.

He was testing me.

So, I lifted my chin.

Refusing to shrink away.

Refusing to break.

His grip tightened, just enough to make me gasp.

"You need to leave," he said. "I'm not asking."

A seriousness laced within his tone and that told me he wasn't playing games.

I should have run right then, but I didn't, because I needed to have the final say.

I stood there, locked in his storm, unable to pull away.

I didn't want to leave.

I wanted to stand my ground and call his bluff.

Instead, I exhaled shakily, and whispered, "Be careful what you ask for, Reich."

His name on my lips like it was something forbidden.

His jaw clenched with a smirk across his face and fingers flexing at his sides.

Then— Softer. Rougher, he replied, "You too, Sage."

He loosened his grip at that point and when the space between us shattered, I ran.

The bouquet slipped from my fingers in the process.

Forgotten.

When I looked back, he was gone, everything how it was, except the wildflowers that now scattered over the field like broken pieces of myself left behind.

By the time I reached home, my lungs burned.

My heart thundered, but it wasn't fear.

It was something else.

Something I couldn't name.

I collapsed onto my bed, staring at the ceiling.

His voice still echoed in my mind.

His touch still burned on my skin.

And I hated how much I cared that it was there.

How I didn't want it to go away, and how much I wanted more.

I told myself I wouldn't go back.

I wouldn't be that girl. I wouldn't be reckless.

Then, I couldn't stop remembering.

His voice. His hands. The look in his eyes.

Like he was destined to break me or save me.

Maybe both.

I should be afraid. I should stay away.

But fear and desire?

They live too close together inside me, and I didn't want to run.

I wanted him to chase me.

Chapter Twelve

REICH

THE REVELATIONS FROM THE night before with Castor twisted my thoughts into knots, each one pulling tighter, amplifying the confusion already simmering just beneath the surface of everything I thought I knew.

Sage.

She was a mystery since the first day she showed up on my field.

An equation I couldn't solve, no matter how many times I tried to work through the variables.

But now?

Now, she was tangled in something much bigger than I had expected.

Her connection to Klay changed everything.

It shifted the entire foundation under my feet.

What was she running from?

And more importantly—why did it lead her to me?

I clenched my teeth as I rolled up my sleeves.

The buttons popped free with sharp snaps, like breaking threads.

My slacks were stained, dirt clinging to my knees, but I didn't care.

Not tonight.

Not now.

I drove the shovel into the dirt again, the metal biting deep into the earth with a sound that was all too familiar.

A hollow, wet scrape.

The kind of sound that got under your skin if you thought about it too long.

The sorry bastard lying on the ground next to me had bled all over my shirt hours ago.

Another mess.

Another name checked off the list.

The red stain had already dried to a dark rust at the sleeves.

I should have changed before now.

I should have taken a hot shower, stripped away the blood and grime, burned the evidence like I always did, but I hadn't.

I'd been too irritated.

Too restless.

Too focused on finishing the job and getting the body in the ground before the weight of everything pressed in too tight.

But it was already pressing in, and the pressure hadn't let up.

The anger. The exhaustion. The endless fucking questions.

They piled up inside me like a sickness I couldn't purge no matter how deep I dug.

I paused for a moment, staring at the line of trees ahead.

My grip on the shovel tightened, the handle slick with sweat.

I was shaking.

Not from the work.

From everything else. From how I ended up in this fucking mess in the first place.

They say life is all about your choices.

But not for all of us.

Some of us were born into losing hands and told to play them anyway.

Some of us didn't get to choose anything.

And if you'd seen what I've seen, you'd understand.

The innocent ones stripped of their dignity.

The futures stolen right out of their hands.

The screams...the ones from children are what haunt me the most.

Their voices are sharp, unrelenting echoes that slice and rip through my nights like broken glass on thin sheets.

Some sounds you can't unhear, but I tried to bury those thoughts the same way I buried these sick men.

Deep.

Forcefully.

Making sure they never claw their way back up to find any form of forgiveness.

Not like forgiveness or salvation exists for men like this, or hell even men like me.

I had stopped believing in that a long time ago.

The day Castor and I were branded like cattle and handed over to the ENA like property.

We were trained, broken, rebuilt into something they felt useful.

Weapons that didn't ask questions, didn't feel and didn't think beyond the job.

We weren't men anymore.

We were tools and yet... some part of me still asked how it got to this.

When exactly had I stopped fighting back?

When had survival turned into servitude?

My thoughts were interrupted when I sensed it, a flicker at the edge of the field.

I stilled.

The shift was subtle, but I knew how to feel for it.

The way the air changed.

The quiet strain in the silence that didn't belong.

I yanked out my earbuds, the music cutting off instantly.

Suddenly, everything around me felt too loud.

The distant hum of insects.

The wind rustling through the dry grass.

Something wasn't right.

I slid my hand to the side holster, fingers wrapping around the cool grip of my gun.

Slow. Silent.

I moved into the shadows of the trees, letting them swallow me in their dark coverage.

Step by step, I closed the distance.

My pulse remained steady.

I had done this more times than I could count.

Hunting. Tracking. Finding. Ending.

And then I saw her.

Sage.

Standing at the edge of the tree line, her hair catching the faint gleam of moonlight, falling in loose waves down her back.

That beautiful shimmer of green at the tips.

The wind tugged at it gently, making it sway like sea grass underwater.

She was so still, but not in fear.

In knowing, like she could sense what I was feeling.

Like she was waiting for me.

I checked my watch.

9:11 PM.

Too late. Too dangerous.

She shouldn't be here.

Was this a setup? Had Klay already found her? Had he sent her back to lure me in?

Panic clawed at my ribs, but I forced it down.

I was going to take her hostage. Get answers from her eventually.

I had a plan. A strategy that was on my terms.

Not like this.

I took another step forward, my boots whispering over dead leaves.

Deliberate. Unhurried.

She didn't move.

Didn't turn. but I saw something else.

The rise and fall of her shoulders.

The tension melting away as I approached, like she knew I was there, and wasn't afraid.

Something about that undid me.

Fear made people tense and brace for impact.

But Sage—she softened.

She submitted to the fear, but the fight was still there.

Beneath the surface.

I recognized it. I knew it too well.

It was what made people dangerous. It was what made me dangerous.

My fingers twitched at my sides.

I needed to stay in control. I needed to walk away.

But I didn't.

I stepped closer.

So close I could feel the warmth radiating off her skin.

I told myself not to touch her, and then I did anyway.

A single stroke down her right side.

Gliding from her shoulder to her hand, slow and deliberate.

Her skin was smooth like a petal beneath my fingertips, and I couldn't help but let my hand linger longer than I should have.

Her breath caught, but she didn't pull away.

Didn't flinch as I leaned in.

Close enough for my breath to graze the curve of her neck.

Close enough to feel the shudder ripple through her.

I let my lips brush the rim of her ear. "You shouldn't take what isn't yours."

She tensed. A tight, coiled reaction, but she didn't speak.

Not right away.

And then— "I—" Her voice was faint and unsteady.

Unsteady.

She started to turn toward me, but my hand shot up, catching her jaw and stopping her.

Not rough, but unyielding. "Stay away, Sage."

"I didn't know," she murmured, her voice stumbling. "I thought this was part of the preserve. The flowers... they're so beautiful... I wasn't trying to take anything or harm anything—"

"Leave." Cold and final. One word because I didn't know how much I would be able to muster out without losing control.

She hesitated. Her voice trembled when she spoke again. "Why are you being like this? I'm just trying to explain—"

And there it was.

The sincerity.

It cut through me like a blade and for a split second, I hated myself.

Hated the man I'd become, but I knew couldn't afford softness.

Not with her and especially not now in my blood-soaked clothes.

I let the cruelty seep into my tone. "Because I don't care."

Her breath hitched.

Her eyes flickered—hurt, then guarded.

She covered it quickly. Too quickly.

Then— "I'm sorry." Soft. Broken in a way that made me want to destroy something.

I exhaled, as the war started to rage inside me.

"You need to leave," I said. "I'm not asking."

She swallowed hard.

Her gaze held mine for a moment longer than it should have.

She didn't want to leave.

I knew it. She knew I knew it. She could say it.

Instead, she exhaled shakily. Her voice a whisper. "Be careful what you ask for, Reich."

My name in her mouth.

Like a fucking prayer or a goddamn curse.

It slammed into me harder than I expected.

A muscle ticked in my jaw. I clenched my fists at my sides, grounding myself. Then, rougher I responded— "You too, Sage."

I let her go and her eyes widened, and for a second, something passed between us.

Something raw and undeniable.

And then— she broke.

Her face crumbled as she turned and ran.

Her footsteps quick and light as they faded into the darkness.

I stood there, breathing hard as I rubbed a hand down my face.

This wasn't how I planned it.

I wanted control and strategy.

Not this.

Not her slipping through my fingers before I was ready.

I stared at the ground where she'd stood.

At the flowers she'd dropped, that were scattered like offerings, or perhaps, warnings.

Did she really not know this was private property?

Did she really not understand what she'd walked into?

I wanted to believe her. I wanted to trust what sounded like honesty in her voice and the purity she somehow portrayed in those green eyes, but I couldn't.

Not with Klay still out there, and not with her name tied to his.

I turned back toward the trees.

Forcing my breathing to even out.

One way or another, she would be under my roof soon enough.

And when that time came— I would get my answers.

But for now?

I needed to send a stronger message.

Something that would break her spirit just enough to keep her away, until I was ready to claim her.

Because when I did... there would be no running.

Chapter Thirteen

SAGE

"*P*LEASE, KLAY... JUST TAKE *me home.*"

My voice cracked on the last word, betraying me more than I wanted it to.

I hated the tremble in it.

The desperation.

I hated giving him even that.

But I was past pride.

I was pleading now, my gaze lifted to his in the hope—no, the need—that he'd see what was written across my face.

How badly I needed to leave.

How wrong this felt.

But he didn't see.

Or maybe he did.

And didn't care.

Aaron—one of Klay's old college friends, the kind of man who wore his cruelty like a badge of honor—stepped closer.

His breath was heavy with stale beer and something sour. The kind of smell that turned your stomach, that couldn't scrub off no matter how hard you tried.

His grin stretched wide and leering, sharp with mockery. "Aw, come on, Sage," he drawled, voice low and sticky, like something rotting. "No need to be scared. Things were just getting good."

Laughter followed his words.

It rippled through the group in jagged waves.

Low. Mean. Predatory.

I wasn't afraid of spending time with Klay's friends.

Not at first.

In the beginning, they'd seemed like any group of guys—loud, reckless, stupid.

But it was the drinking.

It was always the drinking that changed them.

The way it blurred the line between conversation and something darker.

When their jokes dug deeper and their smiles twisted.

When they stopped seeing me as Klay's girlfriend, and started seeing me as something else.

Something to be looked at.

Played with.

Passed around.

Most nights, I forced myself to smile.

I let their jabs roll off my shoulders, pretending they didn't stick, pretending I didn't feel them burrow into my skin.

But tonight was different.

Their words were sharper and hungrier.

Their stares made my skin crawl.

And deep in my gut, something primal twisted, cold and certain.

I had to get out.

But Klay wouldn't move.

He stood, posture as casual as ever, with his one arm slung lazily over the back of his bike, watching me.

Not watching them.

Me.

Like this was a test I was failing.

I swallowed, my throat dry, as panic crawled up the back of my spine, winding itself around my ribs and squeezing tight.

I couldn't breathe.

I couldn't think.

And all I could think of was my father.

How I promised him to check in. Hours ago.

The guilt crashed through me like a wave breaking over brittle glass.

What if something happened?

What if he was waiting?

Needing me?

He was all I had left.

The only person who loved me without condition.

The only reason I kept trying.

I blinked hard, but it was already too late.

The tears slipped free before I could stop them.

One.

Then another.

Warm tracks sliding down my cheeks as I tried—and failed—to hold it together.

And Klay saw.

His gaze sharpened as it snapped to my face, narrowing.

Displeasure carved harsh lines into his features.

I had embarrassed him.

I had made a scene.

And Klay hated scenes he didn't control.

"Are you seriously crying right now?" His voice was sharp, cutting through the night like a blade, loud enough for the others to hear.

He wanted them to hear.

He wanted them to watch.

Their laughter swelled, cruel and raucous, carrying on the smoke-thick air.

It coiled around me, tightening like rope.

I could feel their eyes flicking between us.

Watching him discipline me like a child.

Like a dog.

I dropped my gaze to the cracked pavement as the humiliation burned through me, scalding from the inside out.

I wanted to shrink into nothing.

Vanish.

Klay exhaled sharply, as if he was the one burdened by all this, turning his back to me as he made the signal to leave, "Let's go," he snapped.

He didn't wait to see if I followed.

Didn't offer his hand.

Didn't look back, he just turned toward his back preparing to leave as the others followed suit.

Their laughter turning into jeers now.

Low comments traded between them as they mounted their bikes, engines roaring to life one by one.

Klay was the last to start his.

He sat there astride it, his posture loose and easy, like he had all the time in the world.

But his eyes were on me.

Waiting.

I stumbled forward, panic swelling so big in my chest I couldn't contain it.

He was going to leave me here.

Stranded.

Alone.

Miles from home.

He knew I didn't even have my car because he insisted that I ride with him.

"Klay," I called out, my voice breaking on his name.

It barely cut through the roar of the engines.

"I'm sorry," I said, the words choking out of me.

Tears blurred my vision, hot and helpless, as I repeated, "I'm sorry."

His head tilted, mock-considering.

"I'm sorry you don't know how to have a good time," he said, voice bored. "But I do." His smirk deepened. "And I will."

And then—then came the words that hollowed me out, "So go run home to your daddy and cry to him about your problems."

It hit harder than anything they'd said all night.

Because he knew.

He knew what that would do to me.

But he didn't care.

The engines revved, a wall of sound that rattled my bones.

And then—they started to take off.

Tires screeching and headlights cutting through the night.

One by one, they disappeared into the dark.

But Klay stayed. At least, for a moment.

And then he twisted the throttle, engine growling low.

I took a step forward, reaching out.

"I don't have a car," I said, my voice small. Fractured.

Klay tapped the gas.

"Hmm," he hummed. "How unfortunate."

Silence stretched between us.

And then— "Get on." His voice was flat.

Emotionless.

Like I was an afterthought.

I climbed on the back of his bike because I had no other choice.

My hands hovered before I let them settle on his waist.

Loose. Tentative.

Like I might slip off and not care if I did.

The ride home was hell.

He rode too fast. Cutting across lanes. Ignoring lights. Like he wanted to scare me or perhaps, even kill me.

And maybe it was both.

By the time we pulled up in front of my apartment, my hands were numb from gripping the seat too tightly.

He climbed off the bike, and as I shifted to follow suit, his hand shot out, grabbing me roughly by the collar of my jacket.

I choked on a startled gasp as he dragged me forward, pulling me inches from his face and trapping me tightly between himself and the bike. His breath was cold, but his eyes were colder.

Dead.

He stared at me in heavy silence, like he was weighing something.

Me.

My worth.

Then, abruptly, he shoved me backward.

Hard.

My foot twisted beneath me as I collided painfully into the side of the bike. Metal bit into flesh, and a searing heat exploded across the back of my calf.

I gasped sharply, but the pain was already etched deep into my skin.

The exhaust pipe.

Still burning from the ride.

It hit fast—white-hot and sharp.

I sucked in air that felt like broken glass.

Klay didn't move.

Didn't flinch.

He just watched.

Silent and expressionless.

Like this was punishment.

Or a lesson.

Finally, he let go and I crumpled.

My knees hit the pavement, scraping raw as my hands fumbled for balance but found nothing but concrete.

His voice was colder than the air, low and lethal, "Don't ever disrespect me and my friends again."

And then he was gone.

The engine roared, drowning out everything else.

Until there was nothing.

No sound.

No movement.

Just me.

Slumped on the pavement. Alone.

With my hand pressed against my leg.

The skin was blistered already, starting to peel.

It hurt.

Fuck, it hurt so bad.

But not as much as the truth settling in my chest that I had let this happen.

And I didn't know how to stop it.

I stared down at my burned leg.

At the tremble in my hands.

And I realized— I wasn't sure who I was anymore.

And worse? I wasn't sure I cared.

Because he made me believe this was all I deserved.

As a child, I had always known nightmares weren't real.

No monsters lurked under my bed.

No clawed hands would come reaching from the shadows of my closet.

No sharp-toothed boogeyman waiting to devour me if I left my foot dangling off the mattress for too long.

I knew better.

And that knowledge had kept me calm when the other kids screamed in terror at the dark.

I would lie there, tucked neatly beneath my blanket, listening to the silence, convinced it made me braver.

Safe.

But then I grew up.

And the lines between nightmares and memories blurred into something I couldn't untangle.

The monsters had names.

And faces.

And hands.

And they didn't vanish when the morning came.

They stayed, lingering constantly, and they were worse than anything I'd ever imagined hiding in the dark.

I woke with a start, a sharp gasp tearing from my throat like it had been locked in there for days.

My body was heavy— anchored by something invisible, something suffocating.

Weighted with exhaustion I couldn't sleep off.

For a long moment, I laid there, staring at the ceiling, disoriented, heart racing, my mind trying to unscramble where I was.

Who I was.

I blinked slowly, trying to piece things together and attempting to breathe.

But then—I saw something strange.

Wildflowers.

A small cluster sat neatly on my nightstand.

Vivid against the muted grays of my apartment.

Too bright.

Too alive.

They shouldn't have been here.

I hadn't picked them.

I hadn't brought them in.

My pulse stuttered.

I sat up, slow and stiff, as if moving too fast might shatter the fragile grip I had on reality.

For a second, I told myself it was fine.

Maybe I had left them there.

Maybe I was too tired to remember.

But then I turned my head.

And I saw them.

Everywhere.

Jars. Vases. Cups.

Overflowing with blooms.

Tucked into the spaces between books on the shelf.

Delicate petals spread like tiny, vibrant fingerprints all over my apartment.

I stared.

Frozen.

My heart hammered harder, each beat echoing in my skull.

I was too confused to move and could barely think.

They were beautiful.

And somehow that was what made it worse.

There was something devastating in their beauty.

A deep, hollow sadness settling in my chest as I reached out with shaking fingers and touched a single petal.

Soft. Velvety. Alive.

But not for long.

No matter how delicate. No matter how perfect.

They would wilt and fade, withering into nothing.

Just like everything else.

Just like me.

And that was when it clicked.

The flowers.

I knew where they were from. I had seen them before. Felt them under my fingers and breathed them in.

Reich's field.

My breath caught in my throat, sharp and sudden, as if someone had jammed a fist into my ribcage.

Panic clawed its way up, tight and choking, coiling like barbed wire around my lungs.

I scanned the apartment again, this time seeing the arrangement for what it was.

A message.

I ran my hands through my hair, the uncertainty setting deeper.

How had he gotten in?

I had no spare keys.

No broken windows.

No open doors.

There was no sign of a break-in.

Nothing out of place—except everything somehow was.

And why?

Why would he do this?

He didn't care.

That's what he told me.

What he made sure I believed.

But these flowers...they seemed to tell a different story.

Or maybe they didn't.

Maybe they were just another kind of warning.

A thousand questions crashed through me, splintering into pieces too sharp to hold.

I couldn't stay here.

I couldn't breathe.

I needed answers.

Or maybe I just needed to know if I was losing my mind.

So, I got dressed and I didn't think. Didn't hesitate.

I just ran back to the field.

The second my feet hit the dirt path, I felt it.

That twisting sense of inevitability.

Like I'd stepped into a current I couldn't fight, and it was about to pull me somewhere dark.

By the time I reached the field, my chest was heaving.

Sweat beaded at my hairline and my pulse thudded hard against the base of my throat.

And then—I stopped.

The field.

The one that had once been alive.

Lush.

Untamed.

It was gone.

What was left was ruin.

The flowers had been ripped from the earth.

Uprooted and destroyed.

The soil churned into something raw and exposed.

A wound carved deep into the land itself.

Broken stems and crushed petals lay scattered like corpses across the dirt.

Forgotten and discarded.

Their bright colors faded to bruises in the dying light.

I swallowed hard, my breath came in shallow gasps, and I couldn't make them slow. Couldn't make myself move.

This wasn't just a field anymore.

It was a marker.

A grave with a message carved into the earth itself.

He was stripping it away.

Like he was slowly stripping me away.

Layer by layer.

Until there was nothing left.

The sun bled out as I stood there, streaking the sky in deep reds and purples.

Everything was silent.

Too silent.

The kind of stillness that made your skin crawl.

And then there it was— "Wildflower." His voice cut through the quiet like a knife, sharp and intimate, sliding under my skin.

I froze, as a shiver crawled up my spine.

I turned slowly to see him there.

Reich.

Standing in the ruins.

His dark gaze held mine, unforgiving, like he could see every thought I didn't want him to.

"Were the flowers I gave you not enough?" His voice was soft.

A taunting whisper.

Like we shared something private and dangerous.

I exhaled, but it shuddered on the way out. "Why did you do it? Ruin your field?"

His smirk deepened, slow and deliberate, and something cold unfurled in my stomach. "My field is fine. The flowers were just a departing gift—for staying off my property."

A beat of silence.

Then his head tilted, like a predator curious about its prey, "But did you stay away?"

His voice was a hook, sharp and gleaming.

My stomach dropped.

I didn't and he knew it.

We both did.

He stepped forward, slow, measured.

His presence loomed over me, heavier with every inch he closed.

I told myself that I wanted to move but I didn't.

I let him lean in, close enough for his breath to ghost over my skin.

It was warm and comforting but something about his voice made me shiver. "Exactly."

The word was a verdict.

And I had already been sentenced.

His thumb brushed across my lower lip, slow and possessive.

A silent challenge.

His breath fanned across my skin, stirring something reckless inside me.

Something I hated and yet, still wanted.

"You're dangerous," I whispered. It slipped out before I could stop it.

His smirk was slow, knowing. "And yet, you're still here."

Then his hand closed around my throat.

Firm.

Measured.

Not enough to hurt.

But enough to remind me who was in control.

His lips grazed my ear, his voice rough and low, "You don't like to listen, do you?"

My body betrayed me as I arched toward him—just slightly.

But it was enough to make me hate myself for it and want more.

His fingers trailed down my spine, leaving fire in their wake. "You act like you don't want this," he murmured, dark amusement curling in his tone. "But you keep coming back."

A tremor rolled through me as I spoke, voice barely steady.

"Maybe I'm just bad at staying away."

His smile widened. "Or maybe you don't want to," he said, teasing, as his hand trailed down toward my fingertips.

The soft brush of his skin sent shivers spiraling through me, heat pooling low between my thighs—thick and aching with something I didn't want to name.

I tried to pull away. He only pulled me closer, his grip tightening with intent.

"You like this, don't you?" he asked, smirking, amusement curling at the corners of his mouth.

"You're an ass, Reich." The words were flimsy armor—thin but necessary.

I needed something to hold onto. Something to keep me from closing the space between us.

He saw it. He *felt* it. And he fed on it.

Then his voice dropped, low and sharp. "Do us both a favor and run. We both know you're relatively good at that."

He released me without warning.

I froze as his words sliced clean through me, leaving something hollow in their wake. His gaze flicked down to the ruined patch of earth between us, like it held the damage neither of us dared name.

The torn flowers.

The broken nothingness that remained from the night prior.

"There's nothing here for you anymore." He finished.

The truth behind it hit harder than any physical blow.

I swallowed, my throat tight, raw.

I glanced at the barren ground and then back at him.

His expression was hollow.

Empty.

Like the field.

And like me.

But he was right.

There was nothing left here.

And I wasn't sure if I wanted to run or if I wanted to stay long enough to see what else he could destroy.

Even if it was me.

But something whispered inside that he wouldn't. No matter how much I may have wanted him to.

So, I turned and slowly made my way back, leaving him standing in the field behind me.

Chapter Fourteen

REICH

That was too close. Too damn close.

She came back—just like I knew she would.

Predictable. Relentless.

But still, I had hoped—hoped that this time, she wouldn't.

Not because I didn't want to see her.

Not because I didn't crave her nearness with a hunger that left me raw and restless.

But because every time she did, I made it worse.

Every time she stepped into my space, my world, I lost another piece of the control I'd spent years building.

And every time I pushed her away, every time I drove another splinter into her trust; I could feel something cracking beneath the surface.

In her and in me.

And when it finally broke, I wasn't sure who would survive it.

I didn't want to hurt her.

But it was a lie I told myself to stay sane.

Because I already was.

Every cold word.

Every hollow stare.

Every brutal dismissal.

It wasn't just driving her away—it was dismantling her.

And somewhere deep in the rotted core of me, I knew I was setting the stage for something I couldn't undo.

I was making her brittle and fragile.

Breaking her down into something I could hold in my hands.

And it wasn't for mercy's sake.

It was strategy.

Because when I took her—and I would—I needed her to trust me.

Stripped bare of resistance, pliable enough for me to extract every secret, every truth she had no idea she was keeping.

And I was making damn sure I was the only place she could turn when the bottom dropped out.

Her persistence was admirable.

But also, reckless.

There was something in her, something that wouldn't be dismissed, a hunger for answers so fierce it was consuming her from the inside out.

She didn't just want the truth.

She needed it.

The way a drowning woman needs air.

Like if she could just understand why the world had carved her into pieces, maybe she could stitch herself back together again.

Maybe she thought I was the key.

And maybe, in some twisted, cruel way—she was right.

I thought it was endearing.

But mostly, it was a liability.

And liabilities needed to be controlled.

But she kept saying my name, as if she'd known me for years instead of days.

And I came undone.

Something about the way she said it and what that did to me.

It begged to destroy me.

My control, already hanging by a thread, snapped with a single syllable from her lips.

One look from her and every wall I had constructed with painstaking precision collapsed like sand under a rising tide.

And in that moment, I knew.

She was a danger to me in ways she could never comprehend.

She was the flaw in my system.

The variable I hadn't accounted for.

And I couldn't let her in.

Not until I had answers.

Not until she was mine.

Once she was under my protection, under my roof, in my bed—I would get them.

Every answer she didn't even know she carried.

Every truth she'd buried to survive.

I'd uncover all of it.

Because I knew enough about Klay and his family to understand that their involvement with her was no accident.

The bounty made that clear.

A price on her head high enough to tempt the worst kind of men.

And Klay wasn't just another piece of shit with too much power and not enough conscience.

He had to be obsessed.

Fixated.

And you don't get that way unless there's something you're hiding.

Something you can't afford to lose.

His loose end.

The key to something he was desperate to bury.

And I was going to extract it from her.

No matter what it cost.

Of course, there was always the small possibility—the shadow of doubt gnawing at the edges of my logic—that she was working with him.

That this was a setup from the beginning.

That I was being played.

But even that didn't lessen the pull I felt toward her.

It didn't kill the instinct to protect her.

Even if I didn't know what I was protecting.

Or why.

Because the second Castor showed me that bounty, the decision had already been made.

I didn't need to think.

If I didn't get to her first, someone else would.

And if they got their hands on her before I did...

If she was innocent... she'd never see the light of day again.

So, I made a plan.

Simple. Efficient.

Hold her hostage. Uncover the truth. Keep her alive. Get to Klay. End it.

It should be easy.

It was the kind of thing Castor and I had done a thousand times over.

But my focus was a fragile thing around her.

She had the power to unravel me with a glance.

With a single word.

With every unguarded moment she handed me, I became less of the man I was supposed to be.

And more of the thing I swore I'd never become.

The third time she walked away, I saw it.

The shift.

She didn't run.

She didn't fight.

She lingered.

Just for a second, but long enough for me to see the crack in her armor.

The defeat in her eyes.

Her spirit—once stubborn, feral, wild—was cracked and subdued.

And I hated myself for it.

But it was necessary.

She had to stay away, until I was ready to bring her in for good.

Castor had grumbled about the plan for days. Called me a psycho more than once.

But he knew better than to challenge me outright.

I was the one who got us this far. I was the one who kept us alive. Cleaned up every mess. Fixed every mistake.

This was no different.

I told myself that until I almost believed it but if I was being honest with myself, something about this was different.

Later that night, I found myself in my studio.

The walls lined with shelves of my vinyl collection meticulously ordered. The faint scratch of the needle settling onto black grooves sounded like static in my head as I dropped into the worn leather chair by the window and closed my eyes while the music bled into the air.

I let the words swallow me whole.

The weight of its inevitability.

That beautiful wildflower had no idea what was coming for her.

No clue of the storm I was about to unleash.

I intended to be both her salvation and her ruin.

Her dream and her nightmare.

Because I wasn't just going to take her life apart.

I was going to rebuild it.

Around me.

And if I had to burn everything else to the ground to get what I needed, so be it.

I hoped she was ready for the chaos that was about to erupt.

Because I knew that the next time she tried to walk away from me—it would be the last.

Chapter Fifteen

SAGE

I DIDN'T GET IT.

No matter how many times I turned it over in my mind, no matter how many nights I spent reliving every look, every word, I couldn't make sense of it.

I couldn't understand why Reich hated me.

Why he kept pushing me away.

Why it cut deeper every time he did.

One moment, his touch burned through me—searing and consuming, like he wanted to brand himself into my skin. The next, his words turned sharp, slicing through every fragile piece of hope I dared to hold.

It was a cycle I couldn't predict, a storm I couldn't escape.

And that last night in his field, something inside me broke, causing me to sink.

The familiar pull of depression clawed at my skin, dragging me down into its suffocating depths.

But this time, it was different.

Worse.

Deeper.

Like I was drowning, and no one even realized I was missing.

Days bled into nights. Time lost all meaning.

I stopped keeping track.

I stopped caring.

I moved through the world like a ghost, detached from everything, even myself.

I stopped leaving my apartment.

Stopped walking the trails.

Stopped reaching for the little pieces of normalcy I'd worked so hard to build since leaving Sanele.

Even music—the one thing that had always given me peace—fell silent in my ears.

There was no point pressing play when every note reminded me of him.

When every lyric twisted the knife deeper.

And Sam...Sam was on cloud nine.

Since the festival, she and Castor had become inseparable, orbiting each other with an energy that lit up every room they entered.

Her happiness was a bright, burning thing.

But instead of letting it warm me, I kept my distance.

I told myself I was being kind.

I didn't want to dampen her light.

Didn't want to weigh her down with my darkness.

But the truth was simpler and somehow crueler to me.

Seeing her so fulfilled, so in love, only reminded me of everything I didn't have.

Everything I might never have.

Especially not with Reich.

So, I avoided her.

Every time she would stop by.

Declined her invitations for coffee.

Ignored her texts with excuses about migraines and deadlines.

After the third time, she insisted on coming to me.

I should have seen that as a possibility.

Sam had always been relentless when she wanted something, but this time, I was grateful. Even if I was too hollow to show it.

When she arrived, two to-go cups in hand, she greeted me with the same grin she always had.

As if nothing had changed.

As if it was any other morning and no time had passed since we last spoke.

I curled up in my chair, clutching the latte she handed me like it was a life raft.

"How are things with Castor?" I asked. The question slipped out because it was easier than talking about me.

Sam's face lit up—but only for a moment, then something flickered in her expression.

A shadow of doubt.

"I just can't shake the feeling that he's hiding something from me," she said softly, lowering her gaze to her coffee.

Her words pulled me out of myself, if only for a second.

"What do you mean?" I asked, sitting up a little straighter.

She sighed, dragging her fingers through her hair in frustration. "We've been dating for six months, right?"

I nodded.

"Well..." she hesitated, chewing her bottom lip. "I've never been to his place."

I blinked, confused. "What?"

She arched a brow, visibly exasperated. "Right?"

I shook my head slowly. "How is that even possible?"

Sam gave a small, nervous shrug. "We always meet somewhere or hang out at my apartment. He's never invited me over. And I'm not going to push."

Her smile was thin, brittle. "I've brought it up a few times, but he always changes the subject."

I thought back to the field.

The clearing where the wildflowers once bloomed.

The place that wasn't just beautiful—it was dangerous.

His place.

Reich's home, I realized and probably Castor's, too.

"Do you know if he lives with Reich?" I asked cautiously.

Sam's head snapped up.

Surprise flashed in her eyes and something like betrayal, "He does." Her voice was tight.

I hesitated. Then, quietly, "I think I might know where they live."

Her jaw dropped, and her hands flew to her cheeks in disbelief. "You what?" she demanded. "How do you know where Reich lives?"

Her excitement was sharp, almost manic, but excited, nonetheless.

And despite everything, I found myself smiling.

Just a little.

"It's not what you think," I said quickly, holding up a hand in surrender.

Her face fell, and the sparkle dulled slightly.

"I walk the preserve across the road. About a quarter mile in, there's an opening under the trees that leads to..." I trailed off.

The words caught in my throat like barbed wire.

Memories crashed into me. His hand closing around my throat. His voice in my ear.

There's nothing here for you anymore.

I swallowed the ache down, forcing myself to finish, "It leads to their backyard. I didn't know it was private property at the time. But now Reich probably thinks I'm some kind of thief or stalker."

I forced a hollow laugh. "At least, that's the only explanation I can come up with."

Even as I said it, my mind drifted back to that night at the festival.

The way he touched me like I belonged to him.

The way he watched me like I was a threat or a prize.

I couldn't tell the difference anymore.

The memory clawed at me, dragging a raw, aching sob to the surface.

I barely held it in.

But Sam saw it.

She reached for me without hesitation, wrapping her arms around me and pulling me close.

We held each other tightly, our silent grief tangled together in the quiet of my living room.

Her own eyes glistened, though she didn't let them fall.

When we finally let go, the silence between us was thick.

Heavy with things neither of us could say.

We finished our coffees in that silence.

And then Sam exhaled sharply, "Do you think Castor's cheating on me?"

I stared at her, at the pain she was trying so hard to hide.

"I don't think so," I said gently. "But obviously I can't be sure."

Her face crumpled, and I took her hand in mine, squeezing as I continued, "But If he is, he's a goddamn fool and he doesn't deserve you."

I tried to smile, but it was weak, as I kept going, "And I don't deserve to keep chasing after a man who won't let me explain myself."

Sam wiped at her eyes, shaking her head.

But then, as if struck by sudden clarity, her gaze sharpened, "You know what?"

I raised a brow in question.

She continued, "Castor's at work. And I don't need him to have a good time. We're going out tonight."

Her grin was fierce.

Confident.

"House of Music has a show tonight," she added, nudging me. "And it's been forever since we went to a concert together."

I hesitated.

The weight of my depression clung to me, dragging me down, whispering excuses in my ear.

But Sam didn't budge.

She moved closer, her voice softer, "I know you're hurting, Sage. But I need you tonight. And you need this."

Her hand found mine again.

I wanted to argue. Wanted to crawl back into my bed and disappear.

But instead, I caved, like I always did when it came to Sam.

"Alright," I whispered, letting a small smile tug at my lips, "I guess I owe you after last time."

We both laughed, and it was the first sound in days that didn't make my chest hurt.

And for the first time in days, I felt something I thought I'd lost.

A glimmer of hope.

Fragile, flickering

But alive.

And maybe, just maybe, that was enough for now.

Chapter Sixteen

REICH

I BURIED MYSELF IN work after the night she came back—drowning in tasks, lists, orders, distractions—anything that might keep my mind from circling the same drain it had spiraled into since the moment I met her.

But no matter how deep I buried myself, no matter how many hours I filled with precision and sweat, the truth was always there.

Waiting.

Every morning, without fail, I checked the surveillance feed surrounding my home.

The cameras I'd installed years ago, out of necessity, now served a new purpose.

I told myself it was to make sure she stayed away.

To enforce the distance, I'd created between us.

That was the lie I clung to that was splintering at the edges.

Because the truth?

I needed to know if she would come back.

If I'd left enough of a scar that she couldn't stop herself from coming back.

And deep down—far beneath the cold logic and strategy I built my life on—I wanted her to rebel.

To defy me.

To storm right back onto my property and demand answers.

But she didn't and I knew she wouldn't.

I'd pushed her just far enough away to keep her alive, and just close enough that I could still feel the absence of her eyes on me.

And the hurt in them.

The betrayal that I had caused.

What happened at the festival and the drink laced with God-knows-what, the way she trusted too easily, too fully, was proof enough that she needed protection.

The kind I couldn't give her yet.

The kind I wasn't sure I could ever give her.

Because keeping her alive meant keeping her under control and I wasn't in control anymore.

I told myself she was safer confined to her apartment.

Safer in isolation.

Safer haunted by her own mind than stepping out into a world filled with monsters who wouldn't hesitate to destroy her.

Better to endure silence, loneliness—than to walk straight into the jaws of something she couldn't even see coming.

Even if that meant she hated me.

Even if it hollowed her out.

Even if it hollowed me out, too.

But time wasn't on my side.

And I needed more of it.

Every day I waited, it felt like I was tearing strips of flesh from my own body, piece by agonizing piece.

Eventually, I cracked.

I told myself I'd only check in from a distance.

That I'd stay detached.

That I'd only use the lens I'd hidden behind her headboard in case of emergencies.

But there I was, breaking my own rules.

Again.

Something about her made me do this.

Made me question every line I'd drawn in the sand.

Every boundary I swore I'd never cross.

And then I crossed them.

Every single one.

But the longer I watched her, the harder it became to justify what I was doing.

She wasn't doing anything suspicious.

She wasn't making calls to Klay.

She wasn't plotting.

She wasn't anything I should've feared.

She was just existing.

Barely.

She stayed inside, hidden away, like a ghost haunting her own skin.

The fire I'd seen in her—gone.

Snuffed out.

The woman who had walked my field with peace in her eyes, who had knelt in the wildflowers as if they were sacred—empty.

And maybe she always had been, even before she met me.

She barely left for work.

And when she did, I saw the weight dragging behind her like chains.

She was unraveling and I hated that I was the one who pulled the thread loose.

Sam tried.

I saw her in the background sometimes—her pleading by the door.

Trying to draw Sage out.

Trying to stitch her back together.

But Sage refused.

Again.

And again.

And I felt relief at her refusal because it meant she was safe inside that apartment.

But I still couldn't bear that it was my doing that put her in that state of mind, she wasn't living like she used to.

And she didn't deserve this.

Hurting people like her wasn't what I did.

It wasn't supposed to be who I was.

And yet—here I was.

A stranger in my own skin.

The more I watched, the worse it became.

Every hour that passed made the truth about her clearer.

She was caught in this mess without knowing how deep it ran. A pawn in a game far bigger than anything she could comprehend. She just wanted to survive. Maybe even find peace.

But Klay wasn't going to allow it.

He and his brothers.

Predators.

Men who carved out empires from flesh and fear.

It wasn't just about business with them.

It was about power and control.

My mother's best friend had been one of their father's victims.

Twenty-four years old.

A wife. A mother. Manipulated into debt. Forced into submission and terrorized until there was nothing left but bone and obedience.

She'd tried to run. Tried to break free. And their father made an example of her.

I'd seen what was left and I never forgot it.

My mother told me about the call she got that night.

Her best friend sobbing, begging for help.

Telling her about Harry Ovitt—Klay's father.

About the threats.

And the next morning, she was gone, like she'd never existed.

And my mother grieved her in silence.

But my mother's best friend wasn't the only one. Not by a long shot.

She was just the one I knew.

And that made me swear vengeance.

They became my mission.

Eradicate the line.

Erase them.

Every last trace.

And I'd come so far.

I'd gutted their empire.

One body at a time.

I only needed one last thing. One younger brother left in the line.

Klay was smart—and slippery.

He was always one step ahead.

But I could feel it: his time was running out.

And so was mine.

I couldn't wait much longer. Not for him.

I couldn't keep playing the game the way I had been.

If I wanted a chance at stopping him, I had to become the predator.

I had to outthink him. I had to outmaneuver him at every turn.

And that meant Sage…

She was my last piece.

She was the bait.

She didn't know it, and I hated that she didn't.

But to catch Klay, I had to play his game.

I had to make everything look real.

I had to make it believable.

If Sage suspected anything—if she even hesitated—Klay would see through it.

And she'd be dead before I ever found her again.

This was the gamble I had left.

The only one that mattered.

I had to hope I was right.

Because now, her life was in my hands.

For better or worse, she had become mine to protect.

Even if she ended up hating me for it.

Even if I had to destroy her first.

Because care and affection wasn't what I could offer her.

Not now.

First came survival.

Then came vengeance.

And if there was anything left of us after that,

Maybe she'd forgive me in the end.

Chapter Seventeen

SAGE

T HE HOUSE OF MUSIC was a riot of chaos and charm. A place where everything felt louder—wilder—alive. From the outside, it didn't look like much. Weatherworn bricks. Faded murals peeling from the walls like molting skin. But inside, it pulsed.

A living, breathing thing.

It was as if the walls themselves inhaled every shout, every scream, every bass drop, and exhaled them in raw, eclectic art.

And beneath its unassuming exterior, buried like a secret only the bold could find, was the basement stage.

An intimate den where the ceilings hung low and flickering lights swayed in sync with the pulse of the crowd.

The air was thick and drenched in the scent of whiskey, cheap beer, cigarettes half-smoked, and something else I couldn't quite name.

Something electric.

A charge crackled under my skin, filling the space between each ragged breath.

It hummed through the soles of my boots, up through my spine, until I swore it was becoming a part of me.

And for the first time in weeks—*maybe even months*—I felt awake.

Like I belonged to something bigger than the ache that had been eating me alive.

I had resisted coming here. Sam had practically dragged me out by my wrists, her usual sunshine glow laced with iron determination.

"You need this," she had said earlier that night.

She wasn't wrong.

The suffocating silence of my apartment had become unbearable like a self-made prison with walls that whispered things I didn't want to hear.

But the moment I stepped through the battered entrance to this place, the moment the bass thundered against my ribs, something deep inside me cracked open.

And for a second, just a second, I remembered who I used to be.

Before everything.

This was freedom and I clung to it like it might vanish.

Even now, with the weight of my past pressed tight against my ribs and with the memories waiting to swallow me into the dark, I let myself smile.

At least, for tonight.

Because here, in this dim room humming with life, I could almost believe the past hadn't hollowed me out.

Almost.

But even here—even standing in the thrumming heart of the music where bodies swayed like one living thing— I couldn't outrun him.

Reich.

That name carved itself into me, a brand that refused to fade.

I shouldn't feel this way.

Not after everything I'd survived. Not after Klay. Not after clawing my way out of something that nearly broke me beyond repair.

I shouldn't have space left for another man.

Reich shouldn't be the shadow under every thought, the beat beneath my skin, but he somehow was, and I hated him for it.

But I hated myself more.

He had made his stance clear.

And yet, I still felt his absence like a phantom limb.

A wound that refused to close.

Why did I still want him when he so clearly didn't want me?

I tried to shake the thought and tried to lose myself in the music, in the rush of strangers pressing close, their bodies warm and wild.

Fake it till you make it. That was my mantra for the night.

Pretend I didn't care.

Pretend he wasn't there in the back of my head, like an echo I couldn't silence.

I was getting good at lying to myself.

But deep down, I knew the truth.

It wasn't just about him.

It was about what he made me feel.

That momentary flicker of connection.

The spark that had set something inside me alight, only for him to douse it the second I reached for more.

And still, I wanted it more than anything, even if it destroyed me.

Sam tugged at my hand, pulling me through the crowd.

We threaded our way past groups pressed shoulder-to-shoulder, bodies swaying in a synchronized rhythm that vibrated through the floor.

She left to go get drinks, settling into our routine at concerts.

I would hold our spot while she went to grab refreshments, while I waited for her to return.

The music was deafening, a storm that consumed everything else.

But it was good, and I let it fill me. Let it drown out the gnawing ache in my chest.

Until I felt it.

The shift.

A presence.

Heavy and watching.

I turned before I could think and saw someone I wasn't expecting.

Castor.

Standing just a few feet away.

His gaze locked onto mine like a tether snapping tight between us.

Something inside me stilled.

No longer swaying to the music.

No longer breathing easy.

"Castor?" I forced his name out past the lump rising in my throat, before continuing, "Sam went to get drinks. I thought you were...aren't you supposed to be working?"

I tried for casual, but the words faltered.

His expression didn't soften.

If anything, it hardened, as he answered, "I am."

His tone was low, measured and too careful.

Almost... *regretful*.

My stomach twisted as I realized that something was wrong. *Very wrong.*

"...Do you work here?" I asked slowly, a tremor sneaking into my voice.

His expression didn't change. "Not for the House of Music."

Six words.

And the floor vanished beneath my feet.

"What does that mean?" I demanded, though my body already knew the answer.

Every cell screaming in warning.

Run.

But I didn't move fast enough.

He did.

One second, he was in front of me.

The next, he was behind.

His hand clamped down on my shoulder, his fingers digging in just enough to root me in place.

Not enough to hurt.

His breath was warm against my ear.

And ice cold in his words, "I'm really sorry about this, Sage."

Panic hit me like a tidal wave.

I wrenched against his grip, but it was too late.

I felt the sting.

Something sharp pressed against the side of my neck.

A needle.

The sting blossomed into heat, spreading fast.

Faster than I could fight.

I stumbled, the world tilting on its axis as dizziness slammed into me like a punch. The colors bled together and the bass turned to static, warping into a low, throbbing hum.

I opened my mouth to scream, but nothing came out.

The floor rose to meet me and then the darkness swallowed me whole.

Chapter Eighteen

REICH

The House of Music was a predator's paradise.

A shadowed labyrinth of blind corners, half-hidden exits, and flickering lights that seemed designed to disorient. The walls pulsed with bass-heavy music, vibrating with the chaos of bodies pressed tight in the crush of the crowd. Smoke curled in the air, cloaking everything in a thin haze, and the scent of sweat and spilled liquor clung to every surface.

The security team? *Useless.* Hired for appearances, trained to look the other way.

It was the kind of place where people disappeared without a sound.

Where women like Sage could be swallowed whole before anyone even realized they were missing.

And right now, it was crawling with men just like our target for the night, Lucas Renner.

I moved through the west side of the venue, my hood low over my brow, shoulders loose but ready.

It wasn't hard to blend in.

In a place like this, people were too busy chasing their next high to notice the predator hunting in their midst.

Across the floor, Castor was already in position. I caught a flash of his blonde hair beneath the shifting strobes, his sharp gaze cutting through the crowd like a razor. He scanned everything—threats, exits and obstacles. Mapping the room in real time.

The earpiece crackled softly, as I instructed, "Take the far left. I'll handle the right. Report back if anything stands out."

"Copy that." Castor's voice was light. Too casual, as always. And then, true to form, he gave a lazy salute before melting into the crowd.

I barely registered his antics. My focus was already zeroed in.

I'd found my target.

Lucas Renner.

One of Ali Parrish's most loyal men. And exactly the kind of monster I'd made it my mission to destroy.

A serial rapist, trafficker, and dealer of broken souls.

He operated under the delusion that his money made him untouchable. That power meant no one would ever come for him.

He was wrong.

Because tonight, he was mine.

I tracked him from the shadows as he prowled the edge of the floor, his movements slow and predatory. His gaze slid over the crowd with clinical precision, stripping women bare with a glance. I could practically hear the gears grinding in his skull as he calculated value.

How much? How easy? How fast?

He was choosing and then his attention snapped to something or perhaps, someone.

And my stomach dropped as I followed his vision.

Sage.

She was standing under the edge of the stage lights, completely unaware. Her green eyes sparkled, catching the gleam of the overhead lighting. Even in the dimness, she seemed to glow, radiating a light to her that was untouched and unclaimed.

The kind of light men like Renner sought to snuff out.

I went still.

The earpiece flared again. Castor's voice, sharper this time, "Reich, we've got a problem. Sam's here. And she's with Sage."

"I know." I stated as I felt my teeth grind together. "Lucas is moving toward her."

There was a pause on the other end. Tension bled through the silence.

Lucas Renner never worked alone, and yet, tonight, there was no entourage. No backup. Just him.

Something about that set my nerves on edge.

This wasn't standard procedure but there wasn't time to analyze it.

So, I made the call.

"Castor." My voice was ice. Controlled. "Use the vial on Sage. Get her out of here. Take her to the house. Lock her in the pit until I get back."

Silence.

I could feel his hesitation radiating through the connection.

"Reich..." His tone was lower now. Heavy. Uncertain.

"This is a change of plans," I said, sharper. "Do as I say."

Another beat of hesitation, then he moved.

I tracked him with my eyes as he crossed the floor, not expecting anything to interfere with his plans.

But then Lucas faltered, thrown for half a second as his mark was plucked from under his nose.

He turned, teeth bared and found me.

I didn't give him time to process the mistake.

In one swift movement, I drove the needle into his gut, pressing the plunger with clinical precision.

Recognition flashed in his eyes but it was too late.

The sedative hit fast. His limbs turned into deadweights. His expression twisted, confusion battling with terror.

"Easy, bud," I murmured, catching him before he could collapse completely. My tone was mocking, a cold echo of concern. "Looks like you've had too much to drink. Let's get you some fresh air."

I slung his arm over my shoulder and hauled him toward the back exit.

He was heavier than he looked or maybe I was just running on borrowed adrenaline from seeing Sage.

Outside, the alley was slick with rain. The air was sharp and cigarette smoke hung low, mixing with the faint reek of garbage and diesel.

Lucas groaned against me, his head lolling as he fought the drug.

Annoyance flared within me. I hated when they struggled.

When I reached the car, I drove my boot into his knee, forcing him to drop, then followed up with a brutal elbow to the side of his skull.

He hit the pavement hard, his head cracking against the concrete with a satisfying thud.

Blood pooled slowly beneath him.

He was out cold.

Finally.

I stood over him for a long moment, breathing hard.

Tempted.

It would be easy to end it here.

Quick. Clean. One less predator, but there were too many questions and something about his focus on Sage wasn't adding up.

She wasn't his type.

She wasn't street prey.

She wasn't desperate.

At least, not in the ways they liked.

And yet, there he was.

Tracking her.

With a low curse, I dragged him up the side of the car and shoved him into the trunk.

I took the long way home.

Gave myself time to think.

To prepare.

By the time I pulled into the driveway, the house loomed dark and silent beneath the trees.

Fitting.

A tomb for men like Lucas.

A sanctuary for no one.

Castor was waiting on the front steps.

Arms crossed and jaw tight.

The kind of stillness that screamed fury.

I killed the engine. Stepped out and met his gaze.

He didn't waste time.

"Are you going to tell me what the fuck is going on?" His voice was low and dangerous.

I exhaled, closing the distance between us with slow, deliberate steps.

The tension snapped tight between us.

"Inside," I said.

The words were gravel.

And we both knew it wasn't a suggestion.

It was the beginning of something neither of us could walk away from.

Not now.

Not with Sage locked in the pit downstairs.

And not with Lucas about to wake up in the trunk of my car.

Chapter Nineteen

SAGE

The first thing I noticed was the cold.

It wasn't just the sharp bite of the air; it was the way it seeped into my skin, the metal restraints digging into my wrists, sending a dull ache up my arms with every failed attempt to move. My ankles were bound too tight and unyielding. My legs ached from the strain of sitting too long in one position. There was no slack in the bindings.

No mercy.

I forced myself to take a breath, shallow and ragged, as my head pounded in an unforgiving drumbeat that throbbed behind my eyes. Whatever they'd drugged me with was still there, clinging to the edges of my consciousness like a stubborn fog I couldn't outrun.

For a moment, I stayed still.

Counting the beats of my heart.

Listening. Assessing.

The sound of my own pulse echoed in my ears until, slowly, I became aware of another sound.

Breathing.

Steady. Calm. Controlled.

I forced my eyes open, the dim light stinging until I blinked away the blur. The room was plain but brutal in its simplicity. Cement floors, stained with something I didn't want to think about. Exposed pipes lining the ceiling. The smell of damp earth, old stone, and metal thickened the air, turning every inhale into a fight.

And then I saw my captor.

Castor.

He was only a few feet away, his back to me, rolling his shoulders as though he were working out the kinks from a long day.

No urgency. No concern.

Just... waiting.

I watched him in silence, keeping my body still despite the rising panic building in my chest.

There was no point in struggling. Not yet.

That's when I noticed it.

A mark.

Ink-black and vicious, at the base of his neck where his hair tapered close to his skin. At first, it was just a pattern, but as my gaze sharpened, something ancient stirred in my mind.

Recognition.

It wasn't just ink.

It wasn't art.

It was a symbol.

And something about it felt very wrong.

The shape of it, like something meant to seal something in. Or keep something out. I didn't know how I knew that.

But I knew.

It wasn't merely decoration.

It was a brand and something about it felt familiar. Like something I had forgotten.

My pulse spiked, and the restraints bit deeper into my skin as I involuntarily pulled against them.

The scrape of the chair leg dragged across the concrete, echoing sharp through the room.

Castor moved.

He turned toward me slowly, like he already knew I was awake. Like he'd been waiting for the moment I opened my eyes and realized the depth of where I was.

His expression was relaxed, easy.

Almost amused.

"I was wondering when you'd wake up." He finally said, his voice was silk over glass, smooth but sharp enough to cut.

I stared at him, keeping my breathing even as I fought to swallow against the dryness in my throat.

I didn't answer.

He smiled lazily, but knowing and took a slow step closer, crouching low until he was eye-level with me.

He rested his forearms on his knees like this was a casual conversation. Like I wasn't tied to a chair in a concrete room that stank of rust and rot.

"Say something," he coaxed. "You've got that look."

He said it like I was a puzzle. Like he enjoyed watching me struggle to find the answers.

I clenched my jaw, before I relented, "Where am I?"

My voice came out cracked and hoarse, but steady.

"Somewhere safe." He replied simply, his grin deepened, like it was a private joke he wasn't going to share.

I tugged at the restraints again, making the chains rattle, "Doesn't feel safe to me."

That earned a soft chuckle, before he spoke again, "That depends on how you look at it. But regardless, you have information we need, so your safety is most dependent on how you answer them."

The memories of before I woke up here, came flooding back in a rush—the music pounding at the House of Music, the heat of the crowd, Castor behind me, the sharp sting at my neck... And then nothing.

That's when I connected the dots.

He drugged me and dragged me here.

All for some 'information'?

I wasn't buying it.

"Information?" I scoffed. "You didn't think to just ask?"

The accusation slipped out before I could stop it.

Castor tilted his head, his gaze flickering, "Would you have obliged?"

I didn't answer.

Because we both knew the truth.

His smile thinned as he stated, "Exactly."

My gaze flicked again to the base of his neck.

To the mark.

And this time, he noticed.

"You keep looking at something, sweetheart," he said, voice lower now. Knowing. "What is it?"

I licked my lips and tasted copper as I spoke, "What's on the back of your neck?"

A pause.

The air in the room changed.

Shifted.

Like the wind before a storm.

For the first time, Castor's easy expression faltered. It was subtle—there and gone in an instant—but I caught it.

"That's an interesting question," he said slowly, like he was choosing every word with care.

"I've seen it before," I said.

The truth settled heavy on my tongue.

His gaze darkened, "Have you now?"

I nodded.

But I didn't say where.

Because I still didn't know.

Because the memory of it was buried deep, clawing at the edges of my mind but refusing to take shape.

Castor stood abruptly, running a hand through his hair as he exhaled. "Well," he said. "That's unfortunate."

Ice slithered down my spine, as I forced myself to ask, "Why?"

The word was a whisper.

He turned back toward me slowly, smiling, but his eyes were flat. Empty, as he answered, "Because it means you're asking the wrong questions."

I swallowed hard, the weight of his meaning settling cold and brutal in my chest.

He stepped closer, leaned in until his breath was hot against my ear, "Be careful what you look for, sweetheart. You might not like what you find."

The door creaked open.

I flinched, instinct ripping through me.

And then I saw him.

Reich.

His presence filled the room instantly.

Cold. Heavy. Icy steel wrapped in the shape of a man.

He moved without hurry, every step calculated and predatory.

For a split second, I wanted to believe I was safe.

That he was here to fix whatever this was.

But when the light caught the back of his neck, my stomach dropped through the floor.

The same mark.

Identical.

Branding him as something I didn't understand, but I knew enough to be terrified.

His eyes raked over me slowly, as if taking inventory of what was his.

"How's my wildflower?" He finally said, his voice was low, smooth. Dripping with something dark and indulgent.

Something almost cruel.

I couldn't stop the scoff that broke from my throat, "You're insane."

Reich smiled but it wasn't kind.

"You have no idea." He responded.

And in his eyes, I saw it.

He wanted me to know how much further he could take this if I pushed just enough.

My voice cracked, desperation slipping through before I could stop it, "I'm sorry," I choked out. "I didn't mean to invade your property. I didn't mean—"

He lifted his hand, flicking his fingers.

And I stopped.

Like I didn't have a choice, though I knew I did.

He leaned against the doorframe, casual and relaxed but his eyes were a storm.

Cold, brutal and merciless.

"I warned you," he said.

The panic clawed harder now, rising like bile in my throat, as I tried to plead, "I'll leave! I won't come back! Just—just let me go!"

Reich sighed like I was boring him and then he pushed off the doorframe, slow and deliberate.

Moving toward me like a wave I couldn't outrun.

I pressed back into the chair, chains rattling.

And then his hand was on me.

Not rough, but firm.

His knuckles grazed my cheek before his palm settled there, warm and grounding in the worst possible way.

He crouched until we were eye level, his gaze locked on mine, unblinking. "You think I brought you here to hurt you?"

The question was soft.

Dangerous.

"I..." I tried to speak but I shook my head because I didn't know the answer.

His thumb stroked across my cheek. Gentle.

Too gentle.

"I brought you here to keep you safe." His tone didn't change but I felt the weight of those words all the way to my core.

A whimper slipped past my lips.

He heard it.

And his smirk returned. "Shhh," he murmured. "I'm not going to hurt you."

His voice was soft. Deceptively soothing.

Wrapping around me like silk.

And all I could think was—*liar*.

As he left me alone in the darkness.

Chapter Twenty

REICH

I KNEW BRINGING HER to the Pit was a mistake.

The Pit was never meant to hold someone like her.

But I did it anyway.

Because when it came to her, logic stopped existing. I didn't have a choice. No clean answers. No contingency plan. Lucas had forced my hand, and I wasn't about to leave Sage out there in the open for men like him to circle.

And I sure as hell wasn't ready to let her go.

Still, the moment the steel door sealed shut behind me, I felt it, the slow creep of regret twisting through my gut. This wasn't how I planned it. Not here. Not yet. I had told myself that when I brought her in, it would be controlled. Calculated. Everything on my terms.

But Sage had a way of throwing everything out of balance.

And Lucas Renner... his eyes on her told me there was more to her story. Something deeper. Something dangerous. And if I was going to get answers—*real answers*—I needed her here. Somewhere I could watch her. Keep her close. Keep her safe.

I had her room prepared ahead of time. Surveillance in every corner. Comfortable enough that she wouldn't spiral. A bed. Soft sheets. A dresser. A mirror that wasn't glass. I even chose a warm light instead of the sterile white bulbs Castor swore by. Little details that offered the illusion of safety. Of control. She'd believe it was a trade or a type of comfort for answers.

And maybe it was.

But I didn't think I could give her back when this was done.

I stepped inside, the heavy door slicing through the dark with a hollow groan. The thin beam from the hallway cut through the shadows and landed on her like a spotlight. She was slumped in the chair where Castor had left her, restrained but not to the point of pain.

That had been my stipulation.

She stirred at the sound of my boots on the concrete, her body slow to respond, like she was fighting through a fog. The remnants of the sedative still dulled her movements, but not enough to mask the way she stiffened when she realized she wasn't alone.

Even wrecked, she was stunning.

A disaster I wouldn't mind getting lost in.

Her head turned sluggishly toward me with eyes heavy but burning with something fierce beneath the surface.

Her voice rasped through cracked lips, "Why are you doing this?"

No fear. No begging. Just exhaustion. Defeat.

But I wasn't stupid enough to think she'd given up.

She didn't break easily and part of me respected her for that.

I didn't answer her question. I didn't owe her an explanation.

"Soon enough you'll know," I murmured, keeping my tone flat. Emotionless.

Her gaze sharpened, a dagger aimed straight at me.

"I did what you asked," she said, voice low but hard. "I stayed away."

It was almost funny. She thought this was about my field. A fucking patch of flowers.

I gave her nothing in return but a slow, knowing smile. The kind that seemed to piss her off.

And it worked.

Her frustration snapped like a live wire. "Fuck you," she spat, venom lacing every syllable. "Let me go."

Her chest heaved, breath ragged from the effort. Anger flushed hot beneath her skin, blooming in her cheeks and throat. She radiated fury.

And beneath that...I saw her searching me.

For an answer.

For weakness.

For anything to latch onto.

But I wasn't giving her a thing.

"I'm not your pet, Reich." She spat out. Her voice was sharp, meant to wound. But hearing my name on her lips did something it shouldn't.

Something dangerous.

So, I looked away for a moment and regained control. Barely.

This was going to be a long fucking battle.

I closed the distance between us with slow, deliberate steps. Letting the weight of my presence press against her before I touched her.

When I did, it was almost gentle. A mockery of comfort as I cupped her cheek.

For a fraction of a second, her lashes fluttered closed.

And then—she tried to bite me.

Adorable.

I chuckled softly, my thumb brushing over her jaw as I gripped her throat with my other hand.

"Careful, wildflower," I warned, amusement flickering behind my words. "Don't bite the hand that's about to keep you fed. Or maybe you need me to teach you some manners."

She sucked in a breath, her pulse a frantic drum beneath my fingers.

And still, she fought.

"Manners?" she hissed. "Like taking something that isn't yours?"

Clever girl.

Too clever.

"You don't own me, Reich—"

I didn't answer. Only let my grip tighten slightly, enough to remind her she wasn't in control here.

The air between us thickened, dense with something we both refused to name.

"—so, stop acting like it," she bit out, her eyes flashing.

Her words cut deep.

But I didn't flinch.

I exhaled, slow. Controlled.

"See? That's where you're wrong." I responded.

She scoffed, shaking her head, but I saw the crack in her armor, "You don't get to decide what's best for me."

But I did. When I took her under my roof. When I decided to make her my problem.

I pressed closer, forcing her back into the chair, into me. "No," I murmured, breath hot against her skin. "But it doesn't seem like you knew what was best for you in the first place..."

Her laugh was bitter. Defiant.

I let my lips graze the curve of her jaw, not quite a kiss, but close enough to steal her breath.

"Taking foreign drinks from strangers...trespassing onto someone else's property daily..." I smirked "I bet you didn't even know that there was someone trailing you at the House of Music."

There was silence.

But not the kind I was used to from her.

Her next words were soft.

Hurt.

"Then why... why did you push me away...?"

For a moment, just a breath, I considered telling her the truth.

But truths were dangerous.

Instead, I gripped the back of her hair, tilting her head back until her mouth parted on instinct.

"Tell me why you are the one pushing me away now?" I asked, voice low, curling around her like smoke.

She stilled.

Said nothing.

Just let herself breathe me in.

And I smirked, before giving her praise, "Good girl."

The words dripped between us, heavy and hot.

She shivered and I felt it.

I tilted her chin higher with two fingers, the touch deceptively gentle, belying the steel beneath it. Her skin was soft, trembling faintly beneath the press of my hand. She resisted for a breath—pride warring with curiosity—until her gaze finally met mine.

Those eyes. Fierce, defiant, and burning with something that thrilled me far more than fear ever could.

"Someday," I said, voice low and slow, laced with a promise I had every intention of keeping, "you'll beg to belong to me."

A flicker crossed her face—anger, confusion, something too foreign to name. But she didn't pull away.

I leaned in, close enough that my breath skimmed her lips. I brushed my mouth over hers in the lightest ghost of a kiss—more sensation than contact. A whisper of heat. A warning.

A threat.

"And believe me, wildflower—" I murmured, letting the word bloom with mock affection, the way one might cradle something delicate right before plucking its petals.

"—that day will come sooner than you think."

My knuckles drifted down, slow and deliberate, until they met the hollow of her throat. Her pulse leapt beneath my touch, wild and fast. A war drum behind fragile bone.

She exhaled, shaky and slow, and I smiled—not out of cruelty, but certainty.

The kind of certainty born from knowing what things inevitably bend when the right hands apply pressure.

Her thighs pressed together, subtle but unmistakable. A flicker of tension passed over her features — barely a wince, more like a breath she forgot to hide.

I noticed.

And I couldn't help myself.

"For someone who doesn't want to be my pet—" I said, voice low and curling around the words like smoke around a flame, "—you sure don't mind when I call you a *good girl*."

Her eyes narrowed. A twitch of defiance danced behind the softness of her mouth. "Just because my body reacts to you," she said, quiet but sharp enough to cut, "doesn't mean anything."

I laughed. It came out dark, bitter — like the first drag of a cigarette lit in the ruins of something once holy.

"No?" I stepped closer, slowly but deliberate. Watching how her breath caught in the silence between us. "Then why do you look at me like this is the only thing keeping that spark of yours burning?"

She didn't speak at first. Her jaw tightened. The kind of silence that meant she had too many things to say and none she was ready to admit. Her gaze dropped — not in submission, but in something closer to self-preservation. As if she were afraid of what might come out if she looked at me too long.

"Because you won't stop," she finally whispered, voice brittle with the effort it took to sound unaffected. "And I'm tired of pretending it doesn't get to me."

I moved in closer, letting the tension coil between us like a storm held back by sheer will.

"That's not weakness," I murmured, eyes locked on hers. "That's honesty."

She exhaled — part scoff, part surrender. And in that breath, I saw it: the part of her that hated needing me... and the part that needed me anyway.

She dragged in a breath, "You told me not to take things that aren't mine," she whispered. "Yet here you are."

I leaned closer, fingers weaving lazily through her hair. "And whose are you, wildflower?" I murmured. "A former lover, perhaps? Is that why you came to Providence?"

There it was.

A flicker of fear behind her eyes.

I had found the crack in her wall.

I smiled slowly.

"Remarkable," I murmured, letting my hand drift over her thigh, fingers splayed in warning.

She stiffened, but she didn't pull away.

"Why are you doing this, Reich?" Her voice was quieter now.

Resigned. Raw.

I should've ignored it.

But hearing my name from her lips was too fucking addictive.

I stepped back and straightened.

"I'm going to untie you and take you to your room," I said, flat. "You'll stay there. Understand?"

She said nothing.

So, I waited.

"Say it," I demanded.

Still nothing.

I slid my fingers beneath her chin, tilting her face to mine again.

"Sage," I said, voice low, lips barely a breath away. "Say it."

She swallowed hard.

And then— "I understand."

I smiled, slow and dark.

"Then show me and don't fight me because I don't want to hurt you."

Her breath shuddered out, a surrender she couldn't hide and when I released her, lifting her from the chair, she didn't fight.

I carried her up the stairs, laid her on the bed in the room I'd prepared.

And when she stood, crossing to the door, preparing to leave, I let her.

Let her test the boundary.

Three feet.

And then my hand closed around her wrist.

Hard.

I yanked her back into me.

My voice was a growl against her ear, "Try that again and see what happens."

She glared up at me, but she didn't move.

I smirked, "That's what I thought. Now, get some sleep, we have a job to do."

And then I let her go.

Leaving her standing there.

Breathing heavy.

Trapped in a room with too much space, and nowhere to run.

I slammed the door behind me and smiled to myself.

Because no matter how hard she fought it—she was already mine.

Chapter Twenty-One

SAGE

I STUMBLED AFTER HIM, *every nerve in my body screaming in protest, like each step was another betrayal. My bare feet scraped against the cold, uneven gravel, and every shift of movement sent fresh agony spiraling through me... But it didn't matter. I kept moving. Because stopping meant surrendering.*

And I couldn't.

The sharp tang of blood filled the back of my throat, metallic and bitter. I tasted it with every shallow breath I took. My hands—shaking violently—clutched at my sides, as if I could somehow hold myself together. But my body was splintered. My strength fading with every unsteady footstep.

Still, I followed him.

Klay.

His name throbbed inside my skull, a dull, relentless beat, pounding in time with the pain. He was only a few feet ahead of me, his broad shoulders cutting a jagged line against the horizon. The taillights from his car glowed dimly in the distance as he walked towards them.

And he didn't slow.

He didn't look back.

Like I wasn't there.

Then—his voice.

Cold. Sharp as shattered glass against my already broken spirit, "Sage, you're pathetic."

The words sliced through me with surgical precision, finding every place I was weakest. My breath hitched. Tears blurred my vision until he was just a smear of darkness moving through even more darkness, losing visibility before me.

But I kept going.

Because I had no choice.

"Klay..." My voice cracked, "You have to believe me. It's the truth."

I hated the way I sounded—small. But I couldn't help it because it was what I had been whittled down to.

He stopped.

And for just a second.

Hope flared—stupid, reckless hope.

I should've known better.

As he turned, his stare hit me like a punch to the gut.

Eyes flat and unrecognizable.

There wasn't even anger there anymore.

Just disgust.

"You probably did this shit to yourself," he sneered, his lip curling back in a mockery of a smile. "Is that what this is, Sage? Huh? Some desperate little cry for sympathy? Is that how you get attention now?"

I flinched.

The accusation hit harder than his fists ever could.

I tried to speak.

To defend myself.

But the words stuck in my throat, "I... I just..." The rest of it died on my lips.

Nothing left.

No strength.

No fight.

Klay's expression darkened.

Something primal and vicious lit behind his eyes.

Two steps.

That's all it took for him to close the distance.

And then—he shoved me.

Hard.

The impact was brutal.

I hit the ground with a crack, gravel tearing into my palms, slicing my skin open. Pain flared sharp and hot along my shoulder as it slammed into the dirt. But I barely had time to react before—his knee came down on my throat.

The weight was immediate. Crushing.

A brutal press against my windpipe.

I gasped and choked.

My hands scrambled against his arms, trying to push him off, but it was useless.

I was too weak.

Too broken.

And he was too strong.

He leaned in closer with his face inches from mine.

I could see the dilation in his pupils, the thin sheen of sweat on his forehead. But it was his smile that gutted me.

"You're nothing but a little whore," he hissed, voice low and vibrating with fury. "You hear me? Nothing."

I clawed at his wrist, nails biting into flesh, but he didn't even flinch.

"Mark my words," he growled. "You'll get what's coming to you."

His eyes burned—not just with a threat.

A promise.

Then—release.

His knee lifted and the pressure disappeared. And air came rushing back, ragged and violent. I gasped, coughing so hard it felt like my lungs would tear apart.

I rolled onto my side, hacking, shaking. Tears poured from my eyes, hot and blinding. I didn't even feel the gravel cutting into my cheek anymore.

The pain was everywhere.

And still—I looked up.

He stood over me.

A dark silhouette.

A monster carved out of shadow and venom.

And then—he spit on me.

The wet slap of it landed across my cheek, mixing with blood and tears.

I flinched.

But I didn't wipe it away.

Couldn't.

The shame of it sank deeper than the bruises.

He was already walking away. The slow crunch of his boots over gravel sounded like nails he was just driving further into my coffin.

Then—the roar of his white Mustang cut through the night. The headlights flared bright, blinding. For a heartbeat, I thought he was going to run me over.

End it.

But he didn't.

The tires spun, gravel spraying into the air and then he was gone.

Leaving me broken on a dirt road.

Alone.

Bleeding.

Praying for the night to swallow me whole.

But it didn't. It left me there.

Alive.

With nothing but the wreckage of what was left of me.

And I hated it.

I hated that I was still breathing. Hated that he'd left me alive.

Because in that moment—death would've been a mercy.

I jolted awake, heart pounding as if it had never stopped running, as if sleep had only been a brief blackout. Disoriented, I dragged in a sharp breath that tasted cold and sterile, like metal and antiseptic. My lungs burned as if I'd been underwater too long. Sweat slicked my skin despite the chill that settled deep in my bones.

The silver glow of moonlight spilled through the window across the room, pooling on polished floors and soaking into the muted tones of the walls. It painted everything in ghostly shades, illuminating the stark reality of where I was and what I wasn't.

Free.

How had it come to this?

I thought I'd outrun tragedy. I thought leaving Sanele meant starting over. Surviving. Healing.

But I was wrong.

I hadn't escaped it.

I had run headfirst into its arms again.

And this time, I wasn't sure I had the strength to crawl back out.

My pulse slowed, but not by much. Slowly, I pushed myself upright, every muscle in my body stiff and protesting. It was like surfacing from a nightmare, only to find the nightmare hadn't ended. The room around me was painfully beautiful, a deliberate softness designed to lure me into lowering my guard. Clean lines softened by floral patterns, rich dark woods warmed by amber light fixtures, walls that belonged in a magazine spread. Everything about the space whispered comfort.

Someone who didn't know better might have believed it.

But I didn't.

I knew better.

Comfort was a weapon here.

A deception.

I slid my legs off the bed, feeling the expensive fabric of the comforter fall away from my skin, and planted my bare feet on the cold wood floor. Even the sting of it felt orchestrated—like Reich wanted me to feel the balance of luxury and captivity at once.

I rose on shaky legs and moved toward the bathroom, even though something inside me begged to stay in the bed's embrace. To burrow deep and lose myself in its warmth. It was the best bed I'd ever laid in. Even better than the one I'd had at my apartment, but unfortunately, that wasn't home anymore.

Nothing was.

I passed through a doorless threshold, my reflection catching in the full-length mirror that lined one wall. I looked like a ghost of myself. Hollow eyes, pale skin stretched too tight over sharp cheekbones. My lips were chapped and split from dehydration, my hair tangled from sleep or stress or both.

This was who I had become.

A broken woman in a gilded cage.

And I didn't even know why.

I was kidnapped but treated like an unwilling guest rather than a hostage. And yet, that was exactly what I was.

So why hadn't he hurt me?

He'd had so many chances. So many moments to make me pay for trespassing on his land, for disobeying his orders, for defying him with words and glances.

If he wanted pain, he could have broken me by now.

If he wanted submission, he could have taken it.

But he hadn't.

So why?

What information did they want from me and what was this job he mentioned about?

What did he really want from me?

Inside the bathroom, I reached for the sink and froze as my gaze swept over the counter.

My breath hitched.

My things were here.

My toothbrush. My hairbrush. My perfume.

All carefully arranged as if I had placed them myself, exactly where I always put them at home.

Except this wasn't home.

And I hadn't packed them for some sort of twisted vacation.

A shiver slid down my spine, cold and sharp, as realization dawned.

He had brought them here.

Gone into my life, into my space, and brought these pieces of me to this room.

As if he had always intended for me to be here.

I stepped back, my hand catching on the doorframe to steady myself.

But I didn't stop there.

I turned and crossed to the closet, needing to see.

Needing to know.

I reached for the door, hesitating only a second before I pulled it open.

My clothes hung neatly on matching hangers, arranged in a perfect color gradient. My boots. My sneakers. Everything.

But that wasn't all.

There were others.

Dresses I didn't recognize. Blouses and jeans that I never owned.

Lingerie in delicate fabrics that were never mine.

Items that didn't belong to me.

A sick twist coiled in my stomach.

The last girl, I thought bitterly.

The one who wore these things before me.

I stumbled backward out of the closet, breathing ragged and uneven, my chest tightening like something sharp had lodged between my ribs. I collapsed to the bedroom floor, my legs folding beneath me. The weight of it all pressed down hard, and I couldn't move. Couldn't breathe.

What was happening?

Why had he done this?

I wrapped my arms around myself, but it didn't help. It only made me feel smaller, more vulnerable. The questions clawed at my mind, digging deeper with every passing second.

What had happened to her?

What would happen to me?

I was lost in my mind's spiraling thoughts when I heard a scream.

It was faint. Muffled. Distant.

But it was real.

I stopped breathing.

My head snapped toward the door, eyes wide. My pulse spiked as my ears strained to catch it again. For one agonizing moment, there was nothing but silence.

Then another scream. Softer this time, as if whoever was screaming was already too far gone.

No.

Please let me be imagining this.

But I wasn't.

I knew I wasn't.

The sick churn in my gut turned violent, like nausea twisting through bone and marrow.

It came from below.

Somewhere I couldn't see.

Somewhere I wasn't supposed to hear.

Tears burned behind my eyes, but I didn't blink them away. They slid hot and silent down my face as I curled tighter, biting the inside of my cheek to keep from making a sound.

I couldn't fall apart.

But my body still betrayed me.

Sobs tore through me, raw and ragged, scraping my throat on the way out. I clawed at my skin, nails biting in deep enough to leave crescents, desperate to feel something that wasn't terror or despair.

Desperate to escape this place.

This body.

This life.

Memories crashed over me.

Providence. Sam. All the times I thought I could be free.

I tipped my head back, gasping for air, and my gaze caught something by the window.

Books.

The sight of them sent a jolt through me. I blinked, pushing myself forward on shaking hands and knees to crawl toward them.

Something flickered inside me.

Hope, maybe. Or desperation pretending to be hope.

Some were mine—ones I'd brought with me to Providence.

But others weren't.

The last girl must have had them, I thought.

I touched their covers with trembling fingers, as if they might vanish. Or worse—disintegrate beneath my touch.

I exhaled slow and shaky, dragging myself upright. My hands found the windowsill as I pulled myself to standing, leaning heavily against the cool frame.

I stared out at the field.

It stretched wide, glowing silver under the moonlight.

Wild. Beautiful. Untouched by the chaos it had caused.

It mocked me.

And yet...I smiled.

Maybe Reich was right.

Everything I needed was in this room.

I just had to figure out how to use it.

Chapter Twenty-Two

REICH

"How'd it go, brother?" Castor asked as we hauled Lucas out of the trunk, his limp body thudding onto the cold ground.

I didn't answer. Instead, I grabbed Lucas' hand and bent his fingers back hard.

The sickening pop echoed through the room, followed by a scream that ripped through the air. Raw. Guttural. He thrashed against the restraints, his agony reverberating in the tight space.

Castor sighed, completely unfazed. "That bad, huh?"

I ignored him, my silence deliberate.

"Keeping this stuff bottled up isn't good for you, you know. That's what they say—"

"Who says?" I cut in, voice low. "Your hippie enchantress girlfriend?"

I shot him a look—a clear warning: Don't push me. Not tonight.

Castor only smirked, unbothered. "So much anger. Not good for your soul."

I let the words roll off me, as I responded, "Pretty sure I don't have one."

He exhaled dramatically. "Touché."

Then it was time for business.

We dragged Lucas to the pit. The real work would begin here.

I cracked my knuckles, then sent a hard punch straight to his jaw. His head snapped to the side, lolling forward as he blinked rapidly, dazed. Sweat slicked his face. Panic settled into his features as reality sank in.

Good.

He knew.

"Let's keep this simple," I said, crouching to meet his wild, darting gaze. "I'm tired, and I don't have patience for games. You're still breathing because I believe you have something I need." I leaned in. "Tell me who sent you."

Lucas gulped. His eyes flicked to Castor, then back to me. He hesitated.

Wrong move.

I grabbed the collar of his sweat-drenched shirt and yanked him forward, my voice a quiet snarl. "Who?"

His mouth floundered, his voice shaking. "It was... guys from the casino. They know I do odd jobs. They came to me with a favor—a girl. Green hair. Said I needed to rough her up and take her out of town."

My stomach knotted. "To where?"

"A motel. Three hundred miles west. Sanele." His words tumbled out fast, desperate. "They said she was being... shipped overseas. I don't know where, I swear!"

Shipped.

The word clawed through my brain like rusted wire.

My fists tightened at the thought, as I asked, "How much?"

"Five thousand. Half up front."

Five thousand. That was all it took? A price tag on a human life.

I inhaled sharply through my nose, reining in the violence thrumming beneath my skin.

How many others had they done this to? She couldn't be the first.

"How did you find her?" I pressed, my voice colder now.

"They sent her location the night of." He swallowed hard. "I didn't know until they texted me. Said I had to move fast."

They must have been tracking her. Watching her. Waiting.

But why her?

Why Sage?

It hit me. The bounty. Lucas was nothing more than a pawn. An errand boy for something much bigger.

"Which motel?" My voice was sharp enough to cut.

"I didn't get that far. I was supposed to message them once it was done, but you blindsided me before I could."

I stepped back, my pulse thrumming in my ears.

Behind me, Castor exhaled. "For Klay," he said. "I took the photos we needed of Sage. Proof she's under our control."

"Send them tomorrow," I muttered, exhaustion creeping in. "I don't want to deal with it tonight. I barely want to deal with him." I gestured toward Lucas.

Castor nodded, slipping into the shadows, as I followed to grab what I needed before returning to finish the job.

I turned, heading down the hall, but my thoughts wouldn't slow.

I passed her room, stopping in the process in front of the bedroom door where she was and lingering far too long outside of it.

Sage.

Her boldness. Her defiance. The fire she carried, even in fear. It made her situation with Klay even more baffling.

She wasn't the type to be drawn to men like him.

So why was she involved?

Did she go willingly? Or was she coerced?

The Ovitt brothers didn't date. They were given women. Flashy, affluent, chosen for their status.

Sage didn't fit that mold.

Which meant Klay had kept her a secret.

A woman he couldn't show off but wouldn't let go.
Was that why she ran?
All of it gnawed at me, stealing what little chance I had at sleep.
So, I decided, tomorrow, I'd get my answers.
She had to talk.
For her sake—and mine.

Chapter Twenty-Three

SAGE

I JOLTED AWAKE AGAIN. My heart pounded, frantic and hollow, as though it were trying to escape the cage of my ribs. Cold sweat beaded at my temple, dampening the strands of hair clinging to my skin. My breaths came in shallow gasps, each one stinging my lungs like I'd just surfaced from deep waters.

The moonlight poured in through the window and I blinked hard, struggling to slow my breathing, grounding myself in the reality of where I was.

But this wasn't safety.

This wasn't peace.

I wasn't home.

I stared at the ceiling, the ache in my chest building as the memories clawed their way back up, relentless and cruel. Klay's voice echoed in the hollow space of my skull, a brutal soundtrack on repeat.

"Pathetic."

"You did this to yourself."

"You're nothing but a whore."

Each word reopened wounds I thought had already scarred over. But it seemed there was no end to how deep he could cut me, even when he wasn't here to do it himself.

Each time I woke, I found a moment—a heartbeat—of relief. The disoriented belief that I was free of it all. That I had escaped the hell I'd lived through. But as the fog cleared, the reality settled like lead in my bones.

I was still trapped.

Maybe not by Klay this time.

But by Reich.

By something just as dark. Just as impossible to escape.

I pushed myself up slowly, wincing as the soreness in my shoulders and ribs flared hot and sharp. Swallowing thickly, I forced my legs over the edge of the bed and stood, grounding myself in the task of moving and breathing.

It was all I could do.

I drifted to the bookshelf, fingers trailing along the worn spines of novels I'd once loved. I wanted them to save me again. To pull me out of this place and into another world, one where I wasn't owned by anyone.

But the words blurred on the pages. I couldn't focus. I couldn't outrun the question that had burned in the back of my mind since the moment Reich took me.

What was this job he said we had?

The way he'd said it—it was cold. Detached. Like it was inevitable.

What was he going to do with me?

What was I supposed to do for him?

And why did a part of me still wonder if I was safer here than anywhere else?

That was the darkest part of all.

The door creaked open.

I froze, spine snapping straight as my breath hitched. My pulse pounded against the inside of my throat, wild and fast.

Heavy footsteps crossed the threshold. Measured. Unhurried.

Reich.

He filled the space like gravity itself, dragging my gaze to him whether I wanted it or not. The dim light caught the sharp edges of his face, painting shadows beneath his cheekbones. His hazel eyes glowed faintly, cutting through the gloom.

In one hand, he carried a basic white ceramic plate—filled with breakfast foods. In the other, a glass of orange juice. Beads of condensation clung to the glass, a slow drip of water tracing its path toward his fingers.

He crossed the room without a word, setting both down on the dresser. His movements were fluid. Controlled. As if this was just another ordinary morning.

"Breakfast," he said simply. His voice low and disarming.

I didn't move.

I didn't trust it.

I didn't trust him.

I kept my eyes on the floor, on the empty space between us. But the tension coiled tighter anyway, until it was suffocating.

"I'm not hungry," I said, forcing my voice to stay flat, even as it rasped in my dry throat.

"You need to eat." His tone didn't shift. It was a statement of fact. A quiet expectation. But under it, there was something else. Something that stirred the air between us and made my skin prickle.

I lifted my gaze, searching his face for a reason.

"Why am I here?" I asked.

The silence that followed wasn't unexpected. It was the same answer I always got.

Nothing.

But I still felt the sting.

I stood anyway. My legs wobbled, but I didn't care. I crossed the room in slow, deliberate steps until I stood in front of him, chest rising and falling with shallow breaths.

"How long will I be here?" I demanded. "Can you at least tell me that?"

Again, silence.

A muscle twitched in his jaw, but he said nothing.

I scoffed. Shook my head like it might shake him loose. I turned away, ready to retreat to the only corner of this room that felt like mine.

But he grabbed me.

His hand was a steel band around my arm, spinning me back toward him so fast my balance faltered. His other hand caught my waist, steadying me. Holding me.

His breath ghosted against my cheek as he leaned in. His voice a low murmur. "Stop asking questions you know I won't answer."

I glared up at him, anger burning fresh. "Why not?"

His lips curved—not quite a smile. "Because you won't like the answers."

He let me go, his hand dragging down my arm in a slow, lingering slide before he stepped back. His gaze flicked toward the plate. "Since you're so curious, Sage, let's make a deal."

I didn't like the sound of that.

Still, I asked. "What kind of deal?"

"You answer my questions. Honestly."

"And if I don't?"

The smirk that curled at the edge of his mouth was wicked. Dark. "I'll know."

My stomach twisted. "And what do I get?"

"You get to ask your own."

"You won't answer them," I accused.

"I will," he said, eyeing the plate of food again. "But only if you eat."

I stared at him, suspicion rising like bile. "Why do you care if I eat?"

His eyes darkened. "Sage," he warned. Quiet. Lethal. "I don't want to deal with digging a grave for someone I didn't kill."

My blood ran cold.

"I promised not to hurt you," he continued, his tone measured, almost gentle. "But that promise comes with conditions. So, start eating before I make you regret not doing it yourself."

There was something final about the way he said it. Something that told me he wasn't bluffing.

I hesitated a second too long.

He took a step forward.

I grabbed the toast. Shoved a bite into my mouth.

His expression softened—just barely. His lips curved. Slow. Satisfied. "Good girl."

The words made me shiver. I hated that they made my stomach twist in that familiar, treacherous way.

I chewed mechanically, forcing the food down. Reich watched me the entire time, like a wolf watching his prey, amused by its compliance.

After a few moments, he spoke again. "How did you end up in Providence?"

I swallowed. "I drove."

He arched a brow. "Why?"

"I left home."

"Why?"

I sighed, closing my eyes. "I lost everything."

He was silent a beat. "Everything?"

"My father. My house. My... life."

"And?" he pressed; voice softer now.

I didn't want to say it. I didn't want him to know.

But I was already unraveling.

"My ex."

His expression darkened.

"Tell me about him."

"There's nothing to tell."

"Don't lie to me." His voice snapped around me, dragging the truth out like a splinter beneath my skin. I shook my head, blinking fast, but the tears came anyway.

Memories swelled, crushing me. Klay's voice in my ear. The pain. The shame.

I broke.

The sob tore free of my throat before I could stop it.

And then Reich was there.

His arms wrapped around me, lifting me like I weighed nothing. He carried me back to the bed and sat me down with a gentleness I didn't expect. His hand brushed over my hair, down my spine, soothing in a way that made it hurt worse.

"Don't hide from me," he murmured.

I hated him for saying it.

Hated myself for listening.

For leaning into him.

For letting him hold me like he might put the pieces back together if he just held tight enough.

"You need to stop letting this own you," he said.

I wanted to scream at him. You don't know. You don't understand.

But instead, I sat there. Silent.

Finally, he sighed. "You can answer my questions later." He stood, walking to the door.

My voice cracked as it left me. "Can I ask one?"

He turned. His face unreadable. "A deal's a deal."

I hesitated. "Until I answer yours... I won't get mine."

"Correct."

And then he was gone.

The door clicked shut. I stared at the empty space where he'd stood.

And realized—I wasn't sure if I hated him.

Or if I hated the way he was the first person to ever see me like this.

Chapter Twenty-Four

REICH

C ASTOR STOPPED ME THE moment I stepped out of Sage's room. He was leaning against the hallway wall like he'd been waiting, but his casual posture didn't fool me. His gaze was sharp, something urgent brewing beneath the surface.

"Reich," he said, his tone low but edged with something tight. "Klay called. He wants to talk."

My stomach tightened, but my face stayed still. I held Castor's stare for a breath before extending my hand. "Phone."

He handed it over without question, though his jaw flexed as I took it. He knew what this was. We both did. This wasn't just a conversation. It was a game of inches. A chance to tip the scales or watch everything slip.

I exhaled slowly, rolling my shoulders back as I dialed. One ring. Two.

Klay picked up before the third, his voice sliding through the speaker smooth as oil, but beneath it was the ever-present menace. That coiled threat that lived in men like him. "Reich," he drawled, pleased with himself. "I was starting to think you'd forgotten about me."

I didn't answer.

He chuckled. It was low and cold, a sound that clawed under my skin. "Thank you for finding my little pet," he went on, lazy amusement woven through every word. "I was worried I'd have to send someone to clean up the mess she made. But look at us—working together again. Feels good, doesn't it?"

I kept my tone flat, professional, forcing the bile back down. "All in a day's work."

Klay hummed thoughtfully. "I'll be back in the country next week. I want to collect her myself. Keep her warm for me, would you? You know how I like my things. Broken in, but not broken."

I closed my eyes, grinding my teeth together until my jaw ached. His words slithered like rot in my ears. Broken in. As if she were a toy.

He thought he owned her.

He thought he had every right to.

And for now, I had to let him.

"If you can keep her safe," Klay added, "name your price. Whatever you want, it's yours."

I imagined tearing his throat out with my bare hands. I imagined the crack of his skull against the concrete. I imagined the slow draw of his last breath as he realized too late who he was dealing with.

But I didn't say any of that. I swallowed it all down.

"I'm sure we'll come to an agreement," I said instead, every word carved from stone.

He laughed again. A smug, grating sound that made my skin crawl. "Until then," he said, pausing like he was savoring the moment. "Have fun with her. Test her out."

The phone creaked under the pressure of my grip. I forced myself to release the breath caught in my throat, counting to three before I answered.

"Will do," I said coldly, then hung up before I could hear another word from him. Before I lost the thin thread of control I had left.

Castor was watching me when I lowered the phone. His arms were crossed, his brow furrowed. "You good?" he asked, though we both knew the answer.

"No," I said, handing him the phone. "But I'll manage."

We stood there for a moment in silence, the weight of everything unspoken settling between us.

"You believe him?" Castor asked eventually, his voice low.

I shook my head. "I believe he's obsessed. And desperate." I paused. "Which makes him dangerous."

Castor exhaled through his nose, nodding. "One week, huh?"

"One week," I repeated.

One week to keep Sage safe. One week to keep her in the dark. One week to figure out how to untangle the web she was caught in without getting us both killed.

It sounded simple.

But I knew it wasn't.

I walked with Castor back toward the main room, both of us falling into step without thinking. The house was quiet tonight, but it was the kind of quiet that didn't last. We both knew it.

Later, in my office, we sat across from each other. Castor poured some more of the whiskey while I sifted through files I'd already read a dozen times. My mind wasn't on them.

It was on her.

She was in my house. Sleeping under my roof.

And I had no idea how I was supposed to keep my hands off her.

Castor tapped the edge of his glass against mine. "You seem tense," he said, though there was a sharpness under his words. A knowing. "More than usual."

I ran a hand over my face, scrubbing at the stubble there like I could wipe away the exhaustion clawing at me. "I've spent the last two days trying to pull answers out of someone who refuses to talk."

He laughed under his breath. "Sounds familiar."

I shot him a look. "You're not helping."

He raised both hands in mock surrender. "I'm just saying... you've always had a thing for impossible women."

"She's not impossible," I muttered, draining half my glass. "She's stubborn."

He smirked. "Isn't that what I said?"

I didn't answer. My gaze drifted to the window, to the dark stretch of trees beyond it. Somewhere out there, Klay was planning his next move. Somewhere out there, the world was spinning toward disaster, and I was sitting here, drinking whiskey, wondering how the hell I ended up here.

"You'll figure it out," Castor said quietly, as if reading my mind.

"I always do," I replied, but the words felt hollow tonight.

He left me alone a while later, taking the bottle with him because he knew if he didn't, I wouldn't stop. I'd sit here until dawn, drinking and thinking myself in circles.

I needed something else.

I stood, crossing to the turntable in the corner. My fingers hovered over the records until they settled on the one I needed.

I let the music settle into my bones, closing my eyes as I leaned back against the desk. The lyrics hit too close. I'd built my life on control. On precision. On keeping everyone at arm's length.

And then there was Sage.

I didn't know if she was my rescue or my destruction.

Maybe both.

I checked on her again that night. She was asleep, but not peacefully. Her body twisted beneath the sheets, her face pale and damp with sweat. She was fighting something in her dreams. Something I couldn't touch.

But I wanted to.

I wanted to be the thing that made it stop.

So, I went to her room and I sat down on the edge of her bed and watched her breathe. Watched her fight. Watched her survive.

I reached out, smoothing the damp hair from her forehead, my fingers lingering too long.

"You're safe," I murmured, even though she couldn't hear me. "For now."

But Klay was coming.

And I didn't know if I could keep her safe from him.

Or even from me.

One week.

That's all I had.

One week until this game ended.

Or until it destroyed us both.

Chapter Twenty-Five

SAGE

"**L**OOK WHAT WE HAVE here, gentlemen."

The voice crawled into my skull like smoke slipping beneath a door—thick, suffocating, and impossible to ignore. Muffled at first, distant, but with each word, it sharpened. Clearer. Closer.

I tried to move. I tried to run. But my body... it wasn't mine anymore. It felt foreign. Heavy. As if I'd been submerged in quicksand, dragged under by invisible hands. My limbs refused me, weighted by an unnatural stillness that made my mind thrash in its place, screaming orders that my body would not obey.

I was paralyzed.

A cold surface pressed against the length of me, biting into my skin with a cruel indifference. Dirt. I could feel it now. Damp and gritty beneath my cheek, sapping the warmth from my bones. My breathing rasped out unevenly. Shallow, jagged pulls of air scraped through my throat like broken glass. Every exhale burned.

What happened?

Where was I?

How had I even gotten here?

Fragments of memory flickered in my mind. Footsteps in the hall. Being given some punch from the party. Fingers on my skin. Then nothing. Until now.

A shadow moved in front of the dim, moonlight that shined above me, blotting it out like an eclipse. I blinked, struggling to focus, my lashes sticky with tears I hadn't realized had fallen. And then... a figure crouched beside me, his shape distorted by the haze of half-consciousness. His hand came up, rough fingers prying one of my eyes open. I flinched as much as I could, which wasn't much.

His gaze raked over me—cold, clinical, unfeeling. A predator assessing the weight of its catch.

"She's alive," he said after a beat, his voice dark with something that wasn't relief. It was hunger. Satisfaction. A malicious kind of glee that made my stomach twist violently.

I wanted to close my eyes. To disappear. But I couldn't.

"Where... am... I?" My voice cracked, a ghost of a sound. It hurt to speak, like dragging words across raw flesh. My chest ached under an invisible pressure, every shallow breath a battle I was steadily losing.

"Don't worry about it," another voice snapped from behind him. This one was sharper. Younger. Meaner.

"You'll be in hell soon enough," sneered someone else, this time from my left.

Laughter erupted around me, cutting through the thick air. It was coarse. Harsh. The kind of laughter that wasn't human. It rattled the walls and reverberated inside my skull until I thought I might shatter from the sound alone. The section of woods—wherever I was—felt suddenly smaller. Closer. Suffocating.

I couldn't see them all, but I could feel them.

Four. No—five.

Five dark shapes moving around me like vultures circling something long dead.

I wasn't dead yet.

But they were patient.

"So pretty," one of them said, his voice dripping with mockery. He was close—so close I could feel his breath against my cheek. It smelled like liquor and cigarettes. "How rude of our little brother not to introduce us sooner."

"Our duty," another chimed in, and there was a sickening click as something metallic snapped open. A switchblade? A knife? "We have to vet all his toys."

The word hit me like a slap.

Toy.

That's what I was to them. A plaything. A game. A distraction they would tear apart for fun.

"Please..." I whispered. My voice trembled, breaking on the word. "Don't..."

My legs refused to move. My arms wouldn't lift. I was locked inside my own skin, screaming silently as I lay helpless beneath their shadows. I tried to twist away, but I had nowhere to go. The ground was cold and unyielding. And so were they.

"God, I love it when they beg," one murmured with perverse delight.

The man in front of me—his grin widened, splitting his face into something monstrous. He shared a glance with one of the others, something unspoken passing between them. A plan. A decision.

And then, they moved.

Slow. Deliberate.

Their shadows swallowed the thin slivers of light, plunging me deeper into darkness.

Panic surged, wild and feral. It tore through me with brutal force, a scream trapped in my chest. My pulse thundered in my ears, fast and erratic, drowning out every other sound.

Rough hands closed around my ankles. Another gripped my wrists, twisting them painfully. Their fingers were calloused and cruel, leaving behind bruises I couldn't yet see as they trailed over my skin, touching places they had no right to claim. Fingers slid into my hair, yanking my head back hard enough to snap my vision to the dark sky.

"Shhh," one of them whispered, mock-gentle, as his thumb traced the line of my jaw. "You'll like this part."

I wanted to fight. I wanted to scream and claw and bite. But I couldn't.

I was helpless.

And they were hungry.

Their laughter turned low, almost reverent.

As if this was sacred to them.

As if tearing me apart was their god-given right.

I was prey.

And they were the hunters.

And in that moment, I knew—there was no one coming to save me.

I burst awake, lungs burning, dragging in sharp, ragged breaths like I was clawing my way out of the depths of an endless pit. My heart hammered a brutal rhythm in my chest, my fists clenched so tightly around the sheets they might tear through them. I couldn't stop shaking. Couldn't stop feeling them—their hands. Their laughter. The suffocating weight of being prey again.

I squeezed my eyes shut, trying to force it away, but it was no use. The memories sliced through me like glass, relentless, jagged, and cold. A scream tore from my throat, raw and broken. I clutched at my scalp, nails digging in hard enough to sting, wishing—*desperately*—that I could dig deep enough to rip them out. The images. The sounds. The way their fingers had stripped away my humanity like I was a thing. An object.

I just wanted it gone.

I wanted it all gone.

A thought came to mind, though it seemed like a far-fetched idea.

If I could just replace their touch with someone else's...maybe I wouldn't feel so hollow.

Maybe the scars wouldn't ache so viciously.

Maybe I could breathe again.

A soft creak snapped me out of my spiral, sudden and sharp. My gaze shot toward the sound. My pulse jumped when I saw him.

Reich.

He stood by the window, half-cast in shadow, the morning light bringing a brightening warmth across his features. His frame was casual, deceptively so, leaning against the window frame like he belonged there. An open book hung loosely in his hand, his thumb keeping his place. His presence should've sent me deeper into panic, but instead—it stilled me. Infuriated me. Grounded me in ways I hadn't asked for. And yet... I wasn't sure I wanted him to leave.

"How long have you been there?" My voice was sharp, laced with humiliation. Rawness scraped along every syllable.

He didn't move. Didn't flinch.

He simply closed the book in his hand with slow, deliberate precision, "Long enough."

The silence that followed was thicker than it should've been. A pause loaded with things neither of us wanted to address.

Then softer, he asked, "Bad dream?"

His words shouldn't have mattered. They shouldn't have dug beneath my skin. But the way he said them... not mocking, not dismissive... it disarmed me.

I tugged the sheets tighter around myself, as if they could shield me from him. From the way his eyes never looked away, like he was peeling me open. "I just... can't get certain things out of my mind."

Reich arched a brow, the hint of a challenge flashing behind those unreadable eyes. "The certain things you refuse to talk about?"

I shrugged, trying for indifference. Trying and *failing*. I kept my gaze averted, but it drifted anyway—lingering too long on the sharp cut of his jaw and the way his muscles flexed as he shifted his stance. Even beneath the simplicity of joggers and a plain black t-shirt, he was lethal. Dangerous. And God, help me, my body responded to it.

He smirked like he knew. Like he felt the pull just as much as I did, "I came to check on you after—"

"After my ridiculous meltdown," I cut him off, the words snapping like brittle twigs. The sting of shame made my skin burn.

"No," he said evenly.

His eyes flickered with something I couldn't name. Something I wasn't sure I wanted to.

A silence stretched between us, thick and uneasy.

Then he broke it, his voice low but sharper than a knife, "I have a different question now."

I braced myself for what he was about to say.

"Why are you so scared to tell me what happened?"

I shook my head, but it wasn't enough. "Because..." My voice faltered. I swallowed. "Because you won't see me the same."

He studied me, long and hard, before his tone shifted. Quieter. More dangerous. "And how is it you think I see you now?"

I held his gaze, but it was like holding on to the edge of a blade, "I don't know," I lied.

I knew exactly how he saw me.

As something he wanted.

His lips twitched into something close to a laugh, dark and knowing. "Oh, I think you do."

I bristled. My walls snapped up instinctively, before saying, "As someone you can control."

The accusation flew out like a dagger and I continued with it, "You want to know me because you can't control someone without understanding their weaknesses."

There was no flinch. No defense.

Reich simply tilted his head, amused and infuriating, as he retorted, "You don't need to know someone to control them. People are simple. They just need a little motivation."

The conversation was slipping into dangerous territory, and I knew it.

So, I veered, "How did my things get here?"

Blunt. Deflective. I regretted asking the moment it left my lips, knowing he was probably going to hit me with, "A deal's a deal, Sage."

But instead, he tilted his head again, considering.

So, I added, "Some of the books—"

"Are mine," he interrupted, a wicked smirk playing at his mouth. "I put them here for you."

My throat tightened. "Why?"

"I watched you for months out in my field, you know?" he said, like that explained everything. "And you only ever read the same things. Figured you could use something new."

I clenched my jaw, his admission hitting harder than I expected. *Watching me?* "I don't like new," I snapped.

"Says the girl who ran away from everything familiar just to chase something *new*."

His words landed deeper than they should have, and he let the silence stretch.

Then he added, quieter now, "Maybe you'd actually find what you're looking for if you stopped hiding behind what's safe."

I shot him a glare, sharp and scathing, but he didn't stop.

"You know the definition of insanity, right? Doing the same thing over and over and expecting different results?"

He tilted his head slightly. "Whatever you're doing... it isn't working. I watched you repeat the same routine—day in, day out. And every night, you went home looking just as hollow as you did the day before."

He was right, and I hated that he was.

The conversation was getting too close, too personal. I couldn't let him see it was working—couldn't let him see *me*. So I deflected.

"And the clothes?" I asked, sharpening my tone. "Am I supposed to believe they're yours?"

Reich let out a low chuckle. "They're for you."

"I don't need hand-me-downs from your last house slave," I spat, venom sharp in my voice.

That got him.

His smirk faded. His knuckles whitened against the windowsill, not from anger—but from something worse.

Restraint.

The air thickened between us. My pulse raced.

And even knowing it was dangerous, my gaze drifted lower.

His joggers did little to hide what I shouldn't be looking at.

He noticed but he said nothing. He moved instead. Slow. Purposeful. Like he was stalking something fragile and wild.

Me.

He stepped between my knees, his body heat coiling around me, suffocating. His hand gripped my chin, tilting my face toward his with a slow, commanding touch.

"Look at me," he murmured.

I did.

And it felt like drowning.

He was too close. I could feel every hard inch of him against me, the rough fabric doing nothing to soften the impact. His breath ghosted over my skin, hot and deliberate.

"What is it you need, Sage?"

My pulse stuttered. My body answered before I could.

I wanted him. I needed him to erase everything.

But I forced myself to say, "I... I don't know."

His grip tightened just enough to make me gasp.

"If you keep lying to me," he said, his voice a dangerous promise, "I'll make it so you can't speak... only scream."

A shiver raked through me.

I knew he meant it.

I swallowed hard. "I... need to forget," I whispered.

For a heartbeat, something flickered in his expression. Something unguarded. But it was gone as quickly as it came.

"And what is it you want me to help you forget?"

I hesitated before relenting, "The last time I was with a man... it wasn't a good time."

There.

The truth. *Kind of.*

Silence stretched taut between us.

Then—he laughed. Low. Dark. Dangerous.

"I'm sorry he didn't satisfy you, wildflower," he said, but his voice darkened, before continuing, "But we both know that's not the full story."

His eyes bored into me, stripping me bare.

Then he turned for the door.

Unimpressed by my half-truth.

"Reich—" My voice cracked.

He stopped, glancing back.

"—I haven't heard music since... since coming here," I said, hating how small I sounded. "If it's okay, I'd like to."

His eyes softened. Barely.

But he said nothing.

He just left.

And as the door clicked shut behind him, I wondered if I'd just handed him another weapon to use against me.

Chapter Twenty-Six

REICH

She thinks I want to control her.

The thought kept circling in my head like a vulture. She couldn't be more wrong. If only it were that simple. Control was easy. I didn't need to want it—it was second nature. No, the problem was far worse.

I didn't trust her. And that was why I had to keep her close. Why I had to keep watching her, questioning her, stripping her down until I found something I could believe in.

But Sage... she was all sharp edges and shadowed glances. Half-truths and practiced silences. I could see the effort it took for her to hold herself together every time I asked for something real. It wasn't defiance that kept her quiet.

It was *survival.* That made it harder.

Because even knowing that, it didn't stop me from wanting her.

Not just the feel of her body under my hands—*though, fuck, that haunted me too*—but something deeper.

I wanted to unravel her. Slowly. Intimately.

I wanted to be the one who pulled her apart and laid every piece bare. I wanted to know her. Every flicker of her rage, every crack in her armor, every last bruise on her soul.

I wanted it all.

The parts she wouldn't give anyone.

And when she'd looked at me, those bright green eyes brimming with something raw when she asked for my help... something lit up inside me. A spark of hope that maybe I was finally getting through.

But I'd missed something.

Music.

The one thing that had always tethered me to something real. The one thing that had kept me sane when everything else was nothing but static and ruin. My one escape. It had been hers too. I'd seen it in her eyes that night of the festival and at the House of Music.

She craved it.

Needed it.

Just like I did.

When I left her room, my pulse was wild, like I'd already lost something I hadn't earned yet. I had no choice but to lean into instinct. This was my way in. My way to earn her words, her truths. Music was the door I had to walk through.

I spent hours that night sifting through my collection, something I hadn't done in years with this kind of purpose. Every song held its own kind of history, but I wasn't looking for nostalgia.

I was building a bridge.

One hundred songs. No bullshit. No filler. Each one chosen because I knew the ache behind the lyrics.

Knew what it felt like to need them like oxygen.

And maybe—*just maybe*—it would remind her there was something worth holding on to.

Maybe it would remind *me.*

By the time the sun bled into the sky, I was ready. Playlist queued, meal prepped, hands shaking just a little too much as I knocked once on her door before letting myself in.

She was curled up on the bed, wrapped in sheets that clung to her body like they knew how desperately she needed protection. Her breathing was steady, but the faint crease between her brows told me her mind was still chewing through the nightmares.

She looked almost peaceful.

But I knew better.

I crossed the room, setting the tray on the dresser with quiet precision. I could hear the rustling of sheets behind me. When I turned, green eyes locked on me. Awake. Watching.

Sadness flickered there.

And something else.

Something she didn't want me to see but hadn't figured out how to hide.

"I have something for you," I said, clearing my throat. My voice came out rougher than I wanted. "A few things, actually."

She didn't move right away. She stayed there, frozen in hesitation, like she wasn't sure whether this was another game. I gave her time. Let her take it.

When she finally crawled toward me, clutching the sheets around her like they'd offer her protection, it hit harder than it should've. Even in this room, even with all the things I'd given her, she didn't feel safe.

Not yet.

Maybe not ever.

She eyed the tray warily. "Why are there two plates?"

"Because one's mine," I said, casual. Simple.

I picked up the second fork and took a bite, making sure she saw it.

Her gaze lingered.

There was something about the way she looked at me then. Like I was offering her something she couldn't quite believe was real.

She took the plate. Ate slowly. Carefully.

I arched a brow, catching the shy glances she tried to hide. When our eyes met, she flinched and looked away.

But then she looked back.

Endearing wasn't a word I used often.

But that's exactly what she was in that moment.

"What?" I asked after a while, teasing. "Is there a problem with the food?"

She shook her head quickly, swallowing. "No. I just didn't expect you to eat with me."

"Well," I said, "I am."

I didn't explain it further.

I wasn't even sure I could.

And maybe that was what made this all feel so grounding.

We ate in silence, but it wasn't heavy like I expected. It felt... normal. Comfortable.

By the time I finished, she was still pushing food around. Picking at it, distracted. I let her be. Instead, I grabbed the portable music player I'd set up for her and turned it on.

The first notes drifted into the room.

Soft. Raw.

A melody that spoke of bruises and survival.

It shifted everything.

When I looked back, her eyes were already on me. Bright. Unreadable.

But her breathing had slowed. Her shoulders were looser.

Something about the music was working.

"Music," I said quietly. "As requested," I handed her the controls.

As her fingers brushed mine, the faintest hint of her scent hit me. Sweet. Clean. Always like wildflowers after a rainstorm, just like the night we met.

It shouldn't have made me feel the way it did.

But it did.

"Thank you, Reich."

My name on her lips shouldn't have hit me the way it did either.

But again, it did.

Everything she did was like a punch I welcomed.

"You're welcome, Sage." I stepped back, leaning against the wall to steady myself, before continuing, "Are you ready to talk?"

Her body tensed.

She pulled back into herself.

My patience thinned.

"Sage," I warned. "You're testing me. The longer you hold out, the worse this becomes."

She glared at me then. Defiance sparking hard in her eyes.

"Why does it matter, Reich?" she snapped. "Why does my past matter so much to you?"

I didn't blink, just spoke, all business, "Because you may not trust me. But I need to trust you and knowing all the information is how I do that."

Her jaw clenched.

She wanted to fight.

And maybe she should have.

But I wasn't letting her win this.

"Keep playing this game of hide and seek" I said quietly, almost deadly, "and you'll stay stuck in it."

"I'm not playing your games," she hissed and then pushed her plate off the bed, getting up from where she was sitting.

The plate clattered loudly as it hit the floor.

I didn't flinch.

But something in me snapped.

"You drive me fucking insane." My voice came out low, rough—more confession than accusation. "You can't hide forever, Sage. One day, you'll have to take the mask off...and face who you really are."

I crossed the space in two long strides and backed her against the wall before she could take another step. My hands braced on either side of her head, caging her in—not to trap her, but to stop myself from unraveling.

She stared up at me, breath coming quick and shallow. "If I push you that far," she whispered, "then why keep me here? Why not just let me walk away?"

I sucked in a breath, sharp and tight in my chest. The words slipped before I could stop them. "I've tried."

Her eyes narrowed. "And?"

I met her gaze then—no armor, no mask. Just the truth. "All it did was make me want to know why you keep hiding from me."

The fight drained from her like a wave pulling back. Her jaw slackened, something in her softening—not even surrender, but something much deeper.

"You said I could come to you depending on what I need," she said, her voice lower, watching me through her thick, heavy lashes.

"I did." I swallowed, realizing I may have just fucked up.

"What did you mean by that?" She asked, fidgeting with the edge of her tank top, with her fingers tracing over the hem of her shirt slightly.

Her hands far too close to me.

To my waist.

And then she shrugged, and the strap of her top slid down her shoulder.

My throat went dry.

"What do you need, Sage?" I asked carefully.

But I already knew.

And so did she.

I backed up, putting some more distance in between us, but she surprised me and stepped closer, closing in that space I attempted.

Her shorts slid slowly down her hips to the ground, sending my mind spiraling as my entire body went taut.

"What are you doing?" My voice was rougher than I meant.

She didn't answer.

The other strap fell away.

She turned her back to me, baring the delicate curve of her neck to me like a silent offering.

"Can you untie the knot?" she asked quietly.

I exhaled through my teeth as I stepped in close.

My fingers brushing her skin as I pulled the knot free.

As you wish, wildflower.

Her top slid away.

And then she turned to face me.

Bare.

Exposed.

Unflinching.

Nothing but teasing eyes and a slight smile that said it all.

I was completely, utterly fucked.

And I knew it.

CHAPTER TWENTY-SEVEN

SAGE

MAYBE THIS WAS A mistake.

But deep down, beneath the chaos twisting inside my gut, it didn't feel like one.

I needed this. I needed someone to want me. To touch me like I was something they couldn't bear to lose.

Ever since that last night in Sanele, I'd felt filthy. Stripped down and thrown out. Discarded like something used up and broken. Every time I caught my reflection, it made me shudder. I didn't recognize her—the girl staring back at me with hollow eyes and a brittle smile. She wasn't wanted anymore. She wasn't needed. She was a burden. A story people pitied until they got tired of hearing it.

But then there was Reich.

And God help me against my better judgement, I craved him.

I wanted him with a hunger that burned through my veins, even though every piece of logic in me screamed no. Even though I knew it was reckless and dangerous.

I wanted him because he didn't look at me like I was broken. He didn't flinch away from the shadows clinging to me. It was almost as if he was already darker than they were.

Slowly, I lifted my gaze.

Reich was stiff, rigid as stone, standing like a man fighting a battle he already knew he was going to lose. Every muscle in his body was tense, his jaw locked so tight I could practically hear his teeth grinding together. But his eyes—*God, his eyes*—betrayed him.

They were dark. Hungry.

And when his gaze dropped over my body, lingering at the slope of my shoulders and the curve of my hips, I knew.

I wasn't crazy.

He wanted me just as badly as I wanted him.

And that knowledge gave me courage I didn't know I had.

I let my voice drop into something low, something I hoped sounded braver than I felt, "What do you need, Reich?"

He flinched like I'd caught him off guard.

"What are you doing, Sage?" His voice was a quiet threat, but it was ragged. Frayed at the edges like he was barely keeping himself together.

I pressed a hand to his chest, slow and deliberate, feeling the rapid thud of his heartbeat beneath my palm. It steadied me. Anchored me. And somehow, it also undid me.

I dragged my fingers up. Over his throat. Along the sharp edge of his jaw. My skin buzzed with the heat of him, but I held his gaze the whole time. Testing him. Daring him.

"Just asking a question," I murmured.

My fingertips brushed his mouth.

His breath hitched, lips parting just slightly. His control—*flawless, untouchable Reich*—fractured for a heartbeat. And it made something viciously triumphant swell inside me.

"That's not how this works," he muttered, trying to stay composed, raising a single brow like he was still in charge of this game he insisted on.

But I wasn't playing by his rules anymore.

I took his hand in mine, brought it to my lips, and without breaking eye contact, I slipped two of his fingers into my mouth. Sucking gently and tasting his skin before releasing him.

His pupils blew wide.

And just as the warmth started to seep into his gaze, his other hand snapped out, gripping my wrist hard enough to make me gasp. His fingers tightened slowly, sending a sharp warning through my bones. I should've pulled away. But I didn't.

Instead, a quiet moan escaped me.

Deliberately, almost lazily, Reich parted his lips and took my finger into his mouth. His tongue swept over it, hot, rough and sinfully slow.

And then—*God, help me*—he closed his eyes and moaned, low and dark.

When he pulled back, cool air rushed over my damp skin, and a shiver tore through me, leaving goosebumps in its wake.

I froze, feeling breathless as I spoke his name, "Reich..."

He clenched his jaw, "Don't."

"Don't what?" I swallowed.

His voice was rough, ragged. "Don't make me need you."

And I felt it then. All of it. The war tearing through him. The way he was fighting himself, clawing back control he didn't have anymore. The storm he was keeping contained on my behalf.

But I didn't want him to contain it any longer.

So, I tangled my fingers in his shirt and tugged him toward me. Just enough.

His body pressed into mine, his hardness searing through the thin barrier of his clothes. He caught my hips in his hands, and suddenly I was pinned between him and the wall, his breath hot on my mouth as his lips hovered just over mine.

Waiting.

I felt his pulse pounding in the tips of his fingers as they tangled in my hair, holding me still. His lips brushed mine when he spoke, so soft it was almost gentle.

"I need to taste you."

His confession slipped out like a wound breaking open—bare, unfiltered.

And it hit somewhere deep, somewhere I'd kept hollow for too long.

Like something starved finally speaking.

Like hunger wrapped in ache.

So, I gave him what he was waiting for, "Then taste me, Reich."

His eyes burned—dark, unrelenting.

And in the next breath, my wrists were pinned above my head, as his mouth dragging slow heat down the curve of my throat, breath hot and uneven.

"You have no idea how long I've wanted this," he growled, voice rough against my skin.

My pulse faltered, breath catching. "Then don't hold back."

His smirk was dangerous as he spoke, "Careful what you ask for."

And then his mouth slammed into mine—raw, savage. This kiss wasn't gentle or tentative; it was a claiming. His grip tightened on my wrists, pinning them roughly above me as his tongue thrusted into my mouth, conquering every corner. He pressed closer, grinding his body into mine until I arched into him, starving for more.

My legs instinctively wrapped around his waist, pulling him tighter, anchoring him against me. His hands gripped my hips possessively, lifting me higher until I felt all of him—rigid, scorching and urgent.

When he finally tore himself away, his breath rasped harshly, his eyes were dark and filled with what looked like an insatiable hunger.

"Greedy wildflower," he whispered against my lips.

And I was.

His hands roamed, persistent, rough and reverent all at once, and I let him. Let him take. Let him have me, because in that moment, I wanted to be his.

I needed to be his.

"You want control?" he rasped.

I nodded… before he laughed, "Too bad."

He hauled me to the bed and pinned me there with his body, straddling me, his smile almost sinister and full of dark promises I wasn't sure I was ready to hear, but knew I was ready to feel.

He whispered, dragging his fingers beneath my ribs, "you're mine."

I shuddered at his words. His hands skated over my skin, exploring and memorizing. Every touch felt deliberate, like he was savoring me.

A chill ripped through my entire body. My nipples hardened beneath his palms as he teased them, rolling them between his fingers, watching every twitch and arch of my body.

"So fucking beautiful," he murmured against my skin, his mouth leaving a trail of heat as he moved lower.

He trailed his mouth lower. The heat pooling between my thighs as his fingers traced the inside of my leg.

I trembled.

I tried to close my legs, but he held them open.

Pinning me down harder, as I fought.

I pressed my palms to his chest, not to push him away—just to ground myself. His heartbeat pounded beneath my fingers, a mirror of my own.

His fingers teased the inside of my thigh, making me gasp. I tried to clench them together, using my pathetic attempts to block him from access.

He knew I was testing him, fighting him on purpose.

His eyes glowed with dark amusement. "Too late now, wildflower… I'm getting my taste," he promised, a determination in his voice. "So why don't you keep those pretty legs open... or I'll tie you back up to that chair in my basement. Understood?"

A shiver ran through me at his persistence and his seeming need for me.

I nodded. Desperate. Willing.

Because I wanted this. Without any hesitation.

"Good girl," he whispered.

When his fingers slid between my thighs, I gasped, my hips jerking into his touch.

He held my legs apart with ruthless ease, his gaze never leaving mine as he circled my clit slowly, deliberately, driving me to the edge one excruciating stroke at a time.

And then—he pushed two of his fingers inside me. Slow. Deep.

I whimpered, back arching, hands clawing at the sheets.

"So perfect," he growled, pulling his fingers back as his tongue trailed fire down my thigh before taking me completely into his mouth.

The moan that tore from me was *desperate*. I fisted the sheets, my body bucking against his mouth, his fingers, and the rawness of him. I was flying, drowning and burning all at the same time. Somehow, he made all of that possible.

But just as I reached the edge—he stopped and I came whimpering back down.

"Reich," I cried out, trembling beneath him. "Please."

He pulled himself to meet my face, as he hovered over me, his breath hot against my ear. "You're clever," he said softly. "But I'm not giving you what you want until you give me what I want."

Tears pricked at the corners of my eyes. "I... I don't know what you mean." I acted dumbfounded. Knowing full well, the answers he wanted. The shame he wanted bare before him.

He pulled back, his warmth gone. His absence a cruel shock to my system.

"Why won't you answer me?" I whispered.

He said nothing. His eyes were hard. Closed off.

And it hurt. More than I thought it would.

But I knew that the only way out of this was giving him what he wanted. No matter how much I wanted to hide.

But I wasn't going to give it to him on his terms.

"Fine." I relented. "But I'll only tell Castor what happened" I blurted out.

I continued, "He can convey it to *you* after."

Reich stilled. Something flickered in his gaze, but his face stayed cold.

"Okay," he said flatly.

And then he turned and walked out.

Just like that.

Leaving me aching. Empty.

Chapter Twenty-Eight

REICH

CASTOR ARRIVED THE NEXT day after I told him Sage was willing to give him the answers we needed. I knew why she was drawing another invisible line between us. She wasn't ready to let me in. Maybe she never would be.

I told myself I was fine with that.

But as I paced the length of the room, burning off restless energy before Cas showed, I knew it was a lie. I wasn't fine. I wasn't anything close to fine.

And letting Cas handle this? Well, that was a recipe for disaster.

I needed to give him a pep talk first—make sure he wouldn't fuck it up. That was the problem when I let other people handle things. I never trusted them to get it right. It was why I'd trained myself to rely on only me. My hands. My decisions. My control.

I was the one who kept things together.

At least, that's what I'd always believed.

But Sage... Sage had wrecked that certainty. She had already dragged me into a tangled mess of doubt, forcing me to second-guess my choices, my instincts—*my entire damn life*.

And now?

After tasting her, after feeling her body melt beneath mine... there was no walking away.

I was hooked.

And for the first time in a long, long while, I was scared.

Not of her.

Of myself.

Because I wasn't sure I could protect her. Not the way she needed.

And worse... I wasn't sure she wouldn't turn on me and ruin everything my brother and I had built.

A system in place to keep us safe within the confines of the life we had chosen.

When Cas finally showed, he looked like hell. The dark circles beneath his eyes told me he hadn't slept. His clothes were wrinkled, his jaw shadowed with days-old stubble. The usual easy swagger he wore like armor was gone. In its place was something rawer, stripped bare.

I grabbed two whiskey glasses from the cabinet and poured generously. Liquid gold caught the dim light, gleaming like something that might save us both in this endless black void.

Fat chance.

I handed one to Cas as we clinked them in a silent toast.

"Brother," we muttered in unison.

We drank without speaking for a moment. The silence stretched long between us, familiar and heavy. The burn of whiskey down my throat didn't even register. Cas sighed, dragging his palm over his face like he could rub the exhaustion away.

Finally, he spoke, his voice rough around the edges. "I'm a terrible liar."

I smirked faintly. "You're not as bad as you think."

He shot me a look. "Don't humor me."

"Fine." I leaned back in my chair, exhaling slowly. "Then keep it short, Cas. If you don't overshare, you won't have to lie."

His hand tightened around the glass, knuckles blanching. His stare dropped to the swirling amber liquid, watching it the way you watch something you want to drown in.

"What is it?" I asked.

He shook his head once. "Sam."

My gut clenched.

"What about her?"

He exhaled, heavy and tired. "She keeps asking about Sage."

I waited.

"She doesn't buy the story that she just disappeared without a word." His mouth twisted, part amusement, part regret. "Sam's convinced something else happened. She wants *me* to look into it."

I frowned. "Why you?"

He gave me a flat look. "Because she's smart." His voice was bitter and resigned. "Because she's catching on and starting to realize that 'finding people' isn't just some hobby of mine."

That was a problem.

A big one.

I rubbed a hand down my face. "We can't let her in, Cas. You know what happens if she finds out even a fraction about what we do and who we do it for."

His jaw tightened. He stood abruptly, crossing the room like he couldn't sit still anymore. His shoulders hunched, like he was carrying more weight than his frame was built for.

And I knew he was.

We both were.

"Eventually, I'll have to say something to tide her over," he said. "Or I'll lose her for good."

His voice cracked just enough to make me freeze.

When his eyes met mine, they were raw. Desperate.

"She thinks I'm living a double life," he continued. "That I've got a house somewhere. A wife. A couple of kids. Like I'm playing the perfect miserable suburban dad on weekends and banging the hot blonde secretary in my off hours."

I huffed a dry laugh.

Not because it was funny.

Because it was tragic.

That was the kind of life Cas could've had. Hell, maybe even me in another lifetime. But not here. Not now. Not with the ENA's leash tight around our throats.

I pressed my fingers to my temples, feeling the pulse of a migraine building behind my eyes. "Even if you told her the truth, Cas—are you really willing to put her in that kind of danger? You'd lose her anyway. You can't have a normal life with her. Not in this world we've built."

His gaze dropped as I watched his fists clench.

"I don't know," he whispered. "But I just can't lose her."

And that was it.

The line in the sand.

I recognized it because it was the same one that I had already crossed with Sage.

The difference was Cas was still pretending it was a choice.

I wanted to tell him it would be okay. That if he fought hard enough, he could have her. That if he ran fast enough, far enough, maybe they could disappear together.

But we both knew that wasn't true.

"What are you going to do about Sage?" Cas asked, dragging me back.

His voice was steady again. Too steady.

I opened my mouth, only to close it again because for once I didn't have a response.

What was I going to do about Sage?

She was in my head. Under my skin.

Inside every goddamn thought I had.

I couldn't stop reminiscing over the taste of her. Couldn't stop feeling the heat of her breath on my neck. Couldn't forget the look in her eyes when she'd bared herself to me—trust, desperation and defiance all meshed together.

She was chaos. And I craved it.

But more than that...I wanted to protect her.

And I wasn't sure I could until I got this stupid formality out of the way about Klay.

I ran a hand over my mouth, shaking my head. "I don't know, Cas." My voice felt raw and honest. "I've never felt like this before. But I know it doesn't change anything. This life—this is what we're stuck with."

He studied me closely, something softening in his gaze. "Did she say why me? Why not you?"

I shrugged, feigning indifference like it didn't matter.

But it did.

It fucking did.

Why not me instead of Cas?

To call it jealousy would've been an understatement. I wanted to be the one to unravel that side of her—not watch my little brother do it. Yet here I was, tangled up in this stubborn little wildflower who was slowly wrecking every last part of me.

"All right," He said, pushing away from the table with a heavy sigh. "I'll do my best. But knowing you, by the time I get anything useful out of her, you'll already be lurking in the shadows."

I smirked. "What makes you think I'm not already?"

He let out a small laugh. "Some things never change."

I leaned back in my chair, letting the silence settle over us. "Exactly," I murmured. "Just like our arrangement with the ENA."

The temperature in the room dropped.

A heavy, suffocating silence fell between us.

Just saying those three letters out loud was enough to twist my gut.

The ones who owned us.

The ones who controlled every move we made.

They were the reason we couldn't walk away.

The reason we never could.

Cas's jaw clenched. His fists curled at his sides. He didn't say anything. He didn't have to.

We both knew the truth.

We knew too much.

And that meant we would never be free.

Not until we were dead.

And with every move we made, that day felt closer.

I wasn't sure if I feared it anymore.

Or welcomed it.

I stood, knocking back the last of my whiskey. "Go talk to her," I said, my voice quiet.

Cas nodded once and then he was gone.

And I was alone again.

Left with nothing but the echo of her voice in my head and the weight of everything I couldn't say.

Maybe in another life, Sage.

But not this one.

Chapter Twenty-Nine

SAGE

"You wanted to see me?" Castor's voice carried a note of curiosity as he peered through the doorway, stepping inside and closing it gently behind him. The faint click of the lock sliding back into place felt louder than it should have. It echoed in the space between us, reminding me that—no matter how polite he seemed—I was still a prisoner.

I studied him carefully, watching the way his hand lingered on the doorframe before he let it fall to his side. Searching his face for a crack in his armor. Something human. Something I could reach.

There was a softness in his eyes. I didn't know if it was real or something he'd learned to weaponize, but I was desperate enough to hope it was real. Desperate enough to believe I might get through to him—far more easily than I ever could with Reich.

And if there was ever a chance, this was it.

I drew a breath and steadied my voice. "First, I want to know why I'm here."

Castor didn't answer right away. He took a slow, measured breath and exhaled through his nose, like he was bracing himself for something he didn't want to say. Or maybe he was preparing to say nothing at all.

"Sage," he said at last, "I can't tell you that."

I wasn't surprised.

But I was tired of running in circles.

Tired of being treated like I couldn't handle the truth.

Frustration prickled under my skin, but I kept it tightly leashed. Exploding wouldn't get me anywhere. It hadn't worked on Reich.

And Castor was different.

More thoughtful.

Or maybe just better at pretending.

I let my gaze drift to the floorboards between us for a moment, collecting myself before I looked back up at him.

"What can you tell me then, kidnapper?"

I kept my voice steady, though it was tinged with something closer to desperation than I wanted to admit.

Castor sighed again and rubbed a hand over his face, dragging it down like the weight of this entire conversation was grinding him down. He paced the room, boots heavy against the wood floor, each step deliberate but aimless—like he needed to move but didn't know where to go.

I watched him. I noticed the way his shoulders slumped a little, the way he hesitated at every turn. I could see why Sam was drawn to him. He was magnetic in a wounded way—the kind of person who felt everything deeply but wore it like a joke so no one ever noticed.

Finally, he stopped in front of the small table by the window and leaned his hands on the surface. His gaze met mine, and for a split second, I saw it.

Hesitation.

And maybe something close to guilt.

"I can tell you" He said quietly, "that you need to answer my brother's questions. Sooner rather than later."

His tone was soft but urgent, the kind of warning you didn't want to ignore.

I stilled. "Why?"

The word was sharp. A challenge.

Castor's expression didn't change. "Because once you do, we can explain everything. We can keep you safe."

The word hit me wrong.

Safe.

I almost laughed.

Instead, I took a slow step forward, arms crossed tight over my ribs. "Safe?" I echoed, disbelief coloring my voice. "Safe from who?"

His fingers flexed against the table. I could tell he was holding back—something dangerous or something painful.

"I can't tell you that," he said.

It was always the same wall.

The same silence.

Frustration surged through me, coiling tight in my chest.

"Well... it didn't work because I don't feel safe here," I snapped, the words tearing out of me sharper than I intended.

But I didn't take them back.

Castor's head lifted sharply. His eyes locked onto mine, and for a moment—just a moment—something raw flickered behind them. Not anger.

Something closer to regret.

"You are, Sage."

And for the first time since we met, there was no hesitation in his voice, "You're safer here than anywhere else."

I wanted to believe him.

But belief was dangerous.

And trust was dangerous.

I learned that lesson before.

I turned away slightly, folding my arms tighter around myself—a small act of defiance, but it was all I had left.

"I don't trust you," I said quietly.

He nodded once, like he understood.

But he wasn't done trying to convince me.

"If nothing else," Castor said, his voice softer, "trust that I love Sam more than anything in this world. And she'd never forgive me if I let something happen to you." He paused, then added, "Because you're her best friend. And she cares about you."

The words struck harder than I expected.

Best friend.

They weren't new words. But hearing them... they hit differently now.

Sam.

The one person who always made the world lighter. Who never let me drown, even when I wanted to. She'd seen me when I couldn't even see myself.

My throat tightened.

And I hated the sting in my eyes.

I stared down at my hands, forcing myself to stay still. "And you think she'll forgive you for drugging me? For kidnapping me?"

Castor flinched. It was slight, but it was there.

For once, he didn't have a comeback.

He just stood there, hands curling into fists at his sides, his expression unreadable.

"Reich is tough," he said finally, his voice heavier now. "I know. He's... complicated. But he's trying to keep you out of harm's way. I wouldn't be here if I didn't think that was true."

I wanted to scream.

I wanted to rip the truth out of him.

But instead... I breathed.

And I made a choice.

"It was the day of my father's funeral—" I said quietly.

The words were fragile. I almost couldn't believe I'd spoken them aloud.

But Castor froze.

His entire body stilled.

And slowly, carefully, he moved toward the bed and lowered himself to sit on the edge. Not too close. Just close enough to hear and at the very least pretend he cared.

"—that night, my boyfriend threw a party," I continued. "I told him I was leaving... We argued... I felt bad... So, I stayed..."

I closed my eyes.

The memory pressed against my ribs like a knife.

"One of his friends brought me a drink."

I drew a slow breath.

"And then I woke up in hell."

Castor didn't move. Didn't say a word.

But the way his jaw tightened... the way his hand clenched against his thigh... he knew.

He already knew how the story ended.

But I finished it anyway.

"I was on the ground. Naked. Surrounded by these men." My voice wavered, but I forced it out. "They wouldn't let me go."

The silence that followed was suffocating.

I could barely breathe.

Castor's knuckles were white now. His mouth was a hard line.

"How did you escape?" he asked, his voice low and rough.

"I waited," I whispered. "I pretended to be unconscious. Let the drugs wear off. If they knew I was awake... they would've given me more." I swallowed hard. "I waited until I had enough strength to run."

My hands were shaking, I realized as I clenched them into fists in my lap.

Castor moved then. Closer. Not to crowd me—but enough that I could feel his presence anchoring me.

"Castor," I asked, my voice smaller than I meant it to be. "How many women have been in this room before?"

He hesitated.

But then he leaned forward, his elbows on his knees.

"You're the first."

I blinked.

Shock flooded through me. "Really?"

He nodded once. "Really."

Something in my stomach twisted.

Tightened.

"To this day," Castor continued, "I've never seen my brother let another woman into his home, how he has decided to let you."

He gave me a look I couldn't read, as he continued, "He's been with women. But he never brought them here—"

I stared at him.

Trying to make sense of it.

"—and as for the holding someone captive part—" He almost smiled. It was faint. "—that's a first too."

I huffed a bitter laugh.

But it didn't make me feel better.

If anything, it made the weight in my chest heavier.

Because deep down, I was starting to believe that if Reich ever knew the truth...

If he ever learned how broken I really was...

He wouldn't want me anymore.

That thought—more than being trapped in this room, more than everything I'd already survived—that thought for some reason filled me with more shame.

Castor watched me for a long moment.

Then he exhaled, dragging a hand over his face. "I'm sorry, Sage. If there was another way, I would've convinced him to take it. But there isn't. This information is more invaluable than you know."

Invaluable?

I gave him a confused look. A look that said I wanted more answers than what he was offering. So I asked, "How is my trauma 'invaluable' to a couple of brothers that decided to kidnap me in a small town 200 miles away?"

He hesitated, then added softly, "That's really not my place to say and some things have to stay with Reich. Just trust me... this is all to keep you safe."

I swallowed hard. "You keep saying that and I'm trying to trust you, but it's hard to trust, especially after everything that has happened."

He nodded.

Then he took my hands in his—gentle, grounding. "If you can find even the smallest piece of yourself that still knows how to trust," he murmured, "put it in Reich."

His voice softened further, "I promise you... he won't take it for granted."

And something in his voice made me want to believe him.

Chapter Thirty

REICH

After Castor finished his conversation with Sage, he rushed to find me.

I could hear the weight in his footsteps before I ever saw his face—the way they echoed down the hall, faster, heavier than usual. He was practically running, and that told me everything I needed to know.

This wasn't good.

I braced myself against the edge of my desk, rolling my shoulders back as if that would keep the weight of this off me.

It didn't.

The second he stepped into my office, he didn't waste time.

"She told me everything." His voice was low. Grim.

I nodded once. Waiting. But part of me already knew.

I had already suspected the truth. Maybe I'd known it the first time I looked at her and saw the broken pieces she tried so hard to hide. Maybe I'd seen it in her eyes from the moment she walked into my field.

But knowing something and hearing it confirmed were two different things.

I had hoped—*fuck, even prayed*—I was wrong.

But I wasn't.

The weight settled in my chest like a concrete slab, thick and suffocating. Rage swelled underneath it, sharp and violent, an ache I couldn't dull.

This was real.

This had really happened.

I stood there for a long moment, staring past Castor like if I stayed still long enough, I could undo it all. Reverse time. Change her past. Rewrite what had happened to her.

But I couldn't.

And I was going to have to face her knowing that.

I stepped out of my office, my boots hitting the hardwood with heavy, deliberate strikes as I made my way toward her room.

Each step was a war.

Each breath, a battle.

I willed my heart to slow, to stay steady. But inside, the storm kept building.

She had trusted us with the worst pieces of herself, and now I had to act like I wasn't breaking under the weight of them.

I paused outside her door, inhaling slowly, grounding myself in that rhythm like I had done a hundred times before going into a fight.

But this wasn't a fight I was ready for.

I reached for the handle.

And pushed the door open.

The fading light of dusk bled through the window, washing the room in a muted glow. She was curled in the corner by the window, knees to her chest, arms wrapped tight around them as if she was holding herself together by sheer force of will.

At the sound of my boots crossing the threshold, her head lifted.

Her green eyes met mine, tired but sharp.

She managed a small smile. Fragile and brittle.

Yet, it cut me deeper than any blade ever had.

I tried to give her one back, but it felt hollow and forced.

I knew it didn't reach my eyes, and she saw it too.

Her gaze dropped.

"Why am I here?" Her voice was quiet, but not weak.

I studied her, watching the way her hands flexed against her arms as if bracing for another blow.

But she wasn't done asking questions.

And neither was I.

"Answer the rest of my questions," I said, keeping my tone steady, "… and I'll tell you everything."

She nodded. Slowly.

And it was like watching the last embers of a fire die out.

Resignation settled in her shoulders, heavier than anything I had put there.

She dropped her head, as if the weight of me knowing was too much to bear.

I forced myself to stay in control.

To stay still and not let it show how much it was affecting me.

"How are you feeling?" I asked.

I didn't know why.

I already knew the answer.

She looked up at me again. Her gaze was empty, hollowed out.

"Good," she said. "Or as good as I can be."

Then she let out a dry laugh.

It made something in me tighten until it was almost unbearable.

But I needed to push forward.

I needed to know.

"How many men do you remember being there?"

I kept my voice low. Even. But the burn in my throat was rising fast.

Her throat worked as she swallowed hard.

Her fingers clenched into the fabric of her pants like she was fighting not to come apart at the seams.

"Five," she whispered.

A cold chill ran through me.

I felt it in my bones.

In my blood.

"Was your ex one of them?"

She shook her head, "No."

That didn't make sense.

Klay's circle was a much tighter knit group three others at max. He didn't let anyone in unless he had a reason. Unless they were bound by blood or debt.

"Did he know what happened?" I hated the way my voice sounded. Dread was creeping in. Poisoning me.

Her breath shook. "Yes."

Unbelievable.

"When I was running away," she continued, "I found him. Told him everything—" Her voice cracked. "—but he didn't believe me."

The words hit harder than I expected.

A blade sliding between my ribs.

I stood there, frozen, as the weight of it sank deep.

Klay.

The man she trusted.

The man who was supposed to protect her.

Had looked her in the eyes and called her a liar.

My stomach twisted violently.

I leaned back against the wall, bracing myself against the sickness that swelled in my gut.

But when I looked at her, it was already too late.

The tears had started falling.

Silent.

Slow.

She buried her face in her hands.

Her shoulders shook, small, violent tremors.

Like she was trying to shake them off.

Shake them out of her skin.

But it wasn't working.

And she was breaking all over again.

I wanted to go to her.

I wanted to cross the space between us and pull her into my arms.

But the air between us was too heavy.

Too fragile.

I didn't trust myself not to shatter her completely.

"Do you remember anything about the men?" my voice was tight. Controlled.

Barely.

She shook her head but spoke anyway, "Just that they said their brother was rude for not sharing me."

I went still.

So still it hurt.

"Their brother?" I said it like it wasn't a loaded question. Like it wasn't tearing through my mind like wildfire.

"Yes."

Her voice was empty.

But her words were not.

They sliced through me, leaving nothing but ruin in their wake.

"Their brother…" I echoed it again.

Trying to make it make sense.

But it wouldn't.

"Did they say who they were talking about?" I asked, already dreading the answer.

She shook her head. "I don't think my ex ever mentioned having brothers."

But I wasn't hearing her anymore.

Five men.

Brothers.

It couldn't be.

No, that wasn't possible.

Because I had killed them.

I had hunted them down, every last one.

I had buried their bodies and burned the evidence.

I had watched the life leave their eyes.

I had made sure they were gone.

Made sure they couldn't hurt anyone again.

But now...now I wasn't sure.

Because if they weren't dead...

Then who the fuck did I kill?

"Reich?" Her voice was small. Wavering.

I barely registered it.

I turned on my heel and walked out of her room without another word.

I couldn't stay there. I couldn't look at her and pretend I had the answers. Because I didn't. Not anymore.

By the time I reached my office, my hands were shaking.

I slammed them down onto the desk, bracing myself against it like it was the only thing keeping me upright.

This wasn't supposed to happen.

This was supposed to be over.

But it wasn't.

And I was drowning in a truth I couldn't comprehend.

I yanked my phone from my pocket and dialed Castor.

He picked up on the first ring.

"How'd it go with Sage?"

His voice was casual.

Unaware.

He had no idea how fucked we were.

"We have a problem."

My voice was gravel. Rough and cold.

A pause.

"What's wrong?"

I stared at the wall, feeling the weight of it all settle in my chest like concrete.

"It was his brothers."

Silence.

A long, stretched moment of nothing.

Then— "What?"

I clenched my jaw so tight I thought it might break.

Forced the words out, "The Ovitt brothers."

Another long beat of silence.

Then Castor said it, "We hunted all of them down."

My throat was dry.

"Unless it wasn't them that we hunted."

A slow, creeping horror settled over me.

Like something ancient and cold, sliding beneath my skin.

This wasn't just about Sage anymore.

This was about every woman after her.

Every person we thought we'd saved.

How many more were there?

How many had suffered because we'd killed the wrong men?

How many had suffered because I didn't finish the job?

"We need to find out what went wrong," I muttered. "Now."

Another pause. Then Castor's voice—low and certain, "I'm on my way."

I hung up.

Stared at the phone in my hand like it was a live grenade.

The weight in my chest was unbearable.

I had failed her.

I had failed all of them.

And now—Sage was in more danger than I'd ever realized.

I needed to get her out of the line of fire.

Because if I didn't—She was going to burn with me.

Chapter Thirty-One

Sage

HE COULDN'T GET OUT of the room fast enough.

As if my presence was unbearable now that he knew the truth.

As if the weight of my past, of what had been done to me, had contaminated the very air between us.

I could almost hear the phantom thoughts circling his mind—She tricked me. She's broken. A filthy whore riddled with disease.

Even though I knew Reich wasn't Klay, that he wasn't built for cruelty in the same way, those words still clawed their way into my consciousness. They wrapped around me like barbed wire, impossible to untangle.

The nightmares had become my only constants—reliving moments that never let me breathe.

But God... would it ever end?

The question haunted me. A low, insidious hum beneath every thought.

I was running out of strength and when that was gone, I wasn't sure what would be left.

The hollow echoes of a girl who used to be alive?

Or maybe... she had already left a long time ago.

I paced the room.

Over and over.

The repetitive rhythm of my bare feet across the cold wooden floor was the only thing keeping me tethered.

Until I caught sight of myself in the bathroom mirror.

I hadn't looked at myself in days.

I hadn't dared.

But now...Now I couldn't avoid it.

The woman staring back wasn't someone I recognized.

Her eyes were dull. Empty.

Her face was thinner, sharper, like all the softness had been scraped away, leaving nothing but harsh edges and shadows.

I took a step closer.

I saw the hollows under my eyes.

The cracked lips.

The faint bruises still lingering across my collarbone like fingerprints pressed too hard.

I looked every inch as broken as I felt.

Even though I felt filthy inside—tainted by things I had no control over—I couldn't bear to see myself reflect that filth.

Not tonight. Not after what just happened with Reich.

I turned away quickly, my fingers trembling as I reached for the small music player he had left on the windowsill.

I scrolled until I found something familiar.

A soft and haunting song, drifted through the speakers, wrapping around me like smoke.

I let it happen.

Let it soothe the jagged edges of my mind until the worst of the shaking stopped.

And then, I stripped off my clothes and stepped into the shower.

The rainfall head sprayed warm water over me, each drop hitting my skin like a silent prayer, cleansing me, like a gentle hand smoothing over my scars, wiping them clean.

I closed my eyes.

I could almost feel him.

Reich.

His hands.

The way they'd touched me—hesitant at first, then reverent.

Like I was something worth holding.

Something worth needing.

I pressed my palms flat against the cold tile wall, my breath catching as I imagined his fingers in my hair, his lips against the nape of my neck, his body bracing me there, keeping me upright when I had no strength left.

God, I could almost smell him.

That intoxicating mix of smoke and cedar, sharp and warm.

The scent that made my knees weak, that made me feel... alive.

I dragged my hands through my hair, pretending they were his.

And for a fleeting second, it was enough.

I stayed under the water until my skin was raw and pink.

Then I dried off, wrapping myself in one of the soft black towels Reich had left in the closet.

It was warmer than I expected.

A cocoon that I didn't want to break out of.

But I did.

I forced myself to move to the closet.

The moment I stepped inside, it was like entering another world.

Rows of clothing—luxury brands I couldn't pronounce—hung in perfect symmetry.

Mostly black, a few grays, a handful of rich, deep tones that hinted at life.

And somewhere in between them, my own clothes were hidden like artifacts from a different existence.

I ran my fingers over the fabrics.

Soft silks, delicate lace, cool leather.

Things I never thought I'd wear.

Things that felt too beautiful for someone like me.

And yet...here they were.

As if they had been bought with me in mind.

As if he wanted me to have them.

I stopped at a dress.

Short, black, fit-and-flare, with a lace slit down the middle that hinted at something sinful.

I didn't have anywhere to wear it. Nowhere I could even attempt to go.

But tonight...tonight I just wanted to feel something other than hollow, if only for myself.

I slipped it on, the fabric whispering over my skin like a lover's touch.

And when I looked in the mirror—*shockingly*—I didn't hate what I saw.

I wasn't whole.

I wasn't fixed.

But I wasn't gone either.

Not yet.

My eyes burned with tears and I let them fall.

Because maybe I was starting to heal. One fractured piece at a time.

I walked to the window, resting my hand against the cold glass.

Below me, the open field swayed in the breeze.

Wild. Untamed.

A reflection of something I used to be.

My gaze shifted to the small stack of books Reich had left by the sill.

One stood out.

Persuasion. Jane Austen.

I picked it up, running my thumb over the worn cover.

Reich had been reading this.

Earlier, when I woke up the other day he was sitting in this very room, lost in these pages.

Austen. Romance.

I didn't understand it.

Reich was all hard lines and brutal precision.

He wasn't softness and second chances.

He wasn't supposed to be reading books about love and regret.

And yet... here it was.

And maybe that's why he intrigued me.

Because he didn't fit into the box I kept trying to shove him into.

He was an enigma.

And I wanted to understand him.

I curled into the window seat, tucking my legs beneath me as I lost myself in Anne Elliot's world.

Hours passed. Maybe more.

And when I finally closed the book, something in me ached.

Because I wanted what Anne had found. I wanted to believe in second chances. Even if I always felt like I didn't deserve one.

A soft creak drew my attention to the door.

And there he was.

Reich.

Polished. Perfect. The wealthy, romance-reading enigma who was quickly becoming my undoing.

He held a tray in his hands.

Food.

The same routine.

But there was something different in the way he watched me.

Our eyes met, and for a moment, the air between us thickened.

I smiled. Small. Wistful.

Then I turned back to the window, hiding the storm brewing inside me.

I heard the tray settle against the dresser.

The faint clink of glass.

And then...his footsteps.

Closer.

Beside me.

His voice was low. Warm. Deliberate. "Sage."

I didn't look at him, as I spoke, "I decided to try something new." The words came out sharp. Defensive. But underneath... I was scared. Afraid of what he might say next.

A flicker of something passed across his face.

Surprise. Curiosity. Concern. I didn't know.

"Why's that?" he asked.

His voice was too careful.

Too controlled.

I gave him a smirk that didn't quite reach my eyes. "Broadening my horizons," I replied, mimicking his earlier words back to him.

A faint smile tugged at the corner of his mouth.

But then he said nothing.

The silence stretched between us like a wire about to snap.

I hated it.

"Sage—" His voice was softer now. As if searching for a place to land.

I didn't let him.

"Thank you," I said abruptly. "For the clothes."

And then— "For everything."

The words felt like glass in my throat. Raw. Shattered.

But they were true.

His lips parted, but I kept going. Kept control.

And then—he said it.

"Klayton Ovitt."

The room tilted. The breath left my lungs. The warmth was gone.

Ripped away.

I turned toward him slowly. Meeting his gaze.

His eyes burned.

Hot. Alive. Unforgiving.

He knew him.

And just like that—the fantasy ended.

Chapter Thirty-Two

REICH

"**K**LAYTON OVITT."

I said his name deliberately, slicing it into the room like a blade.

I knew what it would do to her.

I said it anyway.

And the reaction was instant.

Her body jerked, shoulders tightening like she'd been shot. Her breath hitched in her throat. The flicker in her eyes shifted from cautious hope to something raw, terrified,

and defensive.

Like the mere syllables of his name burned her alive.

She shrank away from me, withdrawing into herself, her hands ghosting through the space behind her like she was trying to measure the distance it would take to disappear.

She didn't find an escape.

Her back hit the wall with a soft, desperate thud.

And still, I saw her calculating.

Still fighting.

Even now, when she didn't know what part of this was a trap and what part was me trying to save her from herself.

I should have stayed where I was.

I should have given her space.

But I couldn't.

I closed the distance between us, my steps measured, deliberate. Careful. Like I was approaching a wounded animal, teeth bared and cornered, ready to lash out or bleed out.

But she flinched anyway—before I even touched her. Before I even breathed too close.

And it killed me.

How fragile she was in that moment. How badly I wanted to pull her into me and never let anything hurt her again. Even though I already had.

"Sage," I said her name low, soft, as if gentling her with sound alone would work.

Her eyes squeezed shut. Her breath stuttered against her ribs. And a single tear slid down her cheek like it belonged there. Like it had always belonged there.

I reached out to tuck a strand of hair behind her ear, fingers grazing her temple.

She flinched again.

I froze.

Felt the tremor in my hand and slowly pulled back.

I didn't force it.

Didn't force her.

Instead, I took a slow breath, letting the air between us settle.

Letting myself settle.

Inhaling the faintest trace of her scent—the one that always unspooled something dangerous in me.

Softness. Warmth. Sweetness I didn't deserve.

"You don't trust me," I murmured.

A truth, not a question.

Her forehead pressed lightly to my chest, as if she wasn't aware she was doing it. As if her body didn't know how to stay away from mine.

"I was starting to." Her voice was rasp, worn thin. "But I don't know anymore."

That hit harder than I expected.

I could've argued with her.

Could've defended myself.

But instead, I gave her what I hadn't before—control.

"Ask your questions," I said, as I kept my voice low. Kept it steady even though my pulse was thrumming inside me as I continued, "and then you can decide."

For a moment, neither of us spoke. Just breathing. A shared space between heartbeats.

And then—her body trembled. Her breath released in a soft exhale.

A soundless surrender.

But she didn't pull away.

She didn't run.

Her forehead stayed where it was—pressed over my heartbeat, as if listening.

Her hands clutched the fabric of my shirt like she didn't trust herself to stand on her own.

And I held her.

Not to control.

Not to trap.

Just to hold.

Her voice broke through the silence again.

Quiet, but resolute.

"Are you really trying to keep me safe?"

"Yes." I didn't hesitate. I couldn't. "I swear it."

I tilted her chin up gently, guiding her to meet my gaze.

Her green eyes were bright, rimmed in red, but clear.

She was looking for something.

And I wanted her to find it.

"I need you to believe that," I said, and the rawness in my own voice surprised me.

Her eyes flickered, studying me. Searching.

Then— "Okay."

Just one word.

But it settled between us like a truce.

I let out a breath I hadn't realized I was holding.

"Okay," I echoed her.

But before I could say more, she spoke again. "I trust you," she said carefully. "And I don't need to ask anything else."

I shook my head slightly, studying her expression. She wasn't just saying it.

She meant it. Or she was trying to.

"I might not understand everything," she continued. "Or why this is happening. But all I can do is trust."

That hit me in places inside of me I hadn't thought were still alive.

And for a second—just one—I wanted to fall into her. But before I could speak, she cut me off.

Her voice sharpened suddenly, slicing through the moment.

"No, Reich. I see the pity." She shook her head, defiant. "And I don't want it. Not for what happened."

I stilled.

Let the weight of her words settle.

She was still protecting herself.

Still fighting to keep her dignity.

"I've told you my truth," she said. "I don't want to revisit it."

She exhaled slowly, regaining her control. "Just tell me what I need to do with Klay, and I'll do it."

Something coiled hot in my gut.

Frustration.

Anger.

Not at her.

At the world that had made her this way.

At myself, for not finding her sooner.

I took another step toward her.

Close enough that she could feel the heat radiating off me.

"Why do you think I pity you?" My voice was quieter now.

Less commanding. More curiosity.

She hesitated. Then she whispered, "The way you look at me."

I let out a slow breath, letting it turn into a quiet, humorless chuckle.

"You think I have pity when I look at you?"

She didn't answer.

Didn't need to.

The walls were going back up.

And I wasn't going to let them.

I closed the final space between us.

Not touching her yet.

But close enough to feel her breath hitch.

My gaze swept over every part of her, I admired.

The way her shoulders stiffened. The slight tremble in her hands. The defiance burning in her eyes. The soft parting of her lips as she tried to hold herself together.

She was breathtaking.

The little black dress she wore clung to her body, teasing me with every curve. Every inch of skin exposed was an invitation I hadn't earned. But I was done pretending I could walk away from it.

I reached out.

My fingers trembled as they brushed her jaw.

She flinched—but didn't pull away this time.

I tilted her chin up gently, my lips hovering close to hers.

"Wildflower," I murmured.

Her pulse jumped. I felt it against my fingertips. Fast. Desperate.

I continued, "There's only desire in my eyes for you."

She shuddered. "I don't understand," she whispered.

I leaned in, brushing my breath against her lips. "What don't you understand?" My voice was soft. Almost teasing.

"I didn't think you'd want me after... everything. I thought you would see me differently." The words were raw. The truth behind them brutal. I traced my thumb along her lower lip. Slow. Deliberate.

"You fought to survive when no one came for you," I whispered. "That's what I see when I look at you."

She tried to look away.

I didn't let her.

I wanted her to feel it.

To believe it.

"I don't pity you," I said. "I admire you."

Her breath broke on a quiet sob. But she didn't move away.

I gave her time. And when I was sure she wouldn't run, I closed the space between us completely.

My lips found hers. Slow. Certain. Devastating.

The kiss was gentle at first—testing, tasting.

But it didn't stay gentle.

Couldn't.

Because I was hungry for her.

Starving.

She melted into me.

Her hands gripping my arms like she needed something to hold onto. And I gave it to her. I gave her me.

The kiss deepened.

Her lips parting beneath mine, letting me in.

My hands slid down her sides, gripping her waist, pulling her flush against me.

Her body was soft, warm.

Perfect.

She gasped into my mouth when I lifted her easily, carrying her to the bed. Her laughter was soft, breathless.

And fuck.

That sound undid me.

I laid her back gently, hovering over her, letting her see everything I felt in my eyes.

She was mine and I was hers.

Even if neither of us could say it yet.

I stripped off my shirt, letting it fall to the floor without care.

Her eyes traced every inch of my body, wide and reverent. And it lit something dangerous inside me.

I reached for the hem of her dress, dragging it slowly up her thighs, watching the way her breath hitched.

She didn't stop me.

Didn't protest.

When I finally bared her completely, I sat back for a moment.

Taking her in.

Committing every inch of her to memory.

"You're beautiful," I murmured.

Her cheeks flushed.

She shook her head.

I smirked. "You are."

And I kissed her again before she could argue.

The heat between us was sharp now.

Every touch, every breath, every sound pushing us closer to something we couldn't come back from.

And I didn't want to come back.

I wanted to burn.

With her.

I slid my hand between her legs, teasing, testing.

She was already wet. Already trembling.

Her hips arched into my touch, her moan soft and needy.

"You're mine," I said against her skin.

She nodded.

And for once in my life—I believed it.

She gasped into my mouth, her fingers digging into my shoulders, clinging to me like she was terrified of what this meant.

And she should be.

Because this wasn't just desire.

This was possession.

I guided her backward, my fingers mapping the soft curves of her body, until we were tangled in a mess of mouths and hands, breathless and desperate.

And then—she laughed.

A quiet, breathless sound.

A laugh that nearly kept destroying me.

I pulled back just enough to take her in, to memorize the way her flushed skin glowed in the dim light, the way her lips trembled, the way her eyes held something uncertain.

Something devastating.

She didn't realize it yet.

But she owned me. Completely.

I brushed my thumb over her cheek, watching the way her breath caught.

The way her body instinctively responded to my every touch.

"I need you," she whispered, her voice shaking and wrecked.

The words settled between us, sinking deep.

I let them linger.

Let them consume me.

Then, slowly, I smirked. "I know, Sage."

My lips brushed against hers, my voice barely above a breath.

"But first—" I traced my fingers along her jaw, tilting her chin up. "I need you to do something for me."

She swallowed, heat flickering behind her gaze.

I leaned in, my voice a whisper against her skin, "I want you to trust me."

She hesitated.

Not because she didn't.

But because she already had.

Because I already owned every fragile piece of her trust—and she knew it.

Her lips parted, but before she could speak, I pressed a finger to them, silencing her.

"No talking." My voice was low, teasing. "Just feel."

Her breath shuddered against my skin.

And then—she did.

Chapter Thirty-Three

SAGE

I STIRRED AWAKE SLOWLY, reluctantly. My body wanted to stay submerged in sleep, weightless, where everything was still so real. I knew the moment I opened my eyes, the truth would be waiting.

And I wasn't ready to face it. Not yet.

The fear coiled tight in my chest, suffocating. What if last night hadn't been real? What if it had only existed inside some fragile dream—one that had splintered the second I woke up? I wasn't sure I could survive the answer. If he was gone—if the weight of his body, the warmth of his skin, had all been some cruel trick of my subconscious—I wasn't sure I'd have the strength to pretend again.

Please, I whispered to no one. Let it be real.

It took everything I had to sit up. My limbs felt heavy, like the air around me was trying to hold me down in the comfort I already knew I couldn't keep. I inhaled, steadying myself before opening my eyes. Slowly. Cautiously.

Golden light spilled over me, catching on the edge of the blanket tangled at my hips. Soft. Warm. A blanket that wasn't the one on the bed I had been in.

I wasn't in my room—not the one I'd been locked in before.

No. This was different.

The bed beneath me was impossibly soft, the sheets smooth against my skin. The faintest imprint of his body still lingered beside me in the mattress, as though he'd only just left. My breath hitched at the sight of it—his absence felt like a ghost beside me. But his presence... his presence was everywhere.

This was his room.

I let that realization sink in. Reich brought me here. He brought me to his bed.

Something warm unfurled in my chest. Not like a spark of relief, but something deeper. Slower. A growing bloom of something dangerously close to hope.

I swung my legs over the side of the bed, taking in the space. The master suite was large, but not in a way that felt cold or impersonal. Every detail was curated—deliberate. Dark wood beams crossed the ceiling, anchoring the room with quiet strength. The color palette was muted: deep grays, soft charcoals, brushed steel. Modern without being sterile. Pristine but not lifeless. It felt like him—impossibly controlled, perfectly organized.

My gaze slid to the left, where two massive French doors stood cracked open, sunlight pooling across the floor in thick golden streaks. The curtains stirred with a lazy breeze. Beyond them, I could see the deck, framed by towering evergreens, their needles catching glints of gold.

The room was peaceful. Too peaceful.

I pushed to my feet and crossed to the doorway; the hardwood floor cool under my bare feet. Stepping outside, I let the sunlight spill across my skin. I tilted my face toward the warmth, breathing it in. The air smelled of pine and cedar and something faintly sweet. It reminded me of him.

I closed my eyes. Let the moment hold me.

Then I saw them.

Twelve windows, dark and heavy with metal bars. They stood in stark contrast to everything else I was seeing, their presence harsh and deliberate. Like sentinels watching me. Like prison cells I hadn't noticed before.

One of them was the old room I came from. I knew it without having to think.

How many rooms did this place have? A dozen? More?

I stepped back inside the bedroom, closing the doors softly behind me. The illusion of safety cracked a little. But it didn't break.

On the nightstand, a black t-shirt was draped over, and beside it, a piece of folded paper sat with my name —his name for me—scrawled across it in sharp, dark ink.

Wildflower.

I picked it up slowly, unfolding it as if it might burn me. His handwriting was precise. Clean. The words simple.

I'll be home this evening. Actions have consequences, Wildflower. Be a good girl.

A shiver slid down my spine. Not from fear.

But from anticipation.

A flush bloomed under my skin. My pulse quickened.

I pressed the shirt to my face, inhaling his scent—amber and cedar, smoke and something else entirely him. It clung to the fabric like a claim. Slipping it over my head, I let it fall past my hips, the fabric heavy, too big for me but perfect in its weight. Like he was still holding me.

But curiosity gnawed at me.

Who was Reich really? And why did I feel this unbearable pull toward him? What was it about this house? These rooms?

I needed answers.

So, I stepped into the hallway, silence folding around me. Everything about this place was deliberate. Quiet. Heavy with purpose.

The corridor stretched ahead of me, bathed in filtered light through tall windows. Beyond them, the forest stood still and watchful. Shadows danced across the floor like restless spirits.

A door caught my eye.

A sliding barn door, rich with cedar grain.

I pressed my palm to it and slid it open.

Inside, the scent of Reich hit me harder.

Woodsmoke. Leather. A faint trace of eucalyptus.

This was his space.

A library.

Floor-to-ceiling shelves lined the room, stacked with books worn at the spines from use. Vinyl records were organized meticulously on low shelves, and original artwork—some of it dark and unsettling—hung on the walls.

I ran my fingers over the spines of the books as I wandered deeper inside.

Physics. Philosophy. Psychology. Religious conspiracies and ideological warfare.

And then literature. Worn. Thumbed through. Well-loved.

But a specified book caught my eye. Black leather-bound. Worn, Heavy and incredibly thick.

Eiloud Naphal Ascendancy.

My pulse jumped.

Something about the book caused my skin to crawl, a burn of something foreign came rising in my throat as I studied the cover. Something ancient and otherworldly about its exterior that gave it an eeriness that I couldn't shake.

As I picked the book up, I swore I saw a shadow move into the peripheral part of my vision. I shrugged it off, that feeling of being watched, as I opened up and peered into the contents of this strange book.

Inside, the pages were filled with symbols—some familiar, most not. But one stood out.

The same symbol inked into Reich's skin. Castor's too. What was this? And why had I felt like I had seen it before meeting them?

I explored into the book farther, a mess of symbols and what looked like complex mathematical problems were littered throughout. An uneasiness settled in the more I tried to decipher the foreign book.

An ice like chill crept behind my back, as I caught more shadows within my peripheral. Something about the book felt wrong. Like something I wasn't supposed to see.

I set the book back, hands trembling, and moved to the record player.

The needle was already set.

I flicked the switch, and the record crackled softly.

Music enveloped the quiet space.

I smiled faintly.

I sank into the leather chair by the window, curling my legs underneath as I let the music wrap around me.

I wanted to understand him.

I wanted to peel back the layers he so carefully controlled.

But how?

A quiet idea slipped into my mind.

I could cook for him.

He had provided for me in that way. He had kept me alive, kept me safe.

Maybe...maybe this was how I could offer him something in return.

A gesture.

A truce.

Some part of me whispered the truth.

This was dangerous.

It wasn't freedom.

It wasn't love.

But it was something.

And for now, I would take it.

I stood slowly and made my way toward the kitchen, Reich's shirt slipping over my thighs like a second skin.

I could still feel his hands. His breath against my throat. His words in my ear.

Actions have consequences, Wildflower. Be a good girl.

I wasn't sure which I wanted more.

To obey.

Or to make him prove what would happen if I didn't.

Either way—*I was ready.*

Chapter Thirty-Four

REICH

I WOKE BEFORE DAWN, the room still cloaked in darkness. The faintest glow of early morning bled in through the French doors, pale and gray. For a long moment, I just laid there, breathing in the quiet. I listened to the slow, steady rhythm of Sage's breathing beside me—soft and delicate, like the whisper of wind through leaves.

She was still asleep, her body curled toward mine in the most trusting way, her cheek pressed against my shoulder, her hand resting over my ribs like I was her anchor. The heat of her skin seeped into me, a warmth I hadn't realized I'd been craving until now.

It was dangerous, how much I wanted to stay. How much I wanted to let her keep holding on like this.

But if I didn't move now, I wouldn't move at all.

Slowly, carefully, I peeled myself away from her, shifting my weight so the bed wouldn't creak. Her hand slid from my chest with the faintest graze, and my throat tightened at the loss. I ran a hand down her bare back, my fingers trailing along the curve of her spine once more—softly, like I was memorizing it.

I pressed a kiss to her shoulder. She stirred but didn't wake.

It felt... wrong to leave.

But I did.

Because that's who I was.

I crossed the room silently, grabbing the t-shirt I'd left on the floor and pulling it over my head as I went. My movements were precise. Practiced. Years of slipping out of places unnoticed left their mark. But this wasn't the same. I wasn't running.

I wasn't escaping.

I was just... getting ready for the day.

I slipped into the bathroom and closed the door behind me with a soft click. I stood there for a long minute, staring at myself, tracing the faint scar beneath my jaw with my thumb. A ghost from another life. Another version of myself.

The man staring back at me was a stranger.

I splashed water over my face, rubbed the rough edge of my jaw. Shaved. Pulled on dark clothes.

Routine. Clean lines. Precision.

But I could feel it under my skin.

A restlessness.

A hum in my blood that hadn't been there before.

By the time I made it to the kitchen, the house was already alive with faint sounds. The quiet murmurs of life, carefully orchestrated beneath my roof.

But something about today felt different.

I felt different.

I moved toward the counter, letting instinct guide me. I grabbed a glass, filled it with water from the tap, drank half of it before setting it down.

Then I saw the bowl of fruit on the counter.

Bright, fresh oranges.

I never ate them in the morning. Hell, I rarely ate them at all.

But I grabbed one anyway, tossed it into the air, and caught it.

A grin tugged at the corner of my mouth.

It felt easy. Effortless.

Lightness settled over me, and it was foreign. Unfamiliar. Like some piece of myself I hadn't seen since I was a kid had clawed its way back up from the depths.

And then, of course, Castor showed up to ruin it.

He emerged from the hallway, his presence filling the space with the same old swagger and sharp-edged awareness that had always been there. His gaze found me immediately.

Sharp. Calculating. Curious.

His lips curved into a smirk that made it clear he was about to be an asshole.

"What's going on?" His voice was casual, but there was a thread beneath it. Suspicion.

He was reading me.

He always did.

I raised an eyebrow, catching the orange again before setting it down on the counter. "What do you mean?"

He cocked his head slightly, leaning against the doorway like he had all the time in the world. His arms crossed over his chest; sleeves pushed up to reveal the tattoos inked deep into his skin.

"You've got this stupid-ass grin on your face," he said, nodding toward me. "And unless I'm mistaken, you've never had a woman in your bed until this morning." He tipped his chin toward my room. Making his meaning very clear.

I lowered my head, trying to school my expression.

But it was useless.

The grin slipped through anyway.

Unbidden. Unchecked. Real.

I was happy.

No—more than happy.

I was fucking alive.

The feeling cracked me wide open, and it was dangerous.

But I couldn't seem to care.

For a moment, it was like I was back in the world before all of this—the one I'd barely dared to remember.

Mom in the kitchen, flour on her hands.

Dad's laugh booming through the house.

Cas and me in the snow, boots kicking up powder as we raced toward the sled hill.

Mom's pizzelles baking in the oven.

The twinkling lights of Christmas strung haphazardly over the porch, casting their own quiet magic.

And that last morning.

Before it all changed.

Waking up before dawn.

That warmth—that feeling of being tethered to something real, something good—that's what I felt now.

Because of her.

I lifted my gaze to Castor's.

He was still watching me. Waiting.

"I'm just living life, brother," I said, smirking. "Enjoying the beauty of today before I go to work and do it all over again."

He stared at me.

And then his face twisted, somewhere between horror and disgust. "Brother? Is that you? Have you gone mental? Do you need a doctor?"

I snorted, flipping him off without looking. "Fuck off, Cas."

"There he is," he muttered, shaking his head. But his smirk faded a little, as his eyes began to darken.

And then he was serious, "But really—what the hell possessed you to let Sage into your bed?" His tone wasn't mocking now.

It was a warning.

"You're not the type to make reckless decisions," he continued. "So, what was your thought process there?"

I opened my mouth.

But nothing came out.

How could I explain it? How could I tell him that Sage had pulled something out of me I didn't even know was still alive? That she made me want something dangerous? Something real?

I raked a hand through my hair, blowing out a slow breath.

"I made a decision," I said finally.

Cas studied me in silence.

A beat. Then another.

Then he nodded slowly, his mouth pulling into something that wasn't quite approval. "A reckless one," he said. But his voice was less judgment now.

He pushed away from the doorway, stretching his arms over his head with a low groan.

"I'm just making sure you're not being stupid like Keenan."

The name landed like a brick in my stomach.

Keenan. Reckless. Careless.

The ENA didn't forgive mistakes like his.

And they didn't offer second chances. Not ever.

I stiffened, but Cas let it go.

He didn't press. Didn't need to.

We both knew the rules.

And the consequences.

Still, I felt it in my chest—the flare of something stubborn. Something primal.

I wasn't going to lose Sage.

Not to them.

Not to anyone.

Cas shot me a look before turning away, muttering under his breath, but I caught it anyway.

"She's got you fucked." He stated.

And he wasn't wrong.

I watched him leave, my mind already turning toward the next step.

The next move.

The next risk.

After last night—after having her—I wasn't the same man. I didn't want to be.

She was mine now.

And I would burn the world down before I let anyone take her from me.

Klay hadn't called.

The silence was louder than it should have been but I couldn't focus on that now.

I had to survive this day.

Had to get through it.

So, I could go back to her. To the only place I wanted to be.

And when I got home... I'd remind her who she belonged to.

Chapter Thirty-Five

SAGE

I MOVED THROUGH THE kitchen effortlessly, my fingers trailing along the edge of the marble counter as though tracing the spine of a familiar book. My steps were slow, measured, deliberate. It wasn't just a kitchen—it was a gallery of precision. A curated reflection of him.

Everything had its place.

Everything was immaculate.

Everything about it whispered control.

Power. Restraint.

The appliances gleamed under the soft, diffused light filtering through the large windows. The island stretched like an altar, bare but for a glass bowl of fruit, each piece perfectly ripe, perfectly arranged. Even the cutting boards, stacked neatly by size, looked untouched. Like they were there for show.

It was unsettling.

And impressive.

Not just the order, but the obsessive need for it.

This house wasn't a home.

It was a statement.

An extension of Reich.

A manifestation of discipline and control.

And here I was.

This broken thing.

Standing barefoot on his cold floor in his oversized t-shirt, hair tangled from sleep, skin still marked by his hands, trying to navigate his world as if I belonged here.

But I didn't.

Not really.

Not in a place like this.

I didn't belong anywhere anymore.

And yet, he wanted me here.

I exhaled slowly and caught my reflection in the dark glass of the cabinets. Pale, hollow-eyed. A ghost dressed in his clothes.

What did he see when he looked at me? Was it weakness? Or something else?

I shook my head. I wasn't going to spiral. Not today. I needed to focus.

If I couldn't understand why he wanted me here, then I'd give him a reason. I'd prove I could hold my own in this world. In his world.

Maybe even fit into it.

Maybe even... belong.

I turned back to the stove, adjusting the flame beneath the pan, watching the sauce settle into place with practiced ease. Cooking wasn't new to me. It was grounding, a kind of ritual that reminded me I was still human, even when everything else tried to strip me of that truth.

And then—I felt him.

Before I heard him. Before he spoke.

He was there.

His presence shifted the air, thickened it, made everything in the room bend toward him.

Even me.

Especially me.

He was gravity.

A force I couldn't resist.

"There you are." His voice slid over me, dark and smooth, settling low in my belly like a warning. Or a promise.

I startled, nearly dropping the plate in my hands.

My heart skipped—too fast, too loud.

I turned.

And there he was.

Leaning in the doorway like he belonged in a painting. Effortless and devastating. His shirt was half-buttoned, his sleeves rolled carelessly to his elbows. A few strands of dark hair fell across his forehead, damp from the shower, or maybe sweat.

"One night in my bed," he murmured, his gaze dragging slowly over me, pausing on my bare legs, "and already walking around like you own the place... in my shirt?"

I scrambled to pull myself together, torn between the urge to laugh and the sharp edge of embarrassment prickling beneath my skin.

"I—" I didn't know what to say. I never did with him.

"Relax—" He interrupted.

His grin was slow. Dangerous.

He pushed off the doorway, closing the space between us with those long, easy strides.

"—I'm not complaining about the view."

My breath hitched.

He was close enough now that I could smell him. That faint blend of cedar, smoke, and something darker that always made my knees weak.

I turned away before he could see the heat blooming on my cheeks.

Focusing on the wine rack, I pulled a bottle of a red, more for distraction than anything else. I poured two glasses with hands that weren't quite steady, but I managed.

When I handed him his glass, our fingers brushed.

A shiver shot straight through me, quick and hot, as if I'd been struck.

I hoped he hadn't noticed.

But of course, he had.

He took the glass from me, his eyes holding mine. There was something unreadable there. Something that made my stomach twist in knots.

"Helping yourself to my wine now?" His voice was deceptively light, but the edge was there.

It always was.

I forced a smile, as I responded, "Why? Trying to teach me a lesson about taking things that aren't mine?"

His quiet laugh was low and rich, the sound of it sliding over me like warm honey.

God, this man.

He could unmake me with a single glance.

We settled at the bar; our bodies close but not touching.

The silence wasn't uncomfortable.

It was weighted. Expectant.

Every time his gaze flickered to me, it felt like a touch. Like he was peeling me open without ever laying a hand on me.

And then I asked it.

"Why did you let me stay in your bed?"

The question hung there.

Heavy. Real.

Reich's gaze never wavered, as he asked, "Why do you think?"

I hated when he did this. Made me work for the answers. Made me say things I wasn't ready to say. But I thought about it.

I forced myself to.

"You didn't think I was going to run?" I said it like a challenge, but my voice was softer than I wanted it to be.

His eyes darkened, something flickering behind them. "Were you?"

I shook my head. "No."

And I meant it.

He set his glass down slowly, the sound of it on the counter sharp in the silence. "Then you have your answer."

I swallowed hard.

I could have walked away. I could have left this house. Left him. I could have. But I wouldn't. Not because I couldn't. But because I didn't want to.

I tested him anyway.

"I could walk away."

His expression didn't change.

But his voice—his voice was steel wrapped in silk. "No. You couldn't."

I arched a brow, "You sound sure of that."

He leaned in, his eyes locking onto mine.

"Because if you could," he said quietly, "you would've already."

He was right. God, he was right. And it terrified me how much I didn't care.

My gaze flickered down to the ink coiled around his arms.

The tattoos I'd been dying to ask about.

Symbols. Lines. Stories carved into flesh.

And one, in particular that I couldn't stop thinking about.

The same symbol I'd seen in his library.

On the back of his neck and Castor's. The familiar one I couldn't place.

His voice broke through my thoughts, "Something you want to discuss, Sage?"

I blinked. "I was wondering about your tattoos. They are ... unique." I tried to keep my tone casual.

Failed.

He studied me for a long moment before he smiled.

Slow. Lethal.

"Thank you," he said, amusement in his tone.

I laughed softly, "Which one's your favorite?"

He glanced down at his arms, running his fingers absently along one of the designs. A gesture so intimate, it made me ache. "These are where I feel most vulnerable," he said after a long pause.

I frowned.

"Vulnerable?"

He nodded, the shadow in his gaze deepening. "Yes, I got them to destroy the soft parts of myself. My weaknesses..." He said quietly. "So, nothing can break me."

My eyes drifted to the tattoo over his heart.

"And you think these all make you invincible?"

His smirk was sharp. "No. But I do think they make me look really fucking cool."

I laughed again. This time it was genuine. "I'm sure your concubines agree."

His grin widened. "Wildflower," he murmured, voice thick with amusement, "I'm too preoccupied to entertain any concubines." He leaned in slightly, his breath warm against my skin. "You're the first person to ever ask about them and probably the only one I'd ever tell."

I swallowed hard, absentmindedly playing with the cuticles on my fingers.

His words shouldn't have mattered, but they did.

Too much.

He was letting me in, and it was dangerous.

For both of us.

His gaze softened, "So, what's going on in that head of yours?"

I tried to answer.

But nothing came out, just the constant fiddling of my fingernails. A habit I grew accustomed to when I felt unsure.

"How are you feeling?"

His voice was low. Gentle. Like he was asking for something more than just an answer.

I met his gaze.

"I'm okay," I said, trying to give him more, "Just fine, I guess."

His brow arched.

"Just fine...you guess?" he continued, "You know, in my house, I want my guests to feel better than just fine."

I smiled faintly before responding, forgetting what made me nervous in the first place.

"Got any suggestions?" I teasingly asked.

His gaze darkened. "Why don't you get on your hands and knees and crawl to me?"

My breath stalled in my throat at his directness.

"Why?" My voice was soft, but the heat underneath it was undeniable.

"Because..." he said, his voice rough with promise, "when I'm done with you, you won't feel 'just fine.' You'll feel immaculate."

And before I could stop myself—I sank to my knees ready to let him ruin me again.

The heat between us throbbed, thick and consuming, with every inch I closed between us.

His gaze followed my movements—controlled, unreadable—but I saw it.

The hunger.

I smirked, teasing him, letting the tension coil between us. Letting him watch as I slid closer, inch by inch, my body betraying my mind's futile attempts at restraint.

The moment we met, there was no going back.

And I didn't want to.

Not when it felt this raw.

This real.

But just when I thought I had him—just when I thought he'd let me win this round—he pulled back.

Regaining control.

A wicked thrill shot through me because I already knew—

The more he resisted and held back, the more I wanted him to break.

Reich was the kind of man who would make you beg for what you wanted.

And tonight?

I was ready to plead until he pleaded with me.

His eyes locked onto mine, dark and unrelenting.

He knew.

He knew exactly what he was doing to me.

And I was powerless to resist.

He leaned back, exuding a quiet, absolute dominance, every movement deliberate, controlled.

His gaze flickered to my face, catching something—some tiny slip in my mask—before I could steady myself.

Before I could pretend, I wasn't completely undone by him.

And then—he was already moving, threading his fingers through my hair, his grip just tight enough to send a shiver down my spine.

His lips crashed into mine, a kiss that was electric and devastating.

We moved together, tongues dancing on the edge of surrender, teasing, tasting—but never giving in completely.

Never letting go.

When we pulled apart, our breaths mingled in the heavy silence, ragged and uneven.

We were playing with fire.

His fingers traced my cheek, his touch impossibly gentle for a man who kissed like that.

I shivered, my body reacting before I could think.

Before I could stop myself, a sound escaped—a quiet, breathless moan.

Something flickered in his eyes. Triumph. Amusement. Possession.

Then, without warning—he lifted me effortlessly, his strength unraveling me in ways I wasn't ready for.

I straddled him, my hips moving instinctively against his.

Chasing friction. Chasing him.

But instead of giving in, instead of letting me rush him, he pulled back.

Control. Again.

He carried me with ease, setting me down onto the table, his body slotting between my thighs as he pinned me there.

Every inch of him pressed against me. Hot. Solid. Torturous.

I swallowed hard, barely able to breathe.

"What are you doing?" I asked, my voice unsteady.

His lips curled into a smirk. "So many questions."

His gaze dragged over me, dark and slow, as if drinking me in.

"And never any answers," I teased, my voice laced with defiance.

That smirk widened.

And then he pulled me in again, mouth claiming mine one last time—a promise, a warning and a surrender all at once.

His hands were everywhere.

Gripping. Teasing. Taking.

Staking his claim with every touch, every kiss and every slow drag of his fingers over my skin.

I arched into him, helpless against the way he unraveled me.

His breath ghosted against my ear, sending a shiver straight through my body.

"You knew this was inevitable, didn't you?" he asked.

I couldn't answer.

Not when his lips traced fire down my neck.

Not when I was already too far gone to deny him.

I don't know how much time passed after that.

I just know that we didn't stop.

Didn't slow down.

Didn't hold back.

We made our way across every surface—every inch of space blurred by heat and need and hunger.

The living room.

The dining table.

The kitchen counters.

All of it—devoured.

And it felt endless.

Like the world beyond us had ceased to exist.

Like we had stepped outside of time itself.

That night wasn't just unforgettable.

It was one of the best of my entire life.

Chapter Thirty-Six

REICH

I HELD HER CLOSE, my arm wrapped tightly around her waist, the other hand threading slowly through her hair as we lay sprawled across the cold, hardwood floor of the living room. The fire had long since burned itself down to glowing embers, their light flickering faintly across her skin. She was warm against me, her body molded to mine, fitting as if she'd always belonged there. My fingers combed through the silken strands of her hair over and over, memorizing the texture, needing to do something with my hands because if I didn't... I'd probably lose what little control I had left... again.

The silence between us stretched, heavy but not suffocating. It wasn't the uncomfortable kind that begged to be filled. It was a quiet understanding, a fragile peace I hadn't realized I craved until now.

I dipped my head, brushing my lips across her temple. She exhaled softly, her breath feathering against my neck, and for a moment, it felt like the world outside us didn't exist.

I tilted her face toward mine, needing to see her. Needing proof that this wasn't just some fever dream I'd conjured out of desperation.

Those eyes.

Fuck, those eyes.

Green and wild and devastatingly soft all at once. They carried storms in them, the kind that could destroy, and yet they looked at me now with something gentler. Something raw.

It undid me.

"How are you feeling now?" I asked, my voice low, coaxing, a thread of teasing woven through it, because if I didn't keep it light, I was afraid of how much weight would slip into my tone.

She didn't answer right away. Just studied me with that unwavering gaze of hers, searching for something. I wasn't sure what.

Maybe I didn't want to know.

But then her lips curved faintly, and she gave me a soft nod. "Better," she murmured. Her voice was quiet but certain. "Really."

I let out a breath I hadn't realized I was holding, brushing my fingers along her jaw.

"Good." Because if she was better, maybe I could be too.

"Thank you... for everything," she added, and this time, her hand found mine, her fingers curling around my wrist like an anchor. Like I was the one who needed grounding.

"It's nothing, Sage," I muttered, but my hand lingered on her cheek, my thumb tracing the hollow just beneath her eye.

Her grip tightened just slightly. Not enough to hurt. Just enough to stop me.

"It's not nothing, Reich." Her voice wasn't loud.

It didn't need to be.

There was something resolute in it. Unshakable.

And it hit me like a punch to the gut.

"I was ready to die..." she said after a beat.

No bitterness. No drama. Just truth.

"I was ready to disappear with no one knowing my shame." Her breath shuddered out of her like a ghost she'd been holding in too long. "But you... you didn't let me."

I wanted to argue. Wanted to tell her she'd saved herself. But I stayed quiet.

Because maybe she needed to say this.

And maybe I needed to hear it.

"You showed me how to let that go," she whispered. "You made me see that trusting again doesn't mean giving yourself away." She drew a breath, as though steadying herself, and then her voice dropped, quieter. "I spent so long thinking routine would keep me safe. If I controlled everything, I couldn't be blindsided again. But all I was doing was hiding. From everything. From myself."

I knew what that was like.

I knew it too well.

"You did this," I told her. My voice was rougher than I intended. "Not me."

She shook her head slowly, her eyes shining. "You made me open up."

"Again... that was all you."

Her laugh was faint, but real, as she pointed at herself. "And I thought I was the difficult one."

I smirked, teasing, "You are." then softer, "But you did all the hard work, wildflower."

Her expression changed—something softened, something vulnerable and open that nearly wrecked me.

And then she said it again, "Still... thank you."

I swallowed the lump that suddenly formed in my throat.

It was stupid.

I shouldn't have felt this much over two simple words.

But I did.

Her fingers slid to my chest, resting over my heart. I was sure she could feel how hard it was pounding. And maybe that was the point.

"I know I still have a long way to go," she said after a moment. "But I feel like I'm getting better."

I watched her carefully.

Because there was something else.

I could feel it.

A hesitation.

A shadow.

"What is it, Sage?"

She bit her lip, almost like she was considering lying, but then she sighed, "I found your library today."

My brow arched, "Did you?"

I shouldn't have been surprised.

Of course, she'd been curious.

Of course, she'd gone looking.

"It's beautiful," she added softly.

I nodded once. "It's my favorite place in the house," I said honestly. "It's where I can think. Where I go to feel... normal."

I wasn't sure why I told her that, but it was the truth, and she deserved the truth.

"It suits you," she murmured.

But there was more she was holding back. So, I waited and then I pressed, "Is that really all?"

She hesitated. Just long enough.

Then: "The playlist."

My pulse jumped. "What about it?" I asked, careful to keep my tone neutral.

She swallowed. "It felt like every song understood me on a different level. Every song spoke the words I was too afraid to say... Like whoever made it... knows me better than I know myself."

I sighed, running a hand through my hair. "I just threw some songs together. It's nothing."

A lie. A pathetic one. Her eyes snapped to mine, sharper now, "Stop saying it's nothing."

Her voice was firm. It left no room for argument. She wasn't letting me off easy.

I exhaled slowly. "Maybe," I said, "the person who made it doesn't fully understand what she's been through... but wanted her to know she isn't alone."

Her gaze didn't waver, "Why?"

"Because..." I said, letting the word hang, "Music gives you permission to feel it... The pain... The grief... And maybe—when you're ready—to let it go. It reminds you that you're not alone. That others have felt it too."

"A hundred others to be exact..." I added quietly, "And that's just a fraction."

She looked down and I looked away as I went on, "Every time a song resonates with you, it's because you've poured a part of yourself into it. It becomes a mirror—reflecting what lives inside you, what you've felt but couldn't quite say. It gives voice to the things your heart knows but your own words can't reach."

I glanced back at her. And there it was.

That glimmer of understanding.

"Reich," she whispered. "I don't know how to—"

"You don't have to," I cut in. Because I already knew.

I'd made that playlist for her.

And maybe for me, too.

I couldn't help but silently thank every artist behind those songs in that moment.

The ones who had saved me when I didn't think anything could.

Now, they were saving her too.

"Thank you..." I said quietly.

She blinked, confused. "For what?"

I hesitated, then I let my guard down... "For seeing me."

Her lips parted and I knew she understood.

Because she was seeing me now, in ways no one ever had.

And fuck, it scared me.

It made me want more.

But wanting more meant risking everything.

I was quiet for a long time before I pressed a kiss to her forehead.

Lingering. Soft. Final.

And then I pulled away. Because if I stayed any longer, I wasn't sure I'd be able to let go.

I left her there, curled on the floor by the fire, watching me with those wild, green eyes as I slipped from the room like a coward.

I needed to breathe. To clear my head.

I found Cas in the hall.

And everything changed.

His face was pale, drained of color.

His chest heaved as if he'd just run miles.

His hands shook.

I didn't hesitate.

"Cas?" My voice was sharp, cutting through the silence like a blade. "What happened?"

He struggled to find breath; his body taut with panic.

"She knows," he gasped. "It's all my fault."

"What the fuck are you talking about? Who knows?"

His throat bobbed. And then, barely a whisper—"Sam."

Shit.

Chapter Thirty-Seven

SAGE

The longer I stayed here, the more I could feel it—the past, finally starting to let go of me. It was slow, almost like something peeling off, bit by bit. Layers I didn't even know I was still carrying. Like an old skin I'd forgotten was there. Or maybe I just got so used to it, I thought it was who I was.

It had been part of me for so long—this brittle armor I'd built from every scar, every wound I dragged out of Sanele. Every shame I kept hidden, even from myself.

But now... it was falling away.

And underneath it?

Something I didn't recognize.

But it was... beautiful, too.

I was changing.

Becoming someone else.

Someone lighter.

Someone I thought I'd lost a long time ago.

I woke with that restlessness humming through my bones. A current of energy I hadn't felt in years—raw, electric anticipation sparking just under my skin. Like something was waiting for me. Something important. Something I couldn't ignore anymore.

And before I even realized it, my feet were carrying me toward the library.

When I opened the sliding door, the scent of cedar and old books hung heavy in the air, grounding and intoxicating all at once. Floor-to-ceiling shelves lined the walls, housing stories, knowledge, and secrets bound in leather and ink. There was reverence in the way it was arranged. Not just neatness, but care. Respect for what lived inside these pages.

It was a map of Reich's mind.

And I wanted to explore every inch of it.

I found myself cross-legged on the floor, surrounded by books. Their weight comforting. Their presence familiar. I trailed my fingertips along the spines before selecting one—The Count of Monte Cristo by Alexandre Dumas.

Fitting.

A story of betrayal. Of survival. Of a man who rose from his own grave and became something more than anyone thought possible.

I flipped through the pages. Paused. And then I saw them.

Marks in the margins. Underlines. Notes scrawled in tidy, slanted handwriting. I recognized it from the note he had left me earlier.

Reich's handwriting.

He had left pieces of himself here. Quiet rebellions against untouched pages. Little fragments of thought, insight, sometimes sharp, sometimes sardonic. And sometimes...unexpectedly gentle.

Curious, I pulled another book. Then another.

And another.

Each one bore his imprint.

And something inside me softened.

He left marks. He left proof of his existence. His thoughts. His struggles. His questions.

And I realized—

He wasn't just living in this world. He was trying to make sense of it.

Just like me.

A slow smile curved my lips.

He did things his own way.

It was inspiring.

And it made me want to do more than just exist in someone else's narrative.

It made me want to write my own and become something more.

More than I had ever been in Sanele.

More than I allowed myself to be in Providence.

I was still sitting there when the door creaked open.

I turned, heart skipping, and there he was.

Reich leaned lazily against the bookcase, arms folded across his chest.

His expression unreadable, but his eyes—God, his eyes—burned with something that made my pulse trip over itself.

Effortless. Perfect. Dangerous.

"Having fun?" His voice was low, that smirk of his slicing right through my defenses.

I blinked, caught between embarrassment and something warmer.

I glanced at the mess I had made—books scattered like fallen leaves surrounding me like a tornado. Heat crept up my neck.

"Sorry," I said quickly, fumbling for the closest book. "I didn't realize how late it had gotten. I just... I got caught up."

Caught up in the stories.

Caught up in him.

His gaze sharpened. "Sage," he said slowly, his voice like dark silk. "You don't have to apologize for that."

I hesitated.

But he liked order.

I could feel it in the way he carried himself, in every inch of this meticulously crafted space.

I was disrupting it.

Intruding.

"I'm sorry," I said again, this time softer. "I'll clean it up."

I reached for the books again, but before I could move, he was there.

Sudden. Controlled. I barely registered the space between us closing until his hands closed over mine.

Warm. Firm.

Stopping me.

"If you apologize one more time," his voice was low, rougher now, "we're going to have a problem."

His breath ghosted against my ear, sending a shiver straight through me.

And then he pulled me closer.

I inhaled sharply as his hands slid up to cradle my face.

"You're so beautiful," he murmured. His voice was a rasp. A confession.

Not playful.

Not teasing.

Real.

And something inside me stilled.

Because when he said it, I believed him.

My heart thudded against my ribs as I answered him without thinking—without hesitating—with my lips.

My hands tangled in his hair as I kissed him.

Slow. Fierce and demanding.

And for a moment, he let me take control.

Just long enough to taste victory.

Before he took it back.

His hands slid up my body—slow, deliberate—until they found my throat. His fingers curled there, firm but gentle, holding me in place. Keeping me on my toes. Literally.

"You're so damn greedy," he murmured. His lips grazed mine, feather-light, before he pulled away just enough to leave me wanting.

I made a sound—half protest, half plea—and he chuckled.

"Be patient, wildflower." His fingers flexed. "And you'll get what you want."

He kissed me then. Hard. Consuming.

Until I was dizzy.

Until I was so lost in him that I could barely stand.

When he finally pulled back, his forehead pressed to mine, his breath ragged. "You're going to destroy me," he whispered.

My pulse stuttered as I cupped his cheek, whispering, "Then let me."

I didn't know who moved first.

Our lips met again and that was all that matter. Until he broke the kiss and rested his hands on my waist, steadying me. Grounding me.

"Sage," he said quietly. "Sam's been worried."

The world shifted, as he continued, "She went looking for you."

I drew back, breath catching.

"She doesn't know everything," Reich added. "She only knows you're here because someone tried to go after you."

I swallowed hard.

Why hadn't he told her everything?

"You didn't tell her—?"

"It's not my story to tell," he said simply.

The words sank in and something in me unclenched.

I kissed him softly; a brief thank you pressed against his lips.

He pulled me back in, resting his forehead against mine. "She wants to see you," he murmured. "Is that okay?"

I hesitated, but nodded, "Yes. I think so."

He kissed me one more time before helping me to my feet.

When the door opened and Sam rushed in, I barely had time to brace myself before she threw her arms around me.

Tight. Fierce.

Like she was trying to hold me together.

"You're not leaving me again," she whispered fiercely.

And then she tied a ribbon around my wrist.

One of her endless ribbon bracelets.

"So, I don't lose you." She added.

I laughed softly, but it cracked in the middle.

Because I knew exactly what she meant.

And this time, I wasn't letting go either.

Chapter Thirty-Eight

REICH

After Castor told me everything about what had happened with Sam, I knew how to proceed.

There was no other way.

Letting Sam see Sage wasn't just a concession—it was a necessity.

For Sage, it was about survival.

For me, it was about control.

Sage needed an anchor after the emotional wreckage this week had left her in. A familiar face. Something pure in a world that had shown her nothing but cruelty. And I...I needed to keep Sam close now that she knew.

Because Sam wasn't just a friend.

She was a threat.

Castor didn't understand that part.

Or maybe he did, and he just couldn't bear to think it.

But I could.

And I did.

Because someone had to.

I sat back in my chair, letting Castor spiral in his endless orbit of worry while Sam and Sage talked behind the closed door of the sunroom. His pacing was restless, his steps sharp and unyielding on the hardwood. I could feel the tension radiating off him, thick and wild, like a storm caught inside a man's body with nowhere to go.

"Reich, what the fuck are we supposed to do?" His voice was tight, frayed at the edges.

I let out a slow breath, pressing my fingers into my temples. "We figure it out later," I said, calm despite the violence twisting inside me. "When we have more information."

It wasn't enough.

Not for Castor.

He ran his hand through his hair for what had to be the twentieth time, his jaw clenched so tight I half-expected his teeth to crack.

It wasn't just Sam he was worried about.

It was them.

The ENA.

Their rules were simple.

Unforgiving. Absolute.

Rule number one: No outsiders stay on the premises.

I had already broken that rule. I'd done it carefully—or at least, I thought I had. But now? Now there was another variable I hadn't planned for.

Sam.

Rule number two: No outsider could know what we did.

And Sam knew.

It didn't matter how loyal Castor believed she was.

Even if she swore herself to silence. Even if she carved it into her skin and bled for it.

The ENA wouldn't care.

They would call her a loose thread.

And loose threads had to be cut.

I wasn't sure I trusted her the way Cas did.

I wasn't sure I trusted anyone.

But for now, I had no choice.

I had to let it play out and pray I could keep them all alive long enough to make it mean something.

What worried me more was Sage.

Because it was only a matter of time before Sam told her everything.

If she hadn't already.

And I needed to be the one to tell her.

Not Sam.

Not Castor.

Me.

But my gut twisted with something sharp and ugly.

Not tonight.

Not yet.

There was still too much to unravel.

Later, Castor and I moved toward the sunroom. The door was cracked open, warm light spilling into the hall. Laughter drifted out—soft, familiar, painfully normal.

Sam and Sage.

Their voices tangled together, light and easy, like the sound of something innocent.

Something that hadn't existed in this house for years.

I leaned in the doorway and watched.

And all I could think about was how Sage looked.

The way she smiled with Sam, laughing without restraint. The way she tilted her head, her hair falling over her shoulder like she didn't know the effect it had on me.

The way the light caught in her eyes, softening them, filling them with something close to hope.

For a second, I forgot to breathe.

She glowed.

Not like a woman who had been through hell.

Not like a prisoner in a house ruled by men like Castor and me.

But like someone free.

Someone on the edge of something new.

And it was intoxicating.

"You know what we need to do?" Sam said suddenly, her voice bright, as if the solution was obvious all along. She gestured between the four of us with a grin that felt more dangerous than it should have. "We need to go out."

Castor chuckled. But his eyes flicked toward me with caution.

He was still waiting for my approval.

They all were.

And then Sage turned her gaze on me.

She wasn't asking for permission.

But she was waiting.

And in that moment, I felt it.

The undeniable pull.

Like I was the center of her world.

And God help me, I wanted to stay there.

I wanted to give her everything she asked for.

I wanted to tear the world open and hand it to her, bloody and raw, just to see her smile like that again.

For one insane second, I believed I could.

That I could have this.

Her.

Castor leaned in beside me, his smirk casual. But I could hear the edge beneath it. "What do you say, brother?" he asked, voice lazy and slow. "Shall we get these beautiful ladies out of this house and make sure they are properly fed and entertained?"

There was amusement in his tone. But he wasn't joking.

He was testing me.

Waiting to see if I would do something reckless.

Or if I would remember who the fuck I was.

The others watched me, quiet, expectant.

Like I was the one holding the keys to this entire night.

Maybe I was.

I should have said no.

I should have thought it through.

Taking them out wasn't just risky.

It was dangerous.

Too many variables. Too many things that could go wrong.

Too many people who might recognize Sage.

Too many eyes watching us that we didn't see.

But then I looked at her.

And none of that mattered.

She was looking at me like I was more than what I was.

Like I could give her this one small thing.

And fuck me—I wanted to.

Her quiet anticipation was like a live wire, vibrating in the space between us.

And when she smiled— I was done for.

Her smile was a crack in the armor I'd spent my entire life forging.

A chisel against stone, soft and patient, breaking me down piece by piece.

And all I could do was let it happen.

"Fine," I muttered, the word tasting like surrender.

The light in her face when I said it—it gutted me.

Because I wanted to be the man who could give her that joy without conditions all the time.

And I wasn't sure I could.

But tonight, I would try.

She rose from the couch, moving toward me like she was tethered to me. And when her fingers curled around my arm, grounding me with that quiet, unspoken certainty she always carried— I couldn't breathe.

Her touch wasn't possessive.

It wasn't about control.

It was about something I couldn't quite name.

Her eyes met mine.

And for a moment—Nothing else existed.

A night out with Sage.

It sounded like heaven.

It felt like freedom.

And for the first time in a long, long while—I wanted to believe that it wouldn't be too big of a risk.

Even if I knew better.

Even if I knew what was waiting for us when we got back.

For one night, I'd let myself forget.

For one night, I'd let myself have this.

Her.

And maybe...maybe it wouldn't destroy us.

Chapter Thirty-Nine

SAGE

WE WOVE THROUGH THE quiet streets of town until we reached a restaurant unlike any other—a place swallowed whole by pitch-black darkness.

No flickering candlelight. No dim ambient glow. Just pure, unrelenting black.

It made sense. Reich never did anything without a reason. Everything he did had a purpose.

Dining in the dark was something I had never experienced before, though I'd heard whispers—rumors that when sight is stripped away, the other senses awaken. That without the distraction of vision, flavors become sharper, textures more vivid—every bite an exploration rather than a mere act of consumption.

Maybe that's why Reich had brought me here.

He had a way of expanding my world, pushing me beyond the edges of what I thought I knew, making me step outside my comfort and into the unknown.

And I wanted that.

I wanted him.

Every part of him. The way he heightened my senses, made me crave him in ways I'd never craved another. The feel of his skin beneath my fingertips, the intoxicating taste of his mouth, the piercing intensity of his gaze and the sound of his breath as it tangled with mine. And then there was his scent—*God, his scent*. It filled my lungs like oxygen, becoming something essential, and something I never wanted to live without.

We slipped into a private room at the back of the restaurant, where a table awaited our party of four. Reich settled in beside me, his movements fluid, controlled. As the waitress approached, he leaned back, exuding an effortless dominance.

"The usual."

No menu. No questions. Just a quiet command.

I smirked, my amusement only growing when he caught my eye with a knowing glint, a cocky grin that sent warmth flooding my cheeks.

"Are you two ready?" he asked, voice smooth, laced with something unspoken. His gaze flicked between Sam and me, Cas mirroring his anticipation across the bench.

Sam and I exchanged a look—a silent question passing between us.

Ready for what, exactly?

"Depends on what we're supposed to be ready for," Sam quipped, raising a brow.

I studied Reich and Castor. They were enjoying this. Their eyes gleamed with undeniable mischief, like two schoolboys hiding a secret.

Then, in perfect unison, they pulled out black satin blindfolds.

A ripple of anticipation coursed through me.

"Face each other," Reich instructed.

Sam and I obeyed, exchanging another amused glance before I felt him move behind me. His presence wrapped around me like heat, pressing into every inch of my awareness.

Fingertips grazed my cheek. Trailed down my shoulder. A featherlight touch, deliberate, possessive.

Cas mirrored him with Sam, their movements synchronized and precise.

Then, the silk slid over my skin.

Reich lifted the blindfold, securing it at the back of my head with slow, practiced ease. The world went dark.

His breath ghosted over my ear, low and intimate. "This is going to require that you trust everything I give you."

A shiver licked up my spine.

Then his thumb brushed my bottom lip—a fleeting touch before pressing into my mouth in a silent command.

My lips closed around him instinctively, my tongue teasing the pad of his thumb in a slow, deliberate sweep.

His breath hitched.

"Can you do that, wildflower?" he murmured, his voice a caress. "Can you trust me, even when you're surrounded by darkness?"

I smiled against his skin. "Haven't I already?"

And just like that, the moment between us shifted—tilted toward something deeper and inevitable.

His hands gripped my waist, dragging me closer, his breath warm against my skin.

"Mine," Reich growled.

The word slammed into me, punched the air from my lungs.

"Say it," he demanded.

I should have fought back. I should have resisted.

But the truth was—I wanted to be his just as much as he wanted to claim me.

So, I did the only thing I could—I whispered, "Yours."

His hand slid to the back of my neck, tightening just enough to make my breath catch.

And then he kissed me.

Deep. Consuming. Possessive.

His lips claimed me, owned me, drew me under until nothing else existed.

And I let myself fall.

Because even in the darkness—

He was the only thing I wanted to see.

As we returned from the restaurant, a weight hung thick between us—not silence, but tension.

Something charged. Something unspoken.

Reich's eyes held something I couldn't quite place—a flicker of concern shadowed by something deeper. An unspoken fear.

But if I was being honest, I carried my own unease.

It wasn't just the way he was acting but it was the way his presence, usually so composed, felt subtly off. Like a mask slipping at the edges.

I wanted to ask. The words burned at the back of my throat, demanding to be spoken.

But I knew better.

With Reich, answers always came in their own time—never forced. Never before he was ready.

He disappeared into his office without a word.

By the time he returned, I had lost myself in the pages of The Scarlet Pimpernel by Baroness Orczy. The story fascinated me—a man with a hidden identity, using deception not for his own gain, but to save lives.

A self-made savior.

Moving unseen through the world.

My fingers traced the worn edges of the book, a question gnawing at me.

Would I ever be that kind of person?

Would I ever be capable of saving anyone?

So far, the only person I had ever been busy saving was myself.

I felt his presence suddenly.

Reich lingered at the doorway, his expression softer now. Lighter.

Whatever weight had been pressing on him earlier had shifted. If only slightly.

I offered a small smile, slipping a bookmark between the pages before turning my attention to him.

He stepped into the room, unbuttoning his shirt with a slow, deliberate ease.

"I didn't mean to disturb you," he said smoothly.

"I don't mind." My voice barely above a whisper.

His lips curled in that effortlessly intoxicating smirk.

My gaze flickered to the nightstand. Multiple phones lay there, sleek screens catching the dim light.

I hadn't noticed them before.

"That's one of my favorites," Reich said, nodding toward the book in my hands.

Something in his voice told me he'd been watching me longer than I realized.

I shifted, studying him. "It's inspiring," I murmured. "How he risked himself to save others. Strangers."

Reich lowered his head slightly, the bedside lamp casting sharp shadows across his features. Then, without another word, he climbed into bed beside me.

"Is that why you helped me?"

His gaze met mine—dark, unreadable.

For a moment, I thought he wouldn't answer.

But then, his voice came. Low. Certain.

"I like helping people."

I swallowed, attempting to look away, but his fingers caught my chin, gently yet firmly guiding my gaze back to his.

Then, in a voice edged with something deeper—*something almost possessive*—he murmured, "But I wanted to save you."

His hand traced the curve of my body, slow, deliberate, as if committing every dip and rise to memory. There was something reverent in the way he touched me—like a man worshipping at the altar of his own undoing.

Heat coiled low in my stomach, pooling deep, my pulse a betraying rhythm against the hush of the room.

Reich hovered close, his breath feathering over my lips, thick with unspoken promise. I could almost taste the words he hadn't yet said, could feel them between us, suspended in the charged air.

Instead, I exhaled against his mouth, my voice steady despite the storm inside me.

"I'm going to put this book away. I'll be right back."

His brows pulled together, curiosity flickering in his gaze as he watched me slip from his hold.

I turned away, feeling the weight of his stare like a touch I couldn't shake.

The trip to the library was quick, but anticipation curled in my stomach like a living thing.

By the time I returned, the air had shifted.

It was thick now. Unforgiving.

A silent invitation.

I closed the door behind me, leaning against it for a beat longer than necessary. Reich sat on the edge of the bed, his gaze heavy-lidded, tracking me with the patience of a predator. Hunger burned in his dark eyes—devouring me, waiting.

I let the silence stretch. Let the heat simmer.

Then—*deliberately, slowly*—I let my fingers trail to the hem of my clothes, peeling them from my body piece by piece.

I watched him fight it.

Watched the clench of his jaw, the twitch in his fingers, the sharp inhale as he forced himself to meet my gaze—when every muscle in his body screamed to look lower.

The moment his resolve snapped—when his control fractured—something deep inside me clenched in satisfaction.

"Fuck, Sage," he rasped, his voice rough, breath uneven. "You're asking for trouble that only ends in chaos."

I took a step forward, slow and intentional, my lips curling at the edges.

"Good. I want your kind of chaos."

A challenge.

A promise.

And as his hand closed around my wrist, pulling me down onto his lap, I knew exactly what I was asking for.

And I didn't care.

Because for the first time in years, maybe my entire life, I wasn't afraid of the fire.

I wanted to burn.

With him.

For him.

Because of him.

Chapter Forty

REICH

She moved toward me with a suffocating ease, like gravity itself had shifted—like every molecule of air between us bent and curved in her favor. Each step she took was deliberate. Measured. As if she already knew exactly what it was doing to me. How it was unraveling me one thin strand at a time.

And I allowed it to happen.

No—*wanted* it to happen.

The soft pad of her bare feet against the hardwood made no sound, but I heard her.

Felt her.

Every movement, every inhale synced perfectly with the pounding in my chest.

As if we shared the same rhythm.

As if her pulse was my pulse.

She was poetry in motion—something written by hands that had never trembled, a story unfinished but desperate to be told. And with every step that closed the space between us, the story began to write itself.

Our story.

A narrative I thought I'd burned to ashes long ago, only to find those ashes carried the seeds of something waiting to bloom.

And now?

Now she was standing in front of me, a fire and a vow.

As if the universe had finally stopped to take a breath, only to exhale her back into my life.

To place her right here.

Right where she belonged.

There was nothing accidental about this.

No coincidence.

She was meant to be here.

She was meant for me.

I could see it in the heavy drag of her lashes as her eyes devoured me.

In the way the air between us tightened, thick with the electricity of something neither of us could name but both of us felt.

And I saw something else, too.

Memories flickered on the edges of my mind of moments hidden. Shattered pieces of a past I thought I'd buried, rising up like smoke.

But they hadn't been lost.

They had just been waiting.

Waiting for this.

I pushed up from the bed in one fluid motion.

I didn't want to waste another second.

I met her halfway, right before she could climb in, my hand shooting out to catch her wrist and pull her flush against me.

But this time—this time I didn't push.

I didn't demand.

I let her.

I let her take what she wanted.

Take me.

Her hands slid over my chest, fingers splaying wide as she pressed me back—*slow, sure, undeniable.*

Her palm rested flat over my heart, smirking at me as if she felt the hard thrum of it beneath her skin and was ready to challenge me and make it beat faster.

"What's wrong?" she asked, head tilting slightly. Her voice was a tease, but there was a steel edge to it. "Not used to someone else taking charge?"

I huffed out something that was half a laugh and half a threat, "Careful, Sage."

Her nails traced down my abdomen, following the rigid lines of my skin with deliberate pressure.

Teasing me. Testing me.

And fuck, I was failing her test.

"Or what?" Her question hung there, heavy with expectation.

She wanted to know how far she could push me.

How far I'd let her go.

I let my breath slow, drop by calculated drop, and wrapped my hands around her hips—my grip tight enough to earn me a gasp, as I spoke, "Or I'll remind you who's really in control."

The corner of her mouth quirked up in a grin that was pure sin.

But there was a flicker of anticipation in her eyes, and I caught it.

Held it.

With a flick of my wrist, I tangled my fingers in her hair, dragging her closer.

Just enough to own.

I tugged until our mouths hovered inches apart, her breath spilling into mine, shaky and hot.

Her pulse jumping beneath my touch.

I moved her on to her back toward the bed, forcing her down onto the mattress with my weight pressing her there, my body caging hers completely.

I braced myself on my forearm as I reached for the nightstand with the other, finding exactly what I needed without looking.

The rope felt cool and familiar in my hands.

Soft but unyielding.

She watched me with wide eyes, her breathing uneven, but there was no fear there.

Just a want that was raw and exposed waiting for me.

And I would give it to her.

I pulled her wrists above her head, locking them together with practiced ease. Tying her to the metal hook embedded in the headboard.

A moan slipped from her lips when the rope tightened.

And I felt it—the tremble in her body.

The desperate arch of her back as she sought friction.

She was already breaking.

Already offering herself up on the altar of whatever we were becoming.

She writhed beneath me, every movement a plea, every desperate press of her hips an unspoken surrender.

And her face...God, her face was the most beautiful thing I'd ever seen.

Eyes dark and heavy-lidded.

Lips parted, pink and swollen from my earlier kisses.

A study in pleasure, caught between anticipation and ruin.

And I wasn't finished with her.

Not even *close*.

Her gaze moved to the nightstand, lingering on the candle flickering atop it. The firelight danced over her skin, golden and hypnotic, its flame reflected in the dark pools of her eyes.

"I see... So, that's what you want." My voice was low, edged with meaning.

She turned her eyes back to mine, straining against her restraints, her body taut with anticipation.

"Yes." She whispered.

I couldn't help but oblige. So, I did. I grabbed the candle, my fingers curling around the base.

She held my gaze, unwavering.

"You saved me," she murmured. "Let me burn for you."

I cupped her cheek with my free hand, thumb stroking the soft curve of her jaw before tilting the candle forward—just enough.

The first drop of wax landed on her sternum. She inhaled sharply—*one hard gasp*—and then exhaled on a shuddering moan. Her body jerked, hips lifting, but I pressed my hand to her stomach, keeping her pinned.

I tilted the candle again.

A slow, molten trail ran down her chest, over her ribs, dripping in a pattern that made her shake.

And I watched.

Watched her burn.

Watched her fall apart.

Each drop of wax was a kiss.

Each flicker of pain was a gift.

And she took it with grace and hunger.

By the time I set the candle down, her skin was a canvas of cooling trails, delicate and gleaming.

Radiant.

My hands followed the paths I'd laid, slow and deliberate, melting the cooled wax with the heat of my touch until her skin glistened.

She trembled beneath me, pulling helplessly against her restraints.

And God, I loved it.

Loved her.

Every unraveled inch.

My fingers drifted lower, finding her soft, slick, and trembling on the cusp of surrender.

I stroked her slowly, languidly, savoring the way her breath fractured into broken, desperate gasps.

She was right there.

On the edge.

Mine to tip over.

And I held her there, playing with the line between mercy and madness.

And then I stopped.

Pulled away.

Left her aching.

She whimpered, straining beneath me.

"Reich, please," she breathed.

But I wasn't done.

I climbed over her, pinning her thighs apart with my hips, ready to take her.

I captured her mouth in a brutal kiss just as I thrusted into her—hard, deep and without any warning.

She cried out, the sound caught in my throat as I swallowed it, drinking it down.

Her body arched, bowed, her back leaving the mattress as she took me in.

She was heaven and hell.

And I was undone.

I moved with her, slow at first, deep and claiming, until the rhythm turned sharp, desperate.

Every gasp a plea.

Every thrust a question.

Every moan an answer.

Her body shook with it, her thighs tightening around my hips, her nails digging into my skin, marking me as hers.

And I let her.

I wanted her to.

Because she was mine and I was hers.

Whether we said it or not, whether we survived it or not.

I held her gaze as I moved faster, harder, chasing the edge with her.

And when she shattered, when her body clenched around me and her cry broke free, wild and wrecked, I followed.

Falling with her.

Into her.

When the shaking subsided and air finally filled our lungs again, I stayed there, still inside her, holding her close.

Heart pounding against hers.

I brushed her damp hair from her forehead.

Kissed her temple.

And whispered her name like a prayer I didn't know I believed in until now.

Sage, *my wildflower*.

Blossoming for me.

And I realized then that there was no going back.

Not for her.

Not for me.

This was it.

Our ruin and our salvation.

And I'd take both, so long as I could have her.

Chapter Forty-One

SAGE

THE NIGHT BEFORE HAD felt like a dream—a dream I never thought I deserved, let alone one that could possibly be real.

But it was.

It had happened.

And the proof of it still clung to my skin.

I could still feel him.

His hands tracing every inch of me like he was mapping something he never wanted to lose.

His mouth claiming mine, his breath warm in the spaces where he whispered things, I didn't know how to believe but wanted to.

With Reich, I had found something I hadn't even known existed. A kind of happiness that didn't just fill me, but completed me.

He wasn't just someone.

He was everything I hadn't realized I'd been aching for.

He slipped into the hollow spaces inside me with an ease that was terrifying.

Those empty places I'd long ago made peace with...he made them ache.

And then he made them full.

And for once in my life, I felt... whole.

Not the brittle, patched-together version I'd convinced myself was enough.

No.

Something real.

Something that felt alive.

I hadn't known how hollow I was until he touched me.

Until he saw me.

And now that he had...I wasn't sure I could survive being unseen again.

I had spent so long believing I was beyond saving.

That the fractures inside me were permanent, that the sharp edges would always cut anyone who came too close.

But then there was Reich.

And he didn't flinch.

He didn't pull away.

He reached for the shattered pieces and held them in his hands like they were precious.

Like they weren't broken at all.

And suddenly, all the emptiness wasn't something to mourn.

It was a space, like a blank canvas, waiting to be filled with something worthwhile.

And I was filled with him.

Every look.

Every touch.

Every dark, quiet truth he let slip past those guarded lips.

I loved every piece of him.

Even if I never got to say it aloud.

Even if he could never say it back.

Last night, I had seen more of Reich than I ever had before.

More than anyone, I suspected.

I saw the man beneath the control.

Beneath the steel walls.

Beneath the brutal precision.

I saw his fight.

His love for helping people.

His drive to keep them safe.

His guilt.

His war with something he didn't talk about, something that lived in his bones and weighed him down in silence.

I wondered what it was.

What he carried.

What he thought he had to carry alone.

Was it some boss? His family? Or something deeper and older, clawing at the edges of his soul?

I didn't know.

But I wanted to.

I wanted to know him.

Every fracture. Every fault line.

I wanted to trace his scars with my hands and tell him he was still beautiful.

Still whole.

And maybe—in finding him, I was finding myself, too.

For so long, I had existed in the shadows of my own life.

A ghost walking through the ruins of what had once been.

But now, it felt different.

The emptiness wasn't a grave.

It was a beginning.

And I knew exactly where I needed to be.

I made my way toward the library, the sanctuary that had become something like holy ground to me.

Where the world quieted.

Where my mind could breathe.

Where I started to remember who I was before I was broken.

As I approached the heavy wooden doors, my fingertips brushed over the smooth grain, and a faint, wistful smile curved my lips.

This was where the healing had begun.

The music that once shattered me was now piecing me back together.

Every note a stitch.

Every lyric a thread pulling me tighter into something stronger.

Every melody telling me it was okay to feel again.

And here, in this room, I reclaimed pieces of myself I thought had been lost forever.

No longer broken.

No longer hollow.

Just...imperfect.

And somehow, that was enough.

My scars were proof.

Proof I had survived.

And there were things—*so many things*—that kept me going now.

Through music, I was never truly alone.

Every song whispered that I belonged somewhere.

Through the people in my life.

Sam. Castor. Reich.

I was reminded I was worth something.

More than my scars.

More than the pain I had lived through.

And through myself, I was still here.

And I was breathing.

Every single breath was proof.

I had made it.

Even when I hadn't wanted to.

I wandered through the room, letting my fingertips graze the piano keys as I passed. The faintest sound trembled through the air, a single note breaking the silence.

And then I saw it.

Something sitting on the low table, right beside a half-burned candle.

A pad of paper and a stylus resting on top.

Something inside me stirred.

Something forgotten.

A part of me I had tucked away, locked in some dark drawer and convinced myself I didn't need anymore.

Poetry.

Words had always been my sanctuary.

A place I could pour out the things I couldn't say out loud.

A way to bleed safely.

And I realized that it had been years since I'd let myself write.

But today...today, I picked up the stylus and let my thoughts unfurl across the page like they'd been waiting for this moment all along.

My thoughts inhale you like second nature,

A whisper of fate, a silent wager.

So, I closed my eyes to escape what's real,

Only to open them and begin to heal.

The scars I carried began to fade,

Softened by every promise we made.

Your hand in mine, steady and true,

Guiding me toward something new.

We spoke in silence, hearts aligned,

Leaving the weight of the past behind.

And in that stillness, clear and bright,

We found ourselves bathed in a light.

I stared at the words, feeling them settle inside me, soft and heavy.

They were messy.

Incomplete.

But they were mine.

For a moment, everything was still.

And then the quiet broke.

A creak echoed behind me.

Soft. Barely there.

But it was enough.

I froze, fingers tightening around the stylus.

The door was opening.

And for a breath, I smiled.

Reich.

I could already hear the sharp, clever remark he'd throw at me.

I could already feel the heat crawling up my throat as he made me laugh when I wasn't supposed to.

But the air changed. The temperature dropped. And ice flooded my veins.

Something was wrong.

The footsteps were wrong.

Too heavy. Too fast.

Before I could turn—a hand tangled in my hair.

Fist tight.

And yanked me violently backward, tearing me from the chair with a force that ripped the breath from my lungs.

Pain exploded behind my eyes as my head snapped back.

The room spun. Bookshelves blurred. The table overturned with a crash, the candle shattering as it hit the floor.

I fought.

Kicked.

My nails clawed at unyielding flesh, scraping skin, feeling the sting of impact against my knuckles.

But it wasn't enough.

I slammed into a bookshelf. Then the piano.

Pain lit up my ribs. My arms. My knees.

I tried to scream, but the air was gone.

My body scraped the hardwood, then the cold concrete.

I dug my heels into the floor.

I thrashed.

I didn't stop fighting.

But then we reached the threshold.

The front door flew open, slamming against the wall.

And then, I was thrown.

Hard. Onto the gravel outside.

The air ripped from my lungs.

My palms scraped raw.

The sharp bite of stone tore at my skin.

I rolled, coughing, gasping for breath.

But there was no time.

A heavy boot crashed toward my face.

And the world went black.

Chapter Forty-Two

REICH

HAVE YOU EVER FELT happiness slip through your fingers? Watched it turn to dust before your eyes? Felt that paralyzing helplessness—*the clawing desperation to hold on, to salvage even a sliver of it*—before it's gone?

Before it's too late?

That's exactly how it felt.

That day.

The day they took her.

And I knew.

Long before I saw the wreckage. Long before I tasted the metallic bite of fear in the back of my throat.

I knew.

The second the power cut out—severing the camera feeds I had obsessively monitored for days.

Snuffing out my last tether to her.

A knot of dread coiled in my chest, thick and suffocating.

Each breath I took felt shallow, strained—like trying to breathe through smoke.

Because the house was silent, and Sage was alone.

And I wasn't there.

I'd been sitting with Castor.

Talking about last night.

How it had been everything we'd ever dreamed of.

How, maybe…maybe breaking the rules wasn't always a mistake.

The irony stung like a blade to the gut.

Because breaking the rules was exactly what had led to this.

I told myself it was nothing.

Just a power outage.

Just a glitch.

Just a moment of bad timing.

I told myself she was fine. That she was still curled up in the library, lost in her books. That she was waiting for me. Safe. Protected. Like I promised she would be.

But I knew better.

And the second my tires hit the driveway; I knew I wasn't wrong.

The house loomed ahead—and everything inside me stilled.

Gravel scattered across the doorstep.

The front door open, like a silent scream, gaping wide.

The kind of stillness that meant something terrible had already happened.

And the worst was still to come.

My pulse roared as I stepped inside.

Each footfall echoing in the cavernous silence like gunshots.

The foyer was dark.

Too dark.

And cold.

Not from the temperature but from the absence.

Her absence.

And then I saw it.

Glass shards scattered like ice across the hardwood floors.

A picture frame smashed.

I picked up the broken pieces of it, glass biting into my skin.

Further in I saw strands of her hair tangled in the destruction.

Dark red streaks—*blood*—trailing across the floor.

From the library.

Out the door.

Gone.

And there, in the middle of it all, a notepad.

Her handwriting scrawled across the page.

Words that were just hers.

Words she would have never wanted anyone to see—and she'd written them here.

I picked it up, my hands trembling like they hadn't in years.

She'd been sitting right there. Writing these lines. Feeling something.

Thinking she was safe. Thinking I was coming back.

My throat burned.

I pressed the page to my chest and closed my eyes. Just for a second. Just long enough to promise her I'd fix this.

And then I moved.

Fast. Instinct. Muscle memory.

I headed for my office, pulled up the security system.

But before I could touch the keyboard, I stopped.

Something was on my desk.

Dead center.

A memory card.

Placed there like a gift.

Or a curse.

Ice slicked down my spine.

My jaw locked so tight I felt my teeth grind hard against each other.

I picked it up, slotted it into the reader and hit play.

I should've braced myself.

I should've prepared.

But nothing could have prepared me for this.

The feed was grainy—low quality.

But it didn't matter.

I knew what I was seeing.

Sage.

Standing in the center of a clearing in some woods.

Surrounded by five men.

My lungs seized.

My body locked up as realization punched through me continuously, until I was hollowed out.

This wasn't now. This wasn't today.

This was then.

The night she ran from Sanele. The night she became a ghost.

I watched them circle her like wolves.

I watched them speak to her.

And then I watched her break.

I should've looked away. Should've spared myself.

But I didn't.

Because I needed to see.

I needed to understand exactly what they did to her.

So, I could make them pay. So, I could feed the fire that was already burning me alive.

By the time the footage ended, I was gutted and empty.

But my rage—my rage was alive and breathing. It was crawling beneath my skin like a storm that wouldn't settle.

I had failed her. Once. Twice now.

And I wasn't going to fail again.

I shoved away from the desk, stalking through the house like a man possessed.

Every corner, every shadow, every room—*nothing*.

No sign of her.

Think. Think. Retrace.

I pulled out my phone, fumbling for the last thing I had left.

The only surveillance feed still active.

The master bedroom.

I rewound.

Watched.

There I was.

Kissing her goodbye.

Telling her I wouldn't be long.

And her smile.

Fuck, that smile.

Soft and easy.

Like she trusted me.

Completely unaware of the nightmare about to swallow her whole.

I clenched my teeth so hard I tasted blood.

Then—I saw it.

The moment she tucked the music device into her pocket.

My pulse kicked.

Had she taken it out before they took her?

I zoomed in.

Frame by frame.

It was still there.

I opened the app.

Tracked the signal.

And there it was.

A blinking dot. Not far but moving.

Adrenaline slammed through me like a hammer to the ribs.

I was already moving. Already dialing.

This wasn't a solo job.

This wasn't a quiet extraction.

This was war.

I hit the group call.

Two names. Two men who owed me everything and who I trusted to burn the world down if I asked them to.

Keenan answered on the first ring, his voice lazy. "Bro…. King of the fucking Reich. Look who it is."

Nael wasn't far behind. "No way. You alive or what?"

I didn't answer.

Didn't joke. Didn't breathe.

"I need a favor." My voice was gravel. A blade dragging across concrete.

The line went silent.

They knew.

They heard my tone.

"Where?" Keenan asked, his tone gone steel.

"I have a location." I said.

A beat.

And then Nael, low and cold, "Then let's go."

And just like that—the hunt began.

And God help anyone in our way.

Chapter Forty-Three

SAGE

I WOKE WITH A body that didn't feel like mine.

It felt like I had been ripped apart and stitched back together by unsteady hands. Every bone was out of place. Every muscle screamed in protest. A wrongness radiated from deep inside me, as if something vital had been stolen and I was only just beginning to realize it.

Pain bloomed in sharp, searing waves as I tried to shift, sending lightning through my limbs. My arms were wrenched behind me, tied so tightly they'd gone numb—empty sacks of flesh hanging useless behind the chair. I couldn't feel my fingers at all. It was as if they'd been cut away, leaving phantom echoes in their place.

I sucked in a breath, but even that was agony. My ribs screamed in protest, a hollow cracking sound echoing in my chest. My head pounded with a steady, brutal rhythm, each throb like a hammer crashing into my skull. The light above me was blinding—brutal. Cold fluorescents stabbed at my retinas with ruthless precision, boring holes straight through my eyes and into my brain.

I squinted. Blinked. Failed to focus.

Where am I?

Panic bloomed like fire in my chest. My stomach churned, bile burning up the back of my throat. The sharp metallic sting of it mingled with the heavy weight of fear, thick on my tongue. I swallowed it down because I had no choice.

There was nowhere for it to go.

I tried to move again—willed my legs to shift, to do something—but they felt leaden. Disconnected. Like I wasn't even inside them anymore. The ropes dug deeper into my wrists with each tiny motion, tearing into flesh that was already raw and pulsing. I could feel warm blood slicking beneath the cords. It made no difference. I wasn't going anywhere.

The chair beneath me was metal. Cold. Ice-cold. Its chill seeped into my skin, deeper, until I could feel it leeching through muscle, finding the hollow of my bones. It was a kind of cold that didn't just exist on the outside—it made itself inside you. It hollowed you out. It waited for you to die.

I was drowning.

Not in water but in this.

In helplessness.

In terror.

And then I heard them.

Footsteps.

Measured. Deliberate.

Echoing in a room I couldn't see, couldn't map out.

I didn't need to see it to know.

Concrete walls. No windows. No escape.

The footsteps stopped.

A door groaned open on unoiled hinges.

And then it slammed shut, so violently it sent a physical jolt through me. Pain spiked down my spine, my pulse roaring in my ears as nausea swelled again.

A shadow broke across the floor in front of me.

The door handle turned.

I couldn't breathe.

And then...there he was, my nightmare.

Klay.

My heart didn't even bother to speed up.

It simply skipped beats, sputtering out like it was going to give in.

He stepped through the doorway with a grin that carved its way into my flesh. Slow. Leisurely. His hands tucked into his pockets like we were meeting by accident on the street. His gaze settled on me with a heatless familiarity that turned my stomach to glass. And then he smiled wider.

Like he'd won.

"Good morning, little whore," he drawled, his tone slick with amusement. "Miss me?"

The voice that had haunted my dreams, coated in mock affection, like he was catching up with an old friend.

I shrank into the chair instinctively, but there was nowhere to go. My chest hollowed as his boots dragged a slow, deliberate line toward me.

He circled me, like he was savoring it.

Like a vulture deciding which piece to tear off first.

And then he spat.

Once and then twice.

The third splatter hit my cheek and stuck.

I squeezed my eyes shut.

Don't flinch.

Don't give him the satisfaction.

"What am I going to do with you?" he mused aloud, a performance for his own amusement. His voice turned false-thoughtful, dripping with sickly sweetness. "You really did get yourself into trouble, didn't you?" He bent at the waist, his face lowering closer to mine. "But I have to admit..." His breath washed over me, hot and foul. "...this worked out perfectly for me."

He laughed then.

Short. Sharp.

Each bark like a strike of lightning in my skull.

And then his hand twisted in my hair.

Without warning, he yanked hard, snapping my head back so fast my neck cracked.

Agony exploded through my scalp, my vision flaring white.

I tasted blood.

My throat burned.

The ceiling spun.

"Why?" I croaked, my voice rough, like broken glass scraping down my throat and making me regret even speaking.

I barely recognized the sound.

He let go.

My head sagged forward.

The sudden release made nausea spike so violently I nearly vomited.

Tears stung my eyes, hot and useless.

And then I saw it.

The tattoo.

On the back of his neck.

The same mark.

The one Reich and Castor bore.

My blood turned to ice.

No.

This wasn't happening. This wasn't real.

Were they with him? Had they known? Had they brought me here on purpose? Did Reich leave me at the house for Klay to find me?

I tried to make sense of it. Tried to fight the scream building in my chest.

But doubt was already coiling itself around my spine, cold and sure.

Klay turned toward me again, something black clutched in his hand.

I squinted and my heart lurched.

My music player.

The last piece of Reich I had.

The last piece of me.

He held it up between two fingers, dangling it like a trophy.

"Did you think this was going to save you?" he sneered.

Something inside me cracked.

Not a clean break.

A fracture.

Jagged and deep.

And I knew—I knew—my fate had been sealed a long time ago.

The night those men broke me.

This was just the echo of that destruction.

The aftershock.

Klay crouched low again, his voice sliding under my skin.

"Shaking now, aren't you? Like a child?"

I clenched my teeth. "I'm cold," I said, because it was the truth.

He smiled—but his eyes narrowed just for a second before his fingers tangled in my hair again.

He dragged me close, his lips almost brushing mine.

"You've always had a piss-poor attitude," he murmured. "Good thing I spared Reich from having to deal with you any longer."

The sound of Reich's name—it cracked through me like thunder.

Too loud. Too much.

Klay saw it.

He felt it as he laughed, a cruel and bitter sound. "Oh," he breathed, savoring the realization. "You like him."

Then, with brutal finality—"You know he brought you here, right? For me."

I shook my head.

Because I had to.

Because if I didn't, I'd break apart.

But it didn't matter.

Klay yanked me sideways, the chair skidding across the floor before collapsing beneath me.

The ropes bit deeper.

My ankle twisted.

Pain exploded up my leg, making me scream.

He stood over me, towering, like he had all the time in the world.

And then I heard it.

A second voice.

A laugh.

"Well, well. If it isn't Sage." I turned and my jaw dropped.

It was one of them from that night.

My body went cold.

Numb. Gone.

"You remember Hugh, right?" Klay asked, like he was asking about an old friend.

I didn't answer. I couldn't because I wasn't there anymore.

Not in the present at least.

I was back on the cold ground in the middle of the woods.

My body broken.

My mind screaming.

Klay's fingers closed around my arm.

He dragged me across the floor like I weighed nothing at all.

My skin scraped the tile, burning.

I didn't fight.

What was the point?

Hugh followed closely, grinning the entire time. "Good thing I like them young, brother," he said.

And I knew.

I knew what was coming next.

I sobbed. Completely broken.

There was nothing left of me to save.

They stopped in front of a massive metal freezer.

Hugh opened the door.

Cold air spilled out in a rush, wrapping around me, biting deep.

I didn't fight when they shoved me in.

I didn't move. I barely breathed.

Klay leaned in, close enough I could feel his breath on my ear. "See you soon, whore," he whispered.

I saw something flash in his eyes, something not human.

And then the door slammed shut.

Darkness. Silence. Nothing.

Chapter Forty-Four

REICH

Hanging up with Keenan and Nael should've given me relief. It should've lessened the weight crushing my chest. But it didn't. If anything, it made it worse.

The risk was still there—gnawing, ruthless.

One wrong move.

One second too slow.

And Sage was gone.

Not lost. Not missing.

Gone.

I dragged a hand down my face, inhaling slow through my nose as if that would force air into my lungs that barely worked right now.

Nael had said the plan was solid. Foolproof.

But I knew better.

Nothing was ever foolproof. Not when human lives were involved. Not when your heart was on the line.

And Sage was my heart.

Even if I'd been too fucking blind to admit it to myself until now.

Too busy protecting her in the only ways I knew how—by holding back, by keeping distance, by pretending I could manage this without getting blood on her.

What a joke.

I was drowning in it now.

I wouldn't believe anything until I had her in my arms.

Until I could feel the pulse of her heartbeat under my hands.

Until I knew she was still alive.

I clenched my fists, knuckles popping with the pressure, the leather of my gloves creaking with the force.

Never again.

Those words had become a mantra.

A promise and a curse.

We'd narrowed her location down to three sites, all tucked deep in the forested mountains east of Providence.

Bunkers.

One old one. Two newer ones.

All tied to the Armaros cult—the same cult the Ovitt brothers had aligned themselves with.

The same cult within the ENA that I'd been tasked with dismantling.

I barked a bitter laugh under my breath.

Irony was a cruel bastard.

And I was done playing by his rules.

If there was one thing I'd learned—one thing I kept learning, over and over—it was this: If you want something done right, you do it yourself.

And next time, I would.

Nael.

God. Nael and I went back years.

He was two years younger, but that had never mattered. He'd always carried the weight like he was older. Always seeing things that others didn't. Always planning ten steps ahead.

If I'd ever had another brother—it would've been him.

And maybe, that's why I trusted him now.

Even though trusting anyone else with Sage felt like I was gambling with loaded dice.

Even though the idea of anyone else being responsible for her life made me sick.

He didn't know her the way I did.

He didn't care about her the way I did.

But he was the one I needed.

Keenan was different.

All fire and impulse.

He reminded me of Castor when we were younger and still does.

Felt everything too much. Held nothing back. And sometimes, that kind of recklessness was what you also needed.

Keenan didn't question motives.

He didn't weigh consequences.

He acted.

I needed both of them.

Even if I hated needing anyone at all.

The quiet gnawed at me.

The waiting always did.

But then—I heard it.

The low, hungry growl of Nael's Camaro as it closed in the distance up the drive.

That sound was a time machine.

Took me back to a simpler time.

Late nights. Fast drives. Faster deals.

A brotherhood forged in fire, bone, and blood.

We hadn't always been clean men.

But when we did something, we did it right.

No hesitation. No second guessing.

We got the job done.

The car slid to a stop, headlights cutting through the fog.

They got out together.

Unchanged, but heavier.

Like me and Castor.

Older, wiser and meaner since our days back in college.

Nael was the first to move. Eyes dark and unreadable, but there was something there—a recognition of what this was.

Of whom this was for.

He wasn't here for ENA.

He wasn't even here for me.

He was here to save her. My girl.

He nodded once, the closest thing to an embrace we'd ever shared.

I returned it. He understood. That was enough.

"Haven't seen the old Camaro in a while," I said, forcing something like normalcy out of my throat. It tasted wrong. "She looks good."

Nael smirked. "Thanks. Might actually be done now."

I shook my head. "Every car guy says that."

He huffed a quiet laugh. "And they're all liars."

A voice came from inside the car, "Talkin about this old car again, Nael?"

The passenger door slammed and Keenan stalked toward us, zero hesitation, fire in his eyes. He was a hurricane wearing skin and when he hit me with a crushing hug, I let it happen.

"Still breathing, Reich," he muttered against my shoulder.

It was both a statement and a question.

I nodded, teeth grinding together, "Barely."

Castor was already at my side, arms crossed. His eyes flicked between them. He didn't speak. He didn't need to.

Nael smirked. "Some people actually care about my car, Keenan."

He grinned wide. "Bro, I care. I'm just saying... you talk about her like she's your girlfriend."

Nael didn't blink. "Lyla's never hurt me."

Something in my gut twisted.

"Lyla?" I echoed.

Keenan barked a laugh. "The car, dumbass."

But Nael didn't smile. Not really.

I cut through the air between us with one question, "How's Blythe?"

Keenan stilled and his jaw ticked, as I watched the light dim in his eyes.

"We're going to get her," Nael said, smooth and sure.

But there was doubt in the spaces between his words. There always was when you said something enough times you stopped believing it.

Blythe had been taken because Keenan had gotten too close.

Because he'd loved her too much.

The ENA didn't like love.

Not when it complicated the chain of command.

Not when it made you loyal to someone more than them.

They called it a breach.

And they punished him for it.

"If there's anything we can do," I said, quiet.

Castor nodded, solemn. "Anything."

Nael met my gaze, before he spoke, "We find Sage first."

I nodded.

Because this wasn't about me.

Not anymore.

Every second wasted was another second, they could be hurting her.

"You got the coordinates?" I asked.

Nael tapped the screen of his phone. "Already marked. We hit the primary site first. If they moved her, we have backups."

I forced myself to breathe, "Good."

As the Camaro's doors opened, and we climbed inside, for one sharp second, it felt like the old days.

Before we were broken men..

Before we forgot why we did this.

But this time…this time we weren't hunting for profit.

Or power.

Or vengeance.

This time, we were hunting for her.

And I would burn every last man alive to get her back.

Nael killed the lights as we crept up the path, headlights going dark.

Our tires crunched slow over gravel.

No one spoke. We didn't need to. We were already synced.

Just like always.

Keenan's voice sliced through the silence, "You remember the plan?"

Castor's nod was a shadow. "We take the perimeter."

Nael's grin was pure hell. "We clear the inside. We find Sage."

And I finished, "We end this."

I loaded my gun. Checked my knife. Checked the second gun. Holstered both. And when I spoke again, it wasn't to them.

It was to the men inside that bunker.

To the Ovitt brothers.

And to Klay.

"I'm coming."

And hell was coming with me.

Because I didn't care what the ENA did to me after this.

I didn't care what this cost.

I didn't care if I didn't walk away from it.

She was the only thing I gave a fuck about anymore.

And I was going to bring her home.

Even if I had to bury myself to do it.

Chapter Forty-Five

SAGE

Darkness. Cold.

It pressed in from every side, seeping into my bones, stealing what little warmth I had left.

My body didn't shiver anymore. It was beyond that.

Frozen. Numb.

Silent in a way that felt final.

This had to be it.

The end.

Surely, the universe knew I couldn't take any more.

Surely, it understood that I wasn't made to survive this.

I couldn't breathe. Couldn't think. Couldn't exist.

And maybe that was okay.

Maybe that was all I'd ever been meant for.

To fade away quietly. Forgotten.

To leave no trace. No echo. No mark.

I had fought.

And just when I thought I might have a chance at living again...just when I thought I might be free...my past came for me.

Surging back like a tidal wave of agony and blood and betrayal—crashing over me with the full weight of everything I had clawed my way out of.

Everything I had buried and pretended no longer existed.

But it was still there.

It had always been there.

I didn't want to fight anymore.

I was done. I was ready to let go. To surrender. To die.

And I prayed for it.

I begged for it.

For an end. For release.

For something, anything, that would pull me under and hold me there.

Let me slip away before he comes back. Let me die before I have to endure it again.

But prayers were nothing more than whispers into the void.

And the universe didn't care.

It never had.

The lid creaked open.

That sound...it was too sharp. Too real.

Like metal screaming against metal.

The frozen air peeled back with it, stealing what little warmth I had left.

I braced myself.

For the hands.

Except—there was something different this time.

A flash of silver, followed by a wet, choking gurgle.

And then—warmth.

Not the kind that brought comfort.

But the kind that sprayed across my skin, hot and slick and wrong.

I flinched, my eyes squeezing shut as something wet splattered against my cheek, sliding down in what I knew were crimson trails that I was too numb to wipe away.

I forced my eyes open.

I had to know.

Even if it was the last thing I saw.

But it wasn't Klay's face that loomed over me.

It wasn't the monster I had braced for. It wasn't the nightmare I had begged to avoid.

It was someone else.

A man.

Cold. Detached.

Like he had stepped out of some alternate universe I couldn't comprehend.

There was no anger in him. No joy. Nothing. He was empty. And something about that terrified me more than Klay ever had.

He wiped the blood from his blade with methodical precision, smearing its red streaks across gloved fingers like it was routine. Like none of this mattered.

Like I didn't matter.

And then—he turned.

No words. No acknowledgment.

As if I was nothing but debris in his path.

An afterthought. Forgettable. Insignificant.

I wanted to scream. To demand answers.

But my voice was gone.

I was gone.

I sat there, slumped in a frozen shell, a body too broken to move.

Then—movement.

A shadow at the edge of my vision.

Heavy footsteps, boots scraping against concrete.

I turned my head slowly.

Hugh.

I saw him.

And for a split second, something sparked in my chest.

Not hope. But panic. A pure, primal instinct.

The stranger didn't see him. Didn't know.

And I didn't know how to tell him. How to warn him. How to stop what was coming.

But I looked at Hugh anyway.

I made myself look. Eyes locking on his. A silent signal. A plea I didn't have words for.

Hugh lunged. Fast. But not fast enough.

The stranger was faster.

He turned without hesitation, his hand snapping out and closing around Hugh's throat like a vise.

There was no warning. No struggle.

He slammed Hugh down with such brutal force that the sound cracked through the air like bone snapping in two.

A wet, choking sound followed.

Final.

And then... silence.

I didn't move. Didn't breathe.

I remained there, inside the cold metal of the freezer, my body beyond exhaustion. The cold seeping deeper. Into marrow. Into memory. Even if this was a rescue, it was too late.

I was too far gone.

I had already given up.

My mind had already checked out.

The stranger turned back to me.

Brow furrowed, his gaze sharp as it studied my face.

And he saw it. The hollow in my eyes. The quiet surrender.

And then—he spoke.

Two words. Soft. Like a ghost. "Thank you."

I blinked. Confused. The words didn't make sense.

Who was he talking to? Me? Because of Hugh?

I didn't have time to ask. Because then, there was another voice.

Another name.

"Reich!"

My breath stuttered. My heart stopped.

I knew that name. I knew it better than my own heartbeat.

And then he was there.

Reich.

But not the Reich I had always seen.

This Reich was different.

He wasn't his typical collected self. He was stripped down. Raw. His face was carved from violence and ruin. His eyes wild and feral, gleaming with something I couldn't name. He looked like a man who had lost everything—and was prepared to burn the world to get it back.

Blood coated his hands. Streaked his throat. Spattered across his chest like war paint. His eyes showed that he didn't care. Not about that. Not about anything—except me.

He moved like a predator. But when he reached me—when his hands finally touched me—they were shaking.

He dropped to his knees, gathering me in his arms, as if afraid I'd slip through his fingers if he wasn't careful.

As if I were glass already cracked and he was trying to hold me together with his bare hands.

I collapsed against him, my frozen body melting into his heat.

His heartbeat thundered beneath my cheek.

A living, frantic drum.

Proof.

Proof that I wasn't dead yet.

His fingers tangled in my hair, shaking as they cradled the back of my head.

I clung to him. Or maybe he clung to me. I couldn't tell anymore.

"Sage," he choked.

My name—It sounded like a prayer and a plea. All tangled into one broken breath.

I tried to speak. To tell him I was here. That I was okay. But the words wouldn't come.

He shook his head.

"Don't."

His forehead pressed to mine, his breath ragged and hot against my skin, "Just—don't."

And for once, I obeyed.

Because this wasn't about just me anymore.

This was about him.

His arms tightened around me.

Like he could somehow fuse us together, if by holding me hard enough, he could pull me back from the edge.

Drag me out of whatever grave I had fallen into.

"You don't get to leave me like this," he said. His voice broke on the last word and cracked itself down the middle like a man with nothing left.

I let my body press deeper into his. Let his heat bleed into mine. Let the world fade around us.

And as I gasped against his chest, feeling his heart slam wild and desperate beneath my palm, one truth settled into me like gravity. Heavy. Inescapable.

I would never be able to count the number of times this man had saved me.

And I knew—I would never stop letting him.

Chapter Forty-Six

REICH

S HE COLLAPSED INTO ME, weightless and fragile—as if the last thin threads of her endurance had finally snapped, unraveling with nothing left to hold her upright.

Her body pressed against mine, thin and trembling, as if the effort to stand, to breathe, to exist, had drained every ounce of her strength.

I felt the shallow rise and fall of her chest against me, the sharp, uneven shudders of her breath, the tremor that never seemed to leave her muscles.

She sagged into me like something hollowed out—as if even gravity had lost its claim on her.

I couldn't believe it. She was alive. Against all odds. We found her. She was here.

Breathing.

It was enough to break me.

Relief hit like a sucker punch—violent, unforgiving and sharp enough to steal the air from my lungs.

My knees gave out before I could stop them.

I sank to the damp concrete, the room swallowing us whole, my arms locking around her with a ferocity I couldn't temper.

I held her like she might dissolve in my hands, like something precious and irreplaceable. Like something I was too late to protect.

And maybe I was.

Maybe I always had been.

She'd only been gone twenty-four hours.

One rotation of the earth.

One day.

But when I looked at her—at the pale stretch of her skin, the deep bruises blooming along her throat and wrists, the distant emptiness in her eyes—it was like she'd been gone for a lifetime.

Like a ghost wandering back into a body that didn't fit anymore.

She wasn't just lost.

She was gone.

And yet, she was still breathing.

Somehow.

Her pulse fluttered beneath my fingertips, faint but steady.

I pressed my palm flat against her spine, anchoring her to me, whispering silent pleas I wasn't even sure who I was begging—God, fate, the universe, myself.

Please let her stay.

Please let me fix this.

I tucked her closer. Tighter.

My cheek rested against the crown of her head, breathing her in. The faint scent of blood and cold sweat. And beneath it—her.

The smallest trace of her.

Still there.

Still fighting.

Even if she didn't believe it anymore.

"You're so smart, Sage," I murmured into her hair, the words rasping out like broken glass. "And you're so damn strong."

I swallowed hard, feeling the sting in my throat.

For a long moment, she was still. Too still.

I was about to say her name again, louder, when she stirred. The faintest shift of her lashes. A breath—a real one—caught in her throat. And then her eyes opened.

And they found mine in the dark.

They hollowed me out and made me whole all at once.

The Sage I knew had eyes full of wildfire.

But now?

Now they were a storm cloud heavy with rain, dark and endless.

But they were open. She was here. And for now, that was enough.

For a heartbeat—*just one*—we said nothing.

But there was something between us.

Something louder than words.

A silent thing that pressed into the empty space where language failed.

And I felt it, like a pulse under the skin.

Like the moment before lightning splits the sky.

I wanted to stay there. To live inside that moment and to let time freeze so I could hold her like this forever.

But nothing good ever stays.

And it didn't now.

Keenan's voice broke through the haze, sharp and barking orders.

And then they were there.

The paramedics.

Too quick. Too loud. Too much.

I barely heard what they said.

I barely saw them. I only felt her.

Her hands clutching at my jacket, her fingers digging in, desperate and terrified as they tried to pull her away.

She shook her head, tears slipping down her cheeks, wide-eyed and pleading.

"Don't," she mouthed. "No."

Her voice cracked on that single syllable, but it was enough to gut me.

My throat burned as I let them take her.

As I gave her to them.

It felt like betrayal.

But I knew.

I knew she needed them more than she needed me.

And still—it ripped me apart that I couldn't be everything for her.

I watched them work.

Hands efficient, practiced.

I watched her flinch at every touch. Watched her fight to stay in her skin. Watched her slip away, inch by inch.

And I hated myself.

Because I had done this.

I had failed her. I had let this happen. And I wasn't sure she'd ever forgive me for it.

Hell, I wasn't sure I'd forgive myself.

We took her home. Back to the house. Back to the place she'd fought like hell to make her own again.

But it didn't matter.

Because even though the house was too quiet, she was quieter.

She didn't speak.

Not to me. Not to Sam or Castor. Not to the paramedics when they checked on her again the next morning.

She laid in bed, unmoving.

Her body curled toward the wall, her back to the world.

A hollow shell. Trapped. Gone.

Sam tried but Sage gave her nothing.

Not defiance. Not a fight. Just silence.

Castor hovered in the doorway. Said her name once. Offered to be there if she needed him and then never again.

I watched her fade.

Day by day.

And I knew.

Soon she would start hiding behind a mask again. Soon she would build her walls higher. And this time, I wasn't sure I could tear them down.

Two days passed and I stood outside her door again. Like a fucking ghost.

A bowl in my hands. Soup.

Because I didn't know what else to do.

A bitter laugh scraped out of me as I remember being in this exact same position not too long ago, begging her to eat.

"Some things never change," I murmured to myself.

I took a breath.

And then another.

And I pushed the door open.

She was curled in the corner.

Not on the bed, just on the floor. Like she wanted to disappear into it.

Her arms wrapped tight around her legs.

Her head tucked down.

And the second the door clicked shut I watched as she flinched.

As if I'd struck her. As if she was bracing for it.

I nearly fell apart.

But I didn't. I couldn't. Not now.

"It's okay," I said softly.

The words floated between us, brittle and raw.

I set the plate down.

And I knelt beside her.

Close enough that I could hear the hitch in her breath. See the sheen of tears she hadn't let fall yet.

She didn't look at me at first. Just a flicker of her gaze, peeking over her knees.

Cautious. Guarded. Hollow.

"Sage." Her name was a plea on my tongue. "You need to eat."

Her lips trembled. And when she spoke, it was a whisper, "I can't."

I reached out slowly. Brushed the hair from her face. My fingers were gentle but firm.

I needed her to feel this. To know she was still here.

"Sage... don't make me beg."

Her hands shook. Her breath came faster. I saw the panic tightening around her like a vice.

I didn't think just pulled her into me. Held her tight. Anchored her against my chest.

"Breathe," I whispered against her temple. Soft. Steady.

"I can't," she choked.

"Yes, you can," I said, "With me, you can."

She flinched at the sound of my voice. But she didn't pull away. And I held on.

I wasn't letting her slip.

"Please?" A beg now. "If you won't do it for you... will you do it for me?"

Something cracked. The faintest shift in her walls. A single tear slid down her cheek.

And I caught it with my thumb. Soft. Reverent.

"Thank you," she whispered.

It almost undid me.

I pressed a kiss to her forehead.

Let it linger. Let it mean something.

I reached for the soup. Settled in beside her and lifted the spoon to her lips.

She hesitated.

Her eyes were sharp, almost defiant.

She hated this.

Hated needing. Hated feeling weak.

But she took it.

And when she swallowed— I leaned in, my lips brushing her ear, "Good girl."

Her breath caught.

And then—the ghost of a smile.

Small. Fragile. But there.

"How are you feeling today?" I asked quietly.

Her gaze dropped. Sadness pooling in the hollow of her expression, "I'm not sure how to survive today."

The words gutted me.

I swallowed hard, "What do you mean?"

Her voice was raw.

"I'm still in that room, Reich. Even when I'm here. Even when you're holding me. It doesn't go away. I don't know if it ever will."

She paused before continuing, "I don't know if enduring this is worth it."

It hurt but I wouldn't let her drown.

I tipped her chin up. Forced her to look at me. Made her see.

"It is worth it, Sage." I took a breath. "Because tomorrow always comes. And tomorrow is always a new today. New chances. New choices."

I ran my thumb along her cheek, "Sometimes, it even brings wildflowers."

She stared at me.

Silent. Tear-filled. But something shifted.

"Let today be what it is," I whispered. "Chaos and all. But remember that tomorrow is coming."

Her breath shuddered. But then she finally leaned into me. Her body shaking. Her tears falling as I held her.

Ran my fingers through her hair. Grounded her in something real.

She wasn't okay.

Not yet. Maybe not for a long time.

But she was still here.

And for now that was enough.

Chapter Forty-Seven

SAGE

Everything was a blur when I came back.

A haze thick enough to suffocate me. The air was dense, heavy, pressing in on me like an unseen weight I couldn't shake loose. My body was here—breathing, existing—but I wasn't sure if I was really alive anymore. I was a void wearing my own skin, hollow and cracked.

I had survived.

But survival wasn't freedom.

It wasn't peace. It wasn't relief. It was just existence.

A raw, aching thing you carried day after day until you couldn't remember how to set it down.

And as I lifted my head and met Reich's gaze across the room, that truth settled into me like cold iron in my bones.

This wasn't the end.

It never had been.

And maybe it never would be.

The fear was still there, insidious and suffocating, curling cold fingers around my throat every time I closed my eyes.

Klay's brothers—the ones still alive—they were waiting.

Out there in the dark.

Lurking in the silence, slipping like shadows beneath the hollow recesses of my mind.

Whether I was awake or asleep, they were there—taunting me, promising they would pull me back under.

Promising they would finish what they'd started.

There was no escape. No peace.

Only the slow, crushing certainty that one day they would come for me.

And maybe this time, I wouldn't make it back.

But Reich was always there.

His presence was a tether, an anchor to something real in the middle of all this chaos.

Something solid and warm when everything else was cold.

I found him in the quiet moments—silent, unmoving, watching me like I was something fragile, something he couldn't afford to lose.

Like he didn't trust himself to look away for even a second.

And maybe he didn't.

Maybe I didn't trust myself either.

"I'm going to play some music," he said suddenly. His voice was soft but unwavering, cutting through the haze like a knife. It was gentle. But it was also absolute. There was no argument. No space to protest. Only his voice and the promise inside it.

That he wasn't leaving.

That I wasn't alone.

My mind twisted against it, rebelling the way it always did.

Whispering the lies that had become too familiar.

It won't help. Nothing will. You're tainted. Haunted. Wasted.

I closed my eyes and breathed out the truth I couldn't swallow anymore.

"They're going to find me one day." My voice cracked around the words.

Because it wasn't fear anymore. It was fact.

Reich's jaw tightened, a flash of something dark crossing his expression as his hands clenched at his sides.

He didn't flinch. He didn't soften. But his voice—it was sharper now. Unbreakable.

"I won't let them."

Simple. Final.

As if it was that easy. As if just saying it out loud would make it true.

"Just focus on feeling better," he continued. "Let me worry about them."

The words slammed into me.

They hit like a tide, crashing against the fog clouding my mind.

And for a moment— I wanted to believe him. I wanted to let him carry the weight.

But wanting something doesn't make it yours. And belief is a fragile thing.

Too easy to lose.

Too dangerous to hold.

So, all I could do was collapse into him.

Let my body go limp against his, my eyelids too heavy to keep open as the darkness tried to swallow me whole.

I didn't fight it.

Not this time.

So, I said, If something happens to me—"

"Don't." The word cracked like a whip. Reich's grip on my wrist tightened, almost painful.

He wasn't pleading.

He was commanding.

"I need to say this," I whispered, my throat tight, raw. "You need to hear it."

His eyes burned into mine.

Something desperate. Something close to wild.

"No, I don't," he said. "Because nothing is going to happen to you."

But I shook my head slowly, forcing the words past the lump in my throat. "But if it does…"

He closed the minimal distance between us, his breath hot against my cheek as he lowered his voice to something dark and feral. "Then I burn the world down." His fingers brushed my jaw, tilting my face toward his. "Understand?"

I wanted to hold onto that moment.

I wanted to believe the fury in his voice.

The certainty in his promise.

But it slipped through my fingers like sand, vanishing before I could grasp it.

I was slipping away. Fading.

Being pulled back into the abyss, inch by inch.

But there was his voice again. Rough. Desperate.

"Stay with me, Sage."

I clung to it. To him. To the raw desperation in his tone, letting it anchor me.

Just enough. Just barely. To sink into him. To feel the warmth of his skin and the steady beat of his heart.

"Reich, please," I murmured. My voice was too small. "I just… hold me. Just for a little while."

He exhaled, the sound of it heavy against my ear like he was breathing for both of us and then his arms closed around me, pulling me into the shelter of his chest. Tighter. Grounding me in a way nothing else could.

His head rested against mine and I buried my face in the warm curve of his neck, breathing him in.

Counting his breaths like lifelines.

For a moment, the world disappeared. The chaos quieted. The storm inside me stilled.

Just long enough to make me think maybe it could stay that way. Maybe I could find my way back to myself.

But then—Klay's words echoed in my mind, "Reich kidnapped you to hand over to me."

And a chill swept through me. Tightening my muscles. Banishing the fleeting calm.

The silence stretched between us. Pressed in. Suffocating.

"Reich..." My voice barely made it out. "Klay said you were planning to deliver me to him."

He stiffened instantly like a wire pulled too tight.

"Sage..." His voice was careful. Measured. Like he was choosing his next move on a battlefield.

"There's something I need to tell you." He continued, standing slowly, posture rigid with unease. Guarded but not hiding.

"The men who hurt you... they were never supposed to get that close." He ran a hand through his hair, pacing. "My work... it requires that I handle threats before they become problems."

"Handle?" I asked, already knowing the answer. But needing to hear him say it.

His jaw clenched. "Yes."

"You mean kill," I clarified and there was no question in my voice.

"Yes." He didn't hesitate. His gaze locked onto mine, unwavering, as he continued, "but I made a mistake."

A shadow crossed his features. Something broken.

"I hurt other people," he whispered. Quiet. Haunted. "And I'm sorry, Sage. I've made so many mistakes. But that one..." His throat worked around the words. "That one will haunt me for as long as I'm alive."

I didn't speak.

A million thoughts crashed through me, one after the other.

But none of them came out.

And the fear?

It slipped away for a moment, replaced by something else.

Relief. Recognition.

"So what you're saying is…" I exhaled, letting the reality settle like a stone in my gut.

"I've been kidnapped by a serial killer?"

Reich blinked. Then his mouth twitched into something dangerously close to a smirk. "I guess… if you want to put it that way."

"An orange is an orange," I said with a shrug.

A flicker of amusement crossed his face and I let it ground me. Let it make me feel a little more alive.

"Fair enough." He conceded.

I pushed myself up, pacing. Each step heavier than the last.

He watched me carefully. Like he wasn't sure if I was going to run or not.

"Say something," he pleaded. His voice rough. Fraying at the edges.

I stopped and exhaled shakily, "Well," I said, "it's not exactly an ideal situation. But I think we can work through it."

His laugh was dry. Disbelieving, "Work through it?" He shook his head. "Sage… I just told you—I take lives for a living. I'm the reason this happened to you."

"But you don't kill good people," I said quietly.

His expression darkened, "How do you know that?"

I stepped closer. Pressed my hands to his chest and felt his heart racing beneath my palms. "Because I trust who I've seen you to be."

His eyes searched mine.

Desperate. Conflicted. Wanting.

"Why aren't you scared of me?" he rasped.

"Do you want me to be?" I whispered.

"Sage…"

"Reich…"

The corner of his mouth twitched. And I hadn't seen him smile in days. But there it was. Small. Wrecked.

And it made something inside me feel a little less broken.

He chuckled. Shook his head.

"What?" I asked, watching the way his gaze softened.

"I think I'm in love," he said quietly. Like a secret.

My pulse skittered and my breath caught. I smirked, arching a brow, "And I think you've spent too much time around your brother."

"Perhaps," he murmured. But there was something deeper in his voice now.

Something real.

And before I could talk myself out of it, I closed the minimal space between us letting His lips meet mine and then nothing else mattered.

We fell into each other.

Desperate. Breathless. Hands pulling, clothes falling. Until there was nothing left but skin against skin. And the sharp, sweet ache of belonging.

We collapsed to the floor, and he moved over me like he was made for it. Like I was made for him. His fingers slid between my thighs, teasing, testing. Before pressing inside.

A gasp tore from my lips, and he caught it in his mouth.

"So fucking beautiful," he growled.

And I shattered around him. Lost in the heat of us. In the reckless, brutal need of it.

As we lay tangled together, his breath warm against my skin, I whispered, "I think I'm in love too. I think I don't ever want this to end."

Reich stirred, his voice rough with sleep and something more.

"You're thinking too much, wildflower." He asked.

I met his gaze.

My heart twisting.

Before saying, "But I think we just made everything worse."

He smirked as he pulled me back into his arms. "Perhaps...or maybe," he murmured, "we just finally got it right."

And more than anything—I wanted to believe him.

Because in his arms, the chaos stilled.

The noise in my head faded.

And for the first time, the world felt quiet.

Like maybe peace wasn't a place.

Maybe it was a person.

And somehow, I had found him.

Maybe—just maybe—that's where love begins.

In the wreckage. In the uncertainty.

In the hope that this time... it's real.

Chapter Forty-Eight

REICH

MY HEART WAGED WAR against my head. A ceaseless, merciless battle that tore me apart from the inside out.

Every breath I took was another skirmish, every second another wound, my soul stripped away piece by piece in an endless, unwinnable struggle.

My mind clung to logic.

To reason. To duty. To the ENA. To the cold, ruthless practicality that had governed my life for as long as I could remember.

The work. The mission. The cause.

All of it had been my tether. My reason for existing. My justification for every fucked up thing I'd done along the way.

But my heart?

My heart only wanted to fight for her.

I couldn't let Sage become an obstacle.

I told myself that over and over, as if repetition alone would make it true.

As if I could rewire myself to believe that the right choice was the one, I wasn't used to making.

But it wasn't working.

Not anymore.

Because before her, I had made mistakes—small, fatal errors that still haunted me in the quiet moments when I couldn't run fast enough from the ghosts.

And now?

Now, every breath I took without her close felt like a mistake in itself.

Every decision that didn't end with her safe, with her breathing, with her here, felt like another weight dragging me further under.

I couldn't silence the part of me that saw her not as a distraction—but as a necessity.

Because that's what she was.

Essential. The only thing that made sense anymore.

For so long, I had carried hollowness inside me, convinced that emptiness was my natural state.

That the void was an immutable part of who I was.

A truth I didn't need to fight anymore because it was easier to believe I was built for nothingness.

I had accepted it.

Resigned myself to the cold comfort of silence. Of solitude. Of indifference.

And then she walked into my life. Like a reckoning.

My wildflower.

But there was nothing fragile about her.

She had been scorched. Burned down to the bone.

Thrown through the kind of fire that strips you bare.

But she hadn't let it consume her.

She hadn't let it harden her into something bitter and twisted like the rest of us.

She fought.

Not for vengeance. Not for destruction.

But for understanding. For connection.

Even as she hid the wounds that festered beneath the surface, even as she wore masks so no one would see the pain she still carried.

She was miraculous.

And she had a power over me that I couldn't explain.

Not to myself. Not to anyone.

She slipped into the fractures of my soul, filling them with something I thought I'd lost long ago.

She made me feel whole in ways I didn't think possible. She filled every empty, broken part of me until I wasn't sure where I ended, and she began. And I knew, with brutal, gut-wrenching certainty, that when she left—when I made her leave—she would take every last piece of me with her.

Because she had to go.

And if she didn't, I would have to be the one to walk away.

Even if it meant tearing myself apart in the process.

I didn't want to let her go. I didn't want to leave.

I wanted to be selfish. To keep her. To burn down the world if it meant holding onto her for just a little longer.

But I didn't know how to keep her safe.

And one small mistake could be the difference between her life and her death.

We'd been lucky this last time.

Dumb, reckless luck.

And I wasn't about to risk it happening again.

Not with her.

Not with the woman who had already paid in blood for my failures.

If it came down to it, I would go to the ENA.

I'd pay whatever price they demanded. I'd bleed. I'd burn. I'd break myself into nothing if it meant ensuring her future. Because she deserved that. She deserved a life untouched by the chaos I carried inside me. By the darkness I'd let them carve into me.

I wanted her to shine and I would do everything in my power to make sure she did.

Even if it meant stepping back into the shadows where I belonged. Even if it meant being the monster she'd have to forget. Because she had already suffered enough for multiple lifetimes.

And I would not let her endure any more in this one.

She deserved everything. And I knew I could never give it to her.

But it didn't stop me from wondering—how the fuck was I supposed to walk away from her?

When I loved her and knew with every agonizing certainty that this would break her.

The same way it was already breaking me.

That evening, Keenan stopped by. He was the one person who might understand. The only one who could stand in this emotional upheaval with me and not flinch.

After everything he'd been through—everything he'd lost—there was a part of me that thought maybe he'd already figured out the answers I was still searching for.

It had been a while since we last talked. Really talked—without a crisis looming or a rescue plan on the table.

Longer than I'd thought, if I'm honest.

Time has this way of stretching thin between us, like an old scar you forget about until it starts aching again.

Last I heard, Keenan and Nael were working a trade to get Blythe back.

But the ENA didn't deal in mercy.

They didn't do trades.

If you wanted something from them, you didn't offer leverage.

You offered certainty.

A currency so undeniable they couldn't ignore it and even then, no one really ever made it out once they were under ENA control.

But Keenan refused to accept that.

Six months.

That's how long it had been since they took her.

And I could see it wearing on him now.

The weight behind his eyes. The exhaustion stitched into the corners of his mouth when he thought no one was looking. But he was still here. Still fighting.

And I didn't know if I should respect him or pity him for it.

Maybe both.

But I know that if Blythe had been Sage, I would've done the same thing.

"How are things?" I asked as we sat on the back deck, watching the dusk bleed into night.

Keenan leaned back in the lounge chair, fingers absently peeling at the label of his beer. The silence stretched between us, heavy. Thick with things neither of us wanted to say out loud.

Finally, he sighed, "I don't know." His voice was low. Tired. Stripped of the bravado I usually associated with him. Then, with a bitter, self-deprecating smirk, he added, "But I'd be hopeless if I was someone who gave up. So, thank God I don't ever stop trying."

I offered him a half-smile, letting the silence settle for another few breaths before speaking, "Keenan. Thank you—for everything with Sage."

I met his gaze, meaning every word, before continuing, "If there's anything I can do for Blythe... you say the word."

He lifted a hand, shaking his head as he stared down at his boots, "Thank you, Reich. But no." His voice was flat. Final. "You focus on your girl. If I need you, I'll come to you. But you don't want to get involved in what Nael and I are doing."

I frowned. "What does that mean?"

His jaw worked, muscle ticking in his cheek, "You don't want to get involved," he repeated. "This is high risk. Nael and I... we've got nothing left to lose. You've got your brother. Your girl."

I stared at him, the words twisting in my gut, "You still have Blythe. You still have all of us."

He scoffed, shaking his head like I was missing the point, "I'm trying to protect you."

"I don't need protection, Keenan," I snapped. "You know damn well I can handle myself."

He met my eyes. "I never said you couldn't." His voice was calm. Measured. But there was something in it—something I didn't trust.

We fell silent again.

Old history hanging between us like smoke.

Heavy. Choking.

We had always gotten into shit together.

Always.

Since we were kids. Since the nights we drank cheap whiskey and planned the kind of future that was never going to exist for guys like us. We had bled together. Fought side by side.

So why the fuck was this different?

Keenan leaned forward, elbows on his knees. His voice dropped low. "Nael and I found a way out."

My stomach sank. "A way out of what?"

He held my gaze. Unblinking. "We found a way out of the ENA."

For a second, I said nothing. Then I laughed. A dry, humorless sound that felt foreign in my throat. "You haven't been able to get Blythe out for six months. But now, somehow, you've found a way to do the impossible?"

He didn't flinch. Didn't look away. "It's all or nothing," Keenan said. "We can't get her out unless we get everyone out."

A cold knot twisted in my gut. "Okay," I said carefully. "And how exactly do you plan on getting us all out?"

He exhaled slowly. His expression darkened. And when he spoke again, there was something in his voice I'd never heard before.

Something dangerous.

Something final.

"It involves treason."

Chapter Forty-Nine

SAGE

I spoke with Sam earlier that day, finally feeling steady enough to reach out. My hands hadn't shaken when I texted her. My lungs hadn't seized when I waited for her reply.

For the first time in days, I wasn't drowning in my own head. I wasn't clawing through the dark just to get from one breath to the next.

I was healing. Not perfectly.

But piece by piece. Day by day. Enough to feel something close to hope again.

But I should have known better.

I should have sensed it the moment the energy in the house shifted—subtle, almost imperceptible, like the quiet before a storm tears the sky open. I should have felt it like the ripple in the air before a bomb goes off, but I was too busy convincing myself I was safe.

That we were safe.

But I still should have known.

Hope was fragile.

And fragile things broke when you let yourself believe in them.

The instant Reich appeared in the doorway, I knew something was wrong.

He didn't have to speak. He didn't have to move. His body said it all. Arms crossed like a barricade. Shoulders rigid like he was holding the weight of something impossible. Tension radiating off him in waves, thick and suffocating. A warning shot before the real damage landed.

And then he spoke. Took a breath—slow and heavy, the kind you take when you're about to burn something to the ground, knowing there's no coming back from it.

"I think it's time for you to go home."

One sentence.

Simple.

But they landed like a bullet straight through the hollow in my chest.

His voice was flat. No warmth. No hesitation. Just a death sentence dressed up in casual cruelty.

The words hung there, twisting in the space between us, until they barely sounded real.

But my body registered them before my mind could catch up.

My stomach twisted violently, nausea coiling in my gut like sickness blooming from the inside out.

Home?

He was my home.

How the hell was I supposed to go anywhere when he was here?

I wanted to move. To step toward him. To demand an explanation. But I was frozen.

Trapped beneath the crushing weight of his betrayal.

"No." The word tore free before I realized I was speaking.

A breathless denial.

Desperate and disbelieving.

I shook my head, slow at first, then faster, as if motion alone could erase the moment. "You can't just push me away. Reich."

Reich dragged a hand through his hair, pacing like a man at war with himself.

Like someone who'd already lost. "My carelessness led to this—twice now," he ground out. His voice was rough. Strained. "If it happens again..." He trailed off, his breath hitching before he forced the rest of it out. "I won't let it happen again. That's why you need to leave."

"So that's it?" The words cracked in my throat, hollow and small. "You're just throwing me away?"

He said nothing and that silence was worse than any answer he could've given me.

Fury surged, wild and hot but that heartbreak bled through it, turning everything jagged and raw.

I surged forward, shoving him.

Slamming my fists against his chest like I could break through the wall he was building between us.

"Say something!" I demanded, voice splintering. "Feel something! Anything!"

He absorbed every hit. Every broken plea.

But he didn't move. Didn't flinch. Didn't break.

Only I did.

"Tell me it wasn't real," I begged. The words scraped against my throat, painful, "Tell me. So, I can walk away."

His hands clenched at his sides. His breath came too fast, too shallow. He was unraveling.

And still, I was sure he wouldn't say it. Wouldn't give me the lie I needed to let go.

"Sage—"

"Tell me!" I choked. "Say it didn't matter! That I didn't matter!"

And then— A whisper. Wrecked and raw came from his lips, "I can't."

The words shattered me. My knees buckled. Tears burned hot trails down my face, blurring everything until he was just a smear of color in front of me.

"You know what?" My voice broke open like a wound. "Fuck you, Reich." It came out like a sob. A battle cry. "Fuck you for putting me back together just to break me all over again."

His walls trembled and I saw it: The fracture in his mask he wore so pristinely.

But it wasn't enough.

They didn't fall and neither did he.

"I'm practically Hell's gatekeeper," he said hoarsely. "One day, I won't come back. I'll be dragged under. Six feet down. And you'll be left wondering if you were the reason." His voice cracked, deep and hollow. "Or worse, you'll end up right there with me."

He lifted his eyes to mine, and for the first time, I saw it—the rawness. The fear. The man behind the monster.

"Is that the life you want?" he asked. "A life of worry and fear?"

"Yes." I didn't hesitate. I didn't flinch.

His head snapped up at the word, something breaking behind his gaze.

"Yes," I said again, louder this time. "If it means a life with you, then yes. I accept."

"Sage..." His voice was thick. Choked.

I reached for him. Grasped his hand like it was the only thing keeping me tethered to this world.

"I don't want a life without you," I whispered. "Even a long, safe life wouldn't be worth it. I'd rather have a short, beautiful one—even if it's filled with pain and fear."

I took a shaky breath, steadying myself as I held his gaze. "The only reason people fear losing something is because it means they had something worth keeping. If I don't have something worth losing... what's the point of any of it?"

Silence fell again. Thick. Crushing.

But this time, it wasn't empty.

It was heavy with truth. My truth.

"Life is suffering," I whispered. "It's inevitable. But I'd rather suffer for something that matters than exist everyday in something filled with emptiness." I smiled through the tears, through the ache. "If I'm your wildflower... then that makes you the light. How can I survive without it?"

Reich inhaled sharply. His fingers twitched, reaching for me. Before they hesitated. Before he clenched his fist again, fighting the very thing he wanted.

And that's when I knew. Nothing was going to change.

Even as he pulled me into his arms, the embrace felt hollow.

Not a promise. An apology.

I shoved away from him, the weight of it all collapsing over me. My knees hit the floor.

The sound of bone on hardwood cracked through the room, but I barely felt it. Sobs racked my body, raw and ugly.

I had given him everything.

Every fractured, vulnerable piece of myself.

And he had put me back together.

Only to destroy me all over again.

Why did he have to be everything?

Why did he have to make me whole just to tear me apart?

When our eyes met, I swore I saw forever in them.

But forever wasn't real. Was it?

Maybe this was reckless. Maybe it was madness. But I had to do something.

So, I stood. Wiped my face with trembling hands and walked away—out of the room, down the hall.

He didn't follow.

Of course he didn't. He wanted me gone. Needed me gone.

But I wasn't letting him off the hook that easily.

My fingers curled around an object I had found in the basement a week ago.

Its weight was solid. Cold.

I had no idea what I was going to do.

No plan. No strategy. Only this burning ache that refused to die.

But one thing was certain—this wasn't over.

Not even close.

Chapter Fifty

REICH

I WOKE WITH THE weight of sleep pressing against my skull, the haze of unconsciousness still wrapped tight around my senses. My body ached—not the deep, bone-grinding exhaustion I was used to after long nights in the pit, but something different. Slower. Like my mind and muscles were moving through mud. Sluggish. Off.

But one thing was sharp.

One image burned into my brain like a brand.

Sage. Her face.

Those wild, defiant eyes that had made me reckless from the first moment I saw them.

Fuck.

Pain flared as I flexed my wrists, raw skin catching on leather straps that dug deep enough to sting but not tight enough to keep me down. Sloppy work. Whoever tied me down hadn't known what they were doing. The knots were loose. Lazy. Careless.

I could break out of them blindfolded, asleep.

And I almost did—until I caught the faintest scent in the air.

Not leather. Not sweat. Wildflowers.

A thin strip of light bled in from beneath the door, weak and pale, but it was enough. Enough to make out the walls. The faint outline of the heavy metal chair beneath me. The scuffs on the concrete floors.

Recognition hit like a freight train to the ribs.

My basement. My pit.

The irony was so thick it made my teeth ache.

I turned my head, as much as I could, and caught movement.

Soft. Deliberate.

A figure detached itself from the shadows, emerging with an eerie kind of grace.

And even before she stepped fully into the light, I knew.

I knew every line of her body. Every flick of her hair. Every breath she took into those perfect lips.

My beautiful wildflower.

The one I was supposed to have let go.

And yet here she was.

Owning the room, I'd built to break people in. Wearing red like sin and moving like she had been born to ruin me.

"Good morning, my light." Her voice was syrup-sweet, but there was steel buried beneath it.

A taunt. A dare. A promise.

I stared at her.

At the way her dress clung to her like it belonged there. At the gleam in her eyes, sharp and bright and so fucking alive. And then the realization hit me like a blade between the ribs.

She was in control.

Heat pooled low in my gut, hot and sharp, even as I gritted my teeth.

She had no idea what she was doing to me. Or maybe she did.

Maybe she knew exactly what kind of monster she was going to make me into, and this was her vengeance.

She stepped closer.

Slow. Unhurried.

Her bare feet silent on the concrete and when she leaned in, her lips brushed against my ear, and I felt the tremble that ran through her, even as her voice stayed steady.

"Did you have a nice nap?" she whispered, warm breath fanning over my skin.

I exhaled sharply through my nose, jaw clenched tight, "Sage... what the hell are you doing?"

She tilted her head, watching me like a hunter watches prey that's finally cornered.

"I'm taking something that doesn't belong to me..." She trailed off, lips curving in a slow, wicked smile. "And making it mine."

For a second, I couldn't speak. Couldn't breathe. Because even beneath all the fire and fury she wore like armor, I could see it. The flicker of pain. The hollow ache she hadn't been able to bury. And it gutted me.

Her voice softened, cracking just a little. "You saved me from Klay. Even if it was for your own reasons." She swallowed hard, but her gaze didn't flinch. "I get that. I even accepted it. But what I don't understand..." She took a breath that shook at the edges. "Why did you choose to care? To talk to me? Laugh with me? Cry with me? Heal me?" Her throat bobbed as she forced the words out. "And then you rewired me to you, just so you could leave me?"

I had no words.

None that mattered.

None that wouldn't make this worse.

She stepped back, fingers ghosting over the doorknob like she wasn't sure whether to turn it or rip it from the door. "When I first came here and sat in that same chair, you asked me who I belonged to."

Her voice dropped, low and dangerous, like the calm before a storm.

"I think I finally have the answer."

Then, softer—and deadlier— "I'm not leaving."

My pulse hammered against my ribs, but I stayed silent.

Waiting. Watching. Wanting.

She dragged her gaze back to me, her expression unreadable. "If you didn't want this," she murmured, "you should've let me finish that drink at the festival. Should've let surfer boy take me home." Her smile was sharp as a blade. "Hell, Reich, you should've put me out of my misery yourself." A breath. A beat. "But you didn't."

"Sage—" Her name was a warning on my lips.

But she didn't wait for me to finish. Didn't give me a chance.

She slipped out the door with a quiet click, leaving nothing but silence in her wake.

Except for the muffled sound of her sobs on the other side of the wall causing something inside me to snap.

I flexed against the poor restraints, slipping free in seconds.

She needed to learn how to tie better knots.

I shoved open the door, my pulse a war drum in my ears, and found her at the foot of the stairs. Curled in on herself, arms wrapped tight around her legs like she was holding herself together with sheer force of will. She looked so small. So fucking breakable. Like a gust of wind could shatter her.

I sank down beside her, careful, slow, reaching for her hand. Her fingers were cold.

Trembling. I lifted them to my lips, pressing a slow, deliberate kiss against her knuckles, feeling the way her breath hitched.

"Reich... I'm sorry," she whispered. Her voice was wrecked. Fragile.

"Sage..." I exhaled hard, dragging a hand through my hair, struggling to keep myself steady. "I meant it when I said you were a wildflower. You're this dainty beautiful thing reaching towards the light after having been so long in darkness... but the problem is, I don't have any light left to give."

I closed my eyes for a beat, forcing the next words out. "I only carry shadows. And if you stay, you'll wither beneath them, because I can't give you what it is you need."

She lifted her head slowly, and her eyes—God, her fucking eyes— they were a wildfire.

Fierce. Bright. Unyielding.

"Reich," she breathed, "without you, I wouldn't be living. I'd be decaying. Just like I was when you first met me. So, you're wrong. You give me exactly what I need because what I've needed is you."

Her grip on my wrist tightened. Like a vice. Like salvation.

She continued when I couldn't speak, "So, if I choose you, I'm choosing my own happiness. To feel alive."

My chest tightened, something raw and ragged pulling along the inside of my ribs.

Her words wrapped around me like chains.

Constricting. Suffocating.

And yet— freeing me all at once.

"What makes you happy, Reich?" she asked, her voice almost too soft to hear.

"You." The word came without hesitation.

Without *fear*.

Her lips parted on a sharp breath. Her eyes flickered with something like hope. "Then why won't you choose me?"

Her question hit me like a blade to the gut.

I clenched my jaw, forcing myself to stay steady. "It's not that simple, Sage."

"Then what is it?"

I hesitated. Because once I told her, there would be no turning back.

"I work for some very bad people, Sage. People I committed myself to a long time ago before I even knew you existed." I swallowed hard. "These people. They go by the ENA."

Silence. A long, heavy beat.

Then she straightened. Fire in her eyes. "Then leave them."

I barked a hollow laugh. "You think I haven't tried?"

"Then try harder." Her grip on my wrist was bruising now. "There must be a way. Something even you haven't thought of."

I stared at her.

At the wild, reckless hope in her eyes.

Hope I didn't deserve. Hope I couldn't kill.

"...Okay." The word was gravel in my throat.

She stared at me, breath hitching and I didn't let myself think.

I leaned in, pressing my forehead to hers, breathing her in like oxygen. "I won't leave you."

I didn't know if it was true. Didn't know if I could keep that promise.

But I had to try. Because I couldn't watch the light fade from her eyes again.

I'd rather it consume me instead.

And it did.

That was the first time I ever lied to her.

Chapter Fifty-One

SAGE

I SHOULD HAVE WALKED away.

I told myself that probably a thousand times those last few days. Maybe more. Every breath I took in his presence had felt like a warning.

He was waiting to bolt. I could feel it.

I should have gotten myself out before it got this far—before his name carved into my memory like it had always belonged there. Before his hands knew the shape of me, the pulse of me, better than I did.

But it was already too late.

Reich was a storm I had no desire to escape. A wildfire I was willing to burn in. His chaos had become my sanctuary. And his darkness, a place I wanted to crawl inside of and never leave.

No matter how many times I reminded myself that this was dangerous, that we were dangerous together, I kept coming back. Kept choosing him.

Because the truth was, I didn't want to stop.

Even if it destroyed us. Even if it destroyed me.

I sucked in a shaky breath, my pulse hammering at my throat as I stepped closer. Every inch between us crackled, thick with tension, charged with everything we wouldn't say.

Couldn't say.

I felt the heat radiating from his skin, tasted the weight of the unspoken words hanging between us like smoke that refused to clear.

His jaw was tight, and his hands curled into fists at his sides like he was holding himself together by sheer will. But I could see the tremble in his fingers, the strain in his shoulders as he held me close.

He was breaking.

And so was I.

"You make me insane," I breathed, as my palms fisted against the hard wall of his chest.

I was torn between escape and surrender.

And I feared either would be the end of me.

In a single, fluid motion, he caught my wrists—unyielding, but never unkind. Strength cloaked in softness, like steel beneath silk.

"And you," he murmured, eyes locked on mine, "you make me sane."

His voice was low and rough.

I exhaled a shaky breath, my forehead falling to rest against his. "I don't know how to stop this... I just know I can't leave." I said, the words splintering in the space between us.

The confession was raw. Honest. Terrifying.

He let out a sharp breath, his hands sliding to my waist, his grip possessive as he pulled me flush against him. Like he already knew the answer. "Then don't."

I closed my eyes, pressing my hands flat against his chest, feeling the thunder of his heart under my palms. "This isn't going to work," I whispered, a tremor riding the edge of my voice.

Reich's expression was unreadable, but his body betrayed him. His fists clenched. His chest rose and fell faster than he wanted to show.

"You think I don't know that?" he muttered, his jaw working as he forced the words out. "You think I don't fucking know?"

My throat tightened. "Then why are we still here?" The question was a plea. A demand.

An accusation.

His gaze locked on mine, burning.

Dark. Devastated.

"Because no matter how much it destroys us, I don't know if I can actually let you go. I don't know if I can let go of a life with you. A normal one. But I know one day I'll have to."

And then his mouth was on mine.

Fierce. Unrelenting. Desperate.

Fire and frustration, fury and grief. It wasn't a kiss—it was a collision. It was every word we couldn't speak. Every fear we couldn't silence. It was everything we had fought against crashing down around us.

One second, we were arguing.

The next, we were falling. Together.

His hands were on my body like he was memorizing me—committing every line, every scar, every bruise and hollow place to memory. As if he could anchor himself in my skin. As if he could stay there forever.

And I let him.

My fingers dug into his arms, clinging to him like he was the last steady thing in a world that wouldn't stop tilting.

"We can still make it our own in some way. We don't need those things to have a life together...Please...I can't lose you," I choked against his lips. "Reich, I can't—"

He stilled. Just for a second. Then his forehead pressed hard against mine, his breath ragged.

"You won't lose me" he promised, his voice wrecked. "Because I'll never leave you. I'd let everything crash and burn before that happened."

The way he said it— like it was already a foregone conclusion.

Like he'd already marked the targets and counted the bodies.

Like he'd do it, without hesitation.

And God help me, I believed him. And it shook something loose in me.

Something fragile. Something indestructible.

He pulled back just far enough to see me, his hands trembling as they tightened around my waist.

"Reich..." My voice was low, searching his eyes.

He didn't answer. Just watched me, silent, like I was something he hadn't yet decided whether to keep—or cast out again. A trespasser standing on the wrong side of his walls.

I thought of the field, of the words he'd once given me, sharp as prophecy. I drew in a breath.

"You told me someday I'd beg to belong to you." My gaze caught his, even as he tried to avoid it. "Well... this is me begging."

A beat passed. Then his shoulders lifted in the smallest shrug.

"If you stayed," he said at last, his voice iron-clad, stripped of mercy, "there would have to be rules. Precautions. Lines I can't cross. Things I have to do to keep everyone safe."

The steel in him wavered then, softened into something raw, breaking against the edges of his restraint. "But even then..." His voice faltered. "Even then, I don't know if it would be enough."

I could hear it in his tone—the unbearable strain of needing me and fearing for me in equal measure.

It made my chest ache. Made my heart shatter and rebuild itself at the same time.

His eyes searched mine, wild and desperate, waging a war I couldn't see.

He looked like he wanted to fight me on this.

But instead—his gaze dropped to my mouth and in one breathless second—he kissed me.

His lips crushed mine, his hands threading through my hair, holding me in place as if letting go was impossible. As if I was the only thing anchoring him to this world.

And I kissed him back with everything I had.

With everything I was.

With every broken piece of myself that only he had ever been able to fit against and make whole.

We moved together like we'd done this in a thousand lives before and maybe we had. Maybe this was the kind of story that had always been written into the stars.

Since our paths had collided, our connection had always been undeniable, a perfect harmony in its chaos.

If we were musicians, we'd compose a haunting duet.

If we were writers, a timeless manuscript.

If we were painters, a soul-stirring masterpiece.

But in this world, I didn't know what we were.

All I knew was that when we were together, we had the ability to create something raw and unforgettable.

When we finally broke apart, we were both breathing hard, our foreheads pressed together, our hearts beating in sync.

His hands cradled my face, his thumb tracing slow circles over my cheekbone, grounding me.

"I mean it, Sage," he said, his voice hoarse. "I need you safe. I can't do this if I know you're in danger."

I swallowed hard. "I know," I whispered.

And I did.

"You know?" He smiled briefly, "I've always wanted a normal life... a home... a family... a dog... but the truth is..." He stopped, as he battled against his words. "I can't ever promise that. I can't promise that we won't always be fighting for our lives." His voice cracked.

I held him tightly, trying to ground him with my presence and keep his mind from spinning into flight mode.

"I don't care about any of those things," I told him, steady and true. "Because I only care that you are with me—that in some way, you're always there."

His eyes darkened, a storm gathering in their depths.

"Okay," he said.

He laced his fingers through mine, gripping them tight, his palm warm and solid against mine.

It felt like a vow.

And in that moment, I knew—no matter what came next. No matter the war we were going to have to fight. We were in it together.

And this time, there was no hesitation. No fear. Only certainty—or so I thought.

CHAPTER FIFTY-TWO

REICH

I HELD HER IN my arms, drowning in the depths of those beautiful eyes—eyes I never imagined would be my undoing.

And yet here I was. Unmade by a single glance. Stripped bare by the way she looked at me, like I was something more than the ruin I'd always believed myself to be. Like I was someone worth loving.

Her gaze held no judgment. Just quiet acceptance. The kind that could build worlds—or tear them down.

And God help me, I wanted to build one with her.

For her.

For us.

I wanted to change everything. Rewrite every fucked-up chapter of my life, burn every page that kept me bound to the past. I wanted to give her something better. Something safer.

Something clean.

But there was no clean with me.

I was blood and shadow.

And she was breath and light.

Soft and wild, like the glow of candlelight flickering in the pitch-black void I called my world.

But maybe—maybe it was the other way around.

I had been beyond redemption. A machine built for chaos and destruction.

I was numb. Calloused. Worn down by years of war, both inside and out.

My hands and body had been made to kill.

My heart was nothing but a hollow shell I'd long since given up on trying to fix.

My soul was all rough edges and jagged pieces that didn't fit together anymore on their own or with anyone.

Until her.

She softened the edges of myself I thought were permanent. She breathed life into the hollow places I thought were long dead. Every inch of her chipped away at the walls I'd spent a lifetime building.

Every breath she took made me want to be better.

Every look she gave made me believe I already was.

And she didn't even know she was doing it.

She frustrated me, challenged me and interrupted me. Pushed and pulled until I couldn't tell if I wanted to scream or laugh or crush her against me just to feel her heartbeat pounding in time with mine.

She hated me—until she didn't. Until she trusted me and understood me.

And then—she loved me.

And it wrecked me.

Because she made me feel.

And I hadn't felt anything in years. Not like this.

She had the power to make me feel an unfiltered joy.

A brutal, terrifying, devastating kind of joy.

The kind that was dangerous to want. The kind that was dangerous to need.

But it felt like mine.

Like I was finally alive.

And the only thing keeping me tethered to that life was her and those perfect eyes.

Sparkling like jade diamonds.

Bright. Pure. Fierce. Undeniably the most beautiful thing I had ever seen.

But beauty was cruel when it belonged to something you couldn't keep.

I didn't deserve her, and I knew it.

But knowing didn't make it hurt any less.

I tore myself away from her—every muscle screaming to stay. I left the warmth of her behind like a man willingly walking into a blizzard. Stepping into the cold, where I belonged.

The door closed behind me with a quiet finality, and I found Cas standing there. Leaning against the wall, arms crossed, his expression unreadable at first.

But then his eyes met mine.

And I saw it. The knowing.

He smirked, but there was no real humor in it. Just a sharp edge of something that tasted like grief.

"I thought some things never change," he said, voice casual. Too casual.

He knew. Of course, he knew. He always did.

"I guess I was wrong, Cas," I murmured, the words foreign on my tongue.

His brows lifted. "Woah. Not something I ever expected to hear from you."

I let out a low chuckle. It felt strange. Hollow. Like it didn't quite belong to me.

"People change," I said, quieter now. "Maybe there's some hope for us all."

Cas scoffed. "Optimism?" He shook his head like he was trying to shake off the weight of it. "Fuck, brother. I'm not ready for this new you."

His laugh was warm, familiar.

It cut through the heaviness in my chest for a moment.

And then—he saw it.

The shift. The fracture. The goodbye already forming behind my eyes.

His smile faded, slipping away like a shadow under the door.

And in that moment, I didn't have to say it because he already knew.

"Things aren't changing, are they?" His voice was softer now.

Raw. Dangerously close to fear. Not for himself. For me.

I swallowed hard, feeling it stick in my throat like glass. The weight of what I was about to do pressed into my ribs, heavy and brutal.

I turned away, because I didn't trust myself to hold his gaze. I couldn't let him see me fall apart. Not now. Not when I needed to be steady.

"No," I said, my voice rough and ragged. Final.

Cas exhaled slowly, like he'd been bracing for this all along. He didn't argue. Didn't try to talk me out of it. He just stood there, staring at the space I'd left between us. And maybe, that was worse.

Because this was the hardest thing I'd ever have to do.

Walk away from her. From the life I could've had. From the love I never thought I'd find.

And somehow, still survive it.

I wasn't sure I could. But I would try. For her. For Cas. For whatever pieces of myself I had left to salvage.

Even if it meant dying a little more each day.

Even if it meant living in the shadow of what could've been.

Even if it meant watching her light fade from my life and knowing I was the one who turned away.

Because if this was what would keep her safe...I'd tear myself apart for it.

And I already was.

Chapter Fifty-Three

SAGE

One Month Later

WHEN LIFE FALLS APART, it's rarely just one choice that destroys it. It's never as simple as a single wrong turn or a single mistake. No. It's a tangled mess. A collection of small decisions and sharp words, split-second reactions, and silent omissions. Sometimes they're yours. Sometimes they're someone else's.

And sometimes... it's both.

A chain reaction spiraling out of control, gathering momentum until it crashes into you, and you're left breathless in the aftermath. Staring at the wreckage. Holding out your hands like maybe, just maybe, you can piece it back together.

But you can't.

You can only stand there, hollow and shaking, as the dust settles around you.

And when it does—you don't just see the destruction.

You feel it. You feel it in every crack that splintered your foundation.

Every tremor of betrayal that knocked you off balance. Every whisper of regret that seeps into your bones and makes a home there, as if it had always belonged.

You can't scream it away. You can't cry it out. You just live with it.

Every second. Every breath. Until you forget what it was like to exist without it.

But life is made up of those choices. And choices are never clean.

Each one takes you down a different road but none of which lead to peace.

Some are lined with fire. Some are carved from silence. But all of them come with their own form of suffering.

And when it's time to choose...

The only question left is—*What's worth the pain?*

That's what Reich once told me during one of our many long-winded conversations.

"In the end, it's not about avoiding pain. It's about choosing the kind you can live with."

I never really understood what he meant. Not until the day he left.

I remember it—clearer than anything else. The day I shattered.

I've tried to recall other things since then.

The warmth of his hand in mine. The sound of his voice, low and certain, whispering promises into my hair as we lay tangled in the dark. The way he smiled when he thought I wasn't looking.

But those memories were faded now.

As if my mind is trying to protect me from remembering too much.

As if it's easier to hold on to the ruin than to what was beautiful before it broke.

But that day? The day I lost him?

It's carved into me like a scar I trace with trembling fingers, over and over, hoping one day it'll stop hurting.

It never does.

I had only stepped out for a moment. Just long enough to grab a few things from my apartment. Just a moment.

I told myself he'd still be there when I got back. That he'd be waiting. That we still had time.

I was wrong.

When I returned, the life we were going to build—the fragile little world we'd created from ash and ruin—was gone.

Erased.

Every trace of him, vanished like smoke through my fingers.

All gone.

As if he had never been there. As if we had been nothing. As if I had dreamed it all.

And maybe I could have believed that.

Maybe I would have.

If not for the single folded note left behind. Sitting on the bed we shared like a parting gift I never asked for.

One word scrawled across the front in his uneven handwriting:

Wildflower.

I stared at it for what felt like hours before my hands stopped shaking enough to open it.

Inside, his message was short. Cryptic. Just like him.

One day, when I am someone else, I'll find you.
-Reich

I read it again. And again.

Until the ink blurred and my vision swam with tears I refused to shed.

What did that even mean? When he's someone else?

I didn't want someone else. I wanted him. Exactly as he was.

Dangerous. Flawed. Damaged.

But him.

I needed the man who held me close in the dead of night and whispered that I was the only thing that made him feel alive.

The man who stood between me and the darkness without hesitation.

Who never asked me to be anyone other than exactly who I was.

I needed him to stay.

He had promised he wouldn't leave. He had promised he'd find a way. That we'd figure it out—together. That the ENA wouldn't win. That he'd make it out.

But maybe those were just words too.

Maybe he only said them because he thought I needed to hear them.

Because I wouldn't stop begging him to stay.

And maybe—maybe that's all I was to him, just another job to complete.

Another obligation. Another broken girl who couldn't save herself.

But I didn't believe that.

No matter how much easier it would have been. Because if that were true, he wouldn't have left that note. He wouldn't have called me wildflower. He wouldn't have promised to find me again.

And he sure as hell wouldn't have looked at me the way he did that last night— like I was his salvation and his home.

He once warned me not to take things that didn't belong to me but I think I stole something from him anyway.

Something he wasn't ready to give.

Maybe I stole his peace. Maybe I stole his future.

Maybe that's why now— he's only a memory.

Faded, distant.

A name I whisper when I can't sleep.

A ghost I reach for in the dark, even though I know he's not there.

But I still kept that note.

Tucked in the pages of The Scarlet Pimpernel, the book he told me was his favorite.

I read it sometimes, when the nights get too long and the silence screams louder than I can bear.

I trace the letters he scrawled across the paper.

And I wait.

Because maybe, one day, when he's someone else— he really will find me.

And maybe, just maybe, I'll still be waiting.

Chapter Fifty-Four

REICH

I STILL COULDN'T BELIEVE I let myself do that to her.

Fuck.

The word didn't even come close to the weight of it.

Nothing did.

Not the ache lodged in my throat. Not the fist that felt permanently clenched around my ribs. Not the hollow silence that followed me everywhere, filling every inch of the space where her voice used to be.

None of it came close.

I knew.

God, I fucking knew what it would do to her.

How it would tear her apart. How it would fracture something in her that might never heal again and I still did it.

I did it with my own hands.

I told myself it was the only way.

That maybe—somehow—someday, she'd piece it together. That she'd understand. That she'd look back and realize it was never about hurting her.

Never about wanting to leave. Never about turning my back on her. It was about keeping her alive. Keeping her free.

But that's the problem with choices like mine.

They don't come with explanations. They don't come with second chances.

Only damage.

And she doesn't understand the ENA.

Not the way I do.

She doesn't know what they are. What they're capable of. The lengths they'll go to in order to enforce their control. The things I've seen them do. The things I've done for them.

She thinks she knows pain, but this? This is different.

The ENA doesn't punish you. They erase you. They make you a ghost of yourself before they end you.

And anyone who tries to run? Anyone who tries to break free? They don't just destroy them. They salt the earth where they once stood, as if they never existed.

And if I had stayed... if I had let her stay... They would've erased her, too. They would have taken her from me. They would've taken *everything*.

So, yeah. Maybe I did make a choice.

But it wasn't the one everyone thinks it was.

It wasn't about pushing her away because I stopped loving her. It wasn't about running from her because I was afraid of what we were becoming. It was about choosing her— her life.

Her safety. Her future.

Even if that future didn't have me in it.

I chose to protect her.

Even if it meant ripping us apart. Even if it meant tearing myself in half and living with the emptiness she left behind. Even if it meant I'd lose her completely.

And I did.

God, I did.

But it doesn't stop me from wanting her. From missing her like hell. From waking up at night with her name on my lips and reaching for her out of reflex, only to find cold sheets and nothing but the echo of who we used to be. From standing in the places where we once stood together, pretending she's still there, hearing her voice in the back of my mind like a ghost I can't shake.

If I could just see her like that that again.

Just once.

If I could kiss her forehead the way I used to—when she was half-asleep and safe and warm against me, When the world couldn't touch us and we made promises in the dark that I was stupid enough to believe.

If I could hold her again, feel her head tucked beneath my chin, feel her fingers tracing circles into my skin like she was memorizing me. Like she was branding me in ways I would never recover from.

I'd give anything for that.

Anything to hear her laugh again. That soft, breathless sound that never failed to pull me back from the edge. That spark in her eyes when she was lost in her own head, creating some impossible world that I knew—without a doubt—would always be brighter, better, because she was the one imagining it.

And fuck, the way she reached for me.

Like she knew I'd catch her. Like she never once doubted I'd be there when she fell. Like she believed in me in a way no one ever had. In a way I sure as hell didn't deserve.

I don't deserve that trust anymore. I broke it.

I shattered it into a thousand pieces and left her to pick them up on her own.

I know that. I live with that. Every goddamn day.

But knowing it doesn't stop me from wanting it back. From wanting her back. From aching for her in places I didn't even know existed inside me until she made them real.

And it sure as fuck doesn't stop me from loving her.

Even now. Especially now.

Because no matter how many times I tell myself I did the right thing...no matter how many times I remind myself that walking away saved her life...it doesn't change one brutal, undeniable truth.

I'm still in love with her and I don't know if I'll ever stop.

EPILOGUE ONE

SAGE

"*E*VERYTHING WILL BE FINE. *This will work.*"

His voice was so steady. Like stone polished smooth from years of weathering storms.

Unwavering. Certain.

I wanted to believe him. God, I wanted to let those words be enough.

But they weren't.

"Reich..." His name broke on my tongue, softer than I meant it to be, laced with hesitation. "How can you be so sure? Given everything, you can't possibly know that."

I forced myself to hold his stare, though my chest ached under the weight of doubt, under the unbearable pressure of what if.

"What if it doesn't work?" I whispered.

The question hung between us like smoke, thick and clinging, refusing to dissolve.

And for a moment, just a moment, he was quiet.

Then he exhaled slowly, like a man carrying the weight of the world but somehow still standing tall beneath it.

"Then I'll figure it out," he said, low and unshaken. "Like I always do."

The conviction in his voice made something deep inside me twist painfully. A longing, a grief I hadn't known I was holding until now. Because I wasn't sure how many more times he could figure it out. How many more battles he could fight and still come back whole.

Still come back to me.

I dropped my gaze to the ground, swallowing hard as my heart thundered in my chest. I could feel it—fear, thick and relentless—curling like smoke in my lungs, making it hard to breathe.

Then I heard it.

The quiet shift of his boots against the worn wood floor.

The subtle brush of his coat as he moved closer.

Soft. Unhurried.

His presence loomed in front of me before his fingers reached for my chin. Warm, rough from years of scars and callouses, yet gentle as they tilted my head upward.

And when my eyes met his, something inside me cracked.

His gaze was everything I remembered. Everything I needed. A storm of intensity, tempered by something softer, something that only ever existed for me.

"Don't tell me," Reich murmured, voice dropping to something just above a whisper, as if sharing a secret only meant for the two of us, "that after all these years, you still don't believe me."

He said it like he was smiling, but it wasn't smugness or arrogance. It was a quiet knowing. A steady confidence that had carried him through so many impossible things. A certainty I used to be able to breathe in like air.

My lips parted to answer, but the words tangled behind the tightness in my throat.

And then he smiled.

God, that smile.

Soft, barely there. Just the faintest curve of his mouth, but it shattered me all the same.

It was the kind of smile that said I've got you. The kind of smile that could pull me back from the edge of anything.

His thumb brushed along my cheek, tracing the skin like he was memorizing it. A slow, reverent drag of calloused skin over softness, leaving a trail of warmth I didn't know I was desperate for.

I leaned into it, closing my eyes for the smallest moment. Letting myself fall into the simple act of being touched. Not because I needed to be comforted, but because I needed to be reminded that he was real. That this was real.

That there was still something left of us to hold onto.

When I opened my eyes, he was still there. Close. Steady. Like he'd never let me go.

"I do believe you," I said, my voice shaking but honest. "But sometimes... sometimes I believe in you more than I believe in myself."

His brow furrowed, and he shook his head, his hand slipping to the back of my neck, pulling me closer until our foreheads touched. The warmth of him, the steady rhythm of his breath, the weight of his fingers tangled in my hair—it was almost enough to quiet the storm inside me.

"You don't have to believe in yourself all the time," he murmured. "That's what I'm here for."

And then I woke up.

Always. Just before he kissed me.

As if even in my dreams, I wasn't allowed to have him. As if the universe, cruel and calculating, was determined to deny me even the smallest taste of what it might be like to be his—to really be his.

I woke up reaching for him. Always reaching. Always empty-handed.

It was like some vicious game my subconscious played, teasing me with fragments of a life that could never belong to me.

A life where his lips met mine, where his hands didn't hesitate. A life where he stayed.

But I was never allowed to live in those moments. Only on the edge of them.

Always so close, and then gone.

And every time I woke up, I was hollow again. Grasping for something that slipped through my fingers like sand and all it left behind was the sharp ache of longing.

Since he left, I searched for him everywhere.

In the shifting blur of crowded streets. In the quiet hush of shadowed alleyways. In every low voice that might carry his name, his laugh, his warmth.

But it was never him.

It never would be.

And even knowing that, it didn't stop me from looking.

I still searched.

Like a fool. Like a woman with hope stitched into her arms, even though it bled her dry.

Not that it was any different from the night we first met.

Back then, I wanted him too.

Longed for him in ways I never fully understood. Thought about him constantly, obsessively. Even when he wasn't mine. Even when he was never meant to be.

And then, for one impossible, fleeting moment—it felt like he was.

For one moment, I belonged somewhere. To someone. To him.

And now he was gone again.

The cruel irony of fate played its melody in my ears, soft and sharp, threading its way through my days.

A song of what-ifs and never-weres. A song that never reached its crescendo.

It just... faded. Slow and silent, into something I couldn't quiet. A song I was beginning to think would outlive me.

Sometimes I wondered how things would have turned out if I had never left Sanele. If I had never taken that road that led me to Providence. To him.

Had I stayed, would life have been simpler? Would I have found peace? Would I still be alive?

Or would I have merely kept drifting—empty, silent—haunted by a hollow I never knew existed until I met Reich.

I told myself I didn't regret it. That I wouldn't change any of it.

Not a single second. Not even the hurt.

Because he healed me more than I ever thought I deserved. He put me back together in places I thought would stay broken forever.

But the truth was...he also carved something out of me when he left.

Something vital.

And I couldn't fill the space he left behind.

The emptiness that clung to me.

A ghost that followed each step I took. A shadow that whispered his name in the silence between my heartbeats.

It was quieter than grief but heavier.

It was the kind of absence that hurt because I could still feel him—in every corner of my space. In every thread of my skin. In every memory I wasn't ready to surrender.

So, I knelt and I begged.

Begged that somehow, some way, our paths would cross again. That the same stars that cursed us might show mercy and guide him back. That the universe might give me one more moment.

A breath. A look. Anything.

But those pleas tasted bitter in my mouth.

If there was any gods, I had cursed them for bringing Reich into my life only to rip him away when I finally learned how to live.

I cursed the stars for aligning so cruelly, for weaving our souls together, only to unravel them the moment I began to believe in something more.

He healed me but he also took a piece of me with him.

And I was left empty. Wandering. Searching for the one person who had made me feel alive and wondering if I would ever feel that same way again.

This loss was different than losing my father.

Losing my father left a gaping wound—raw and visible to the world but able to be filled with other things that gave me purpose.

But Reich?

He left something quieter. Crueler.

Because with him, there was anger.

A fire that burned so hot it could consume me from the inside out.

But it was his choice to leave that made it unbearable. That made it a special kind of devastation.

A quiet grief that was consuming and persistent with no understanding of the why.

One that didn't scream or demand, but hollowed me out slowly, leaving me an echo of the person I used to be.

And after waiting too long, I made the decision to find him.

I left a note behind that day.

I pressed fragile hope onto paper, hands shaking as I wrote the words. The ones I didn't think I'd ever have the courage to say to his face.

But pleading, nonetheless, that one day he'd find it.

That somehow, against all odds, fate would be kind enough to place it in his hands.

I didn't know if it ever would.

If he'd ever see it. If he'd ever think of me again.

But I had to believe he might. That maybe—just maybe—he would read the words and remember us.

It was all I had left to offer.

My last tether to him. A whisper in the dark. A soft plea

In case my journey to find him, never led me home.

Reich—

You've always been my safe haven, even if only in my heart, where our playlist still echoes the way you loved me back together.

Thank you, always.

—Sage

REICH

Three Years Later

SOMETHING PULLS AT ME—AN ache, silent yet relentless. It presses beneath my skin like a splinter I can't reach, whispering in a voice I can't silence.

I made a mistake.

With her.

And no matter how many miles I put between us, it follows me.

I can't outrun it.

I can't outrun her.

Her shadow haunts every space I thought I'd reclaimed.

I see her in the empty chair across from mine. I feel her in the silence of my bunker, the kind that burns raw because it's missing the sound of her laughter, the soft cadence of her breathing at night.

She lingers in the cold sheets on my bed, in the echoes of songs that once meant nothing until they meant everything.

And now, they mean loss.

When I close my eyes, I don't find peace.

I find *her*.

Her touch. Her voice.

The way her fingers once laced through mine like they belonged there and maybe they did.

I told myself leaving was the right choice.

That if I let her go, she'd be safe.

And if I repeated it enough times, I'd start to believe it.

But the truth is, I only half-saved her.

The other half of her?

The part I carried with me?

I broke that.

And the burden of that choice is a weight I can't shed.

It crushes onto my ribs when I breathe. It carves at my sanity when I think too long. It makes me question if I ever really knew what I was fighting for or if I lost sight of it the moment I walked away from the only thing in this world that was ever truly mine.

Maybe our story wasn't supposed to end. Maybe this ache is the proof of something unfinished or maybe it's just another cruel game, a reminder that fate doesn't give second chances to men like me.

But when the world is quiet, and I let myself remember...I still wish I could go back.

Back to that first night.

When everything was new, and the wreckage hadn't begun. When her smile was unguarded, and I hadn't yet ruined her trust. When there was still a version of me that could've deserved her.

I wish I could rewrite it all, but I can't and so I live in the hollow of what could have been and the ghost of what was.

The night air was heavy—saturated with the scent of damp earth and rust, the sharp tang of something long dead.

I walked the overgrown path like a man heading to the gallows, my boots crunching over weeds and rotted leaves.

The garden shed loomed ahead. Crooked. Splintered. Hollowed out by time and weather.

But it wasn't the shed I was after.

It was what lay beneath.

I wrenched the door open, its hinges screaming in protest.

Inside, I found the hatch and when I pried it loose, the air that rushed out smelled of decay and secrets long buried.

I didn't hesitate.

I descended into the dark and there she was. My next task.

Curled in on herself, tucked away in the farthest corner like a secret the world was trying to forget.

Her hair was matted, streaked with blood, and her body—fragile, gaunt—barely clung to life.

But she was alive and that was enough to rip something open inside me.

I knelt. I reached for her. Brushed trembling fingers through the knots of her hair.

She stirred. A shallow breath shuddered through her body, her eyelids fighting to open.

And when they did—those eyes.

Fuck, those eyes.

They weren't the same but they were hers.

Still hers. Still mine.

"Wildflower," I whispered, the word cracked and wrecked in my throat.

Her lips parted and I knew.

I had never stopped being hers and she had never stopped being mine.

About Paige Alexandria

I write stories that live in the shadows—where love is tangled, passion burns deep, and healing comes with scars. With a background in mental health, I understand how heavy the past can feel, and I weave that weight into characters who are raw, flawed, and achingly human.

Music is often my refuge and my muse, fueling the rhythm and intensity of my words. My hope is that each story draws you in, offering both escape and connection—reminding us that even in darkness, there is beauty, and within every broken piece, the possibility of redemption.

When I'm not writing, you'll find me lost in music, wandering through new ideas, or savoring the quiet moments that inspire the chaos on the page.

Instagram - @p.alexauthor
Paigealexandria.com

Sneak Peek

In Reich and Ruin
Book Two of
The Black Sigil of Naphal Series

After a year of searching through the wreckage of her past, Sage finally found the one man who had haunted her every thought—Reich Davidian. But their reunion is nothing like the peace she imagined. Time apart has left them both scarred, their bond tangled in unanswered questions, unhealed wounds, and the dangerous pull of a love neither of them could sever.

Reich is no longer the man she remembers. The ENA has its claws in him, reshaping him into something darker, something even he doesn't understand. Every step closer threatens to expose the monster he fears he's becoming. And every step away threatens to break what little is left of them.

For Sage, what once seemed like salvation may now be the greatest risk to her fragile stability. For Reich, protecting her might mean destroying himself. Together, they're caught between the past they can't let go of and the future the ENA is determined to control.